Mulligan

KG MacGregor

Mulligan

ISBN 1-932667-31-8

Edited by Cindy Cresap
Cover Design by Stephanie Solomon-Lopez

Published by
BookEnds Press
Gainesville, Florida

Acknowledgments

Lots of people made important contributions to this book, and I'd like to take a moment to acknowledge them.

It was a tremendous pleasure to work with editor Cindy Cresap for the first time. Her insights and suggestions contributed not only to this book, but to my writing toolbox. I look forward to working with her again.

Also, I thank Jenny for her technical editing and story ideas, and Karen Appleby for her meticulous proofreading.

And last, I thank friends AK, Chris, Helen, Karen, Lynn, Michele, Tami, Teresa, Steph, and Susan for their comments on an early draft.

I'd like to dedicate this book to the memory of Laura, a wonderful woman who passed away in February 2005, much too young.

KG MacGregor
www.kgmacgregor.com

October 1999

"So if Betty is three times as old as her daughter Jane, and four years ago she was four times older, how old is Jane now?" Louise Stevens scanned the room to assess the expected confusion of those in her algebra class as they followed along in their textbooks. Quadratic equations were always tough at first, even for the brightest students. "Who wants to try to write that formula on the board?"

Nearly all of the students in her fifth-period class were sophomores. She was faculty sponsor of this Class of 2002, so their banner—signed by all 506 students—hung above the chalkboard in her classroom. Louise thought them an interesting group. They got along with each other, worked well together in school, and, as freshmen, had set records at the school for fundraising and community service projects. There definitely was something special about the Class of 2002.

A crisp autumn breeze rippled through the blinds, turning pages for those sitting close to the window. Louise draped her cardigan around her shoulders and stood to begin her walk through the aisles. Papers rustled throughout the room, a telltale sign that math texts weren't the only objects of attention in the classroom. She smiled to herself, wondering what secrets she might learn by confiscating a note or two. But that sort of thing wasn't her style.

After thirty-eight years in front of the classroom at Westfield, the sixty-year-old math teacher had no need for a heavy hand when it came to discipline. She commanded her students' respect without ever having to ask for it.

"I see I'm going to have to volunteer someone." That brought a few chuckles, but from the corner of her eye, she saw a tentative hand go up. Michele Sanders, a tall, lanky girl from Louise's homeroom, worked harder in math class than anyone else. The girl was good with numbers, but Louise suspected another motive for her dedication to algebra—Michele had a crush on her. That had been an uncomfortable realization at first, but she tried not to worry too much about it. She did nothing at all to encourage feelings of attraction from her students, and always was careful not to be unkind. Crushes were a normal part of adolescent development and they ran their course in time. Louise didn't mind one bit that they seemed to produce better math students.

She continued her stroll through the aisle, noting with pride that most of her students were dressed today to show their school spirit. It was Friday, and the Westfield Spartans were playing their last football game of the season tonight on the road against Monroeville. Almost everyone in the room—the teacher included—was wearing blue and white; several of the boys on the team had on their game jerseys, and one girl wore a cheerleading uniform. But Louise was partial to those in the "Marching Spartan" sweaters, like Michele. She had a soft spot for students in the band.

"Mike, how would you write that formula?"

Several students snickered as she approached Mike's desk, where the young man was slumped forward, his face buried in the crook of his elbow. He was sound asleep.

"Someone else, then," she encouraged, her voice lower as she walked quietly toward the slumbering student, the only senior in her class. Probably another late night stocking groceries, she thought. Careful not to wake him, she grasped his jacket and spread it over

his shoulders as she rounded his desk to return to the front of the room.

"Miss Stevens, Mr. Meyer's at the door."

Louise looked up to see Ted Meyer, Westfield's principal, looming in her doorway. By the look on his face, he had urgent business.

"Have a look at the problems on page sixty-eight. Michele, will you go to the board and write that formula, please?" Louise could have sworn the girl blushed as her name was called.

Ted waited with his hand on the doorknob and gestured for her to step into the hallway. He then closed the door behind her.

"What's up, Ted?" Louise's stomach knotted as she readied herself for what her boss would say. The last time he came to her room with an expression like this one, he had brought news that two of her students had been killed in a car accident. The principal's grave look told her his message today was also serious.

"I need you to come downstairs with me, Lou," he said softly, placing his hand on her elbow.

His words shocked her and her heart began to hammer. "Rhonda," she whispered, stepping around him toward the stairwell.

Ted hurried behind her, but the stout man couldn't keep up with her long legs and urgent gait. By the time he reached the top of the stairwell, Louise had already turned the corner at the landing, dangerously skipping steps in her heeled shoes as she barreled toward the band room.

When she reached the bottom of the stairs, she saw dozens of students gathered in the hallway outside the band director's office. Their young faces were somber and it was clear that many were crying. All eyes were on her as she turned the corner and charged toward the band room on a dead run.

The scene inside was surreal. A huddled group of teachers parted at once to allow Louise access. She anxiously drew closer to see Rhonda Markosky lying on her back, her beautiful face swollen and purple. The physical education teacher knelt beside her, frantically pumping her broad chest in a mechanical rhythm. After every fifth compression, he would pause to allow another teacher to blow a deep breath into the unconscious woman's lungs.

Louise hurried to kneel alongside the still form, clutching the twisted hand tightly. "Rhonda." She rubbed the hand vigorously, imploring the motionless woman to respond. "Rhonda, I'm here." Please answer me, sweetheart.

No one else spoke as the grim reality of the situation settled among the teachers. Shouts from the hallway announced the arrival of the paramedics, but few in the room held any hope that the band director would survive what was apparently a massive heart attack.

"Stay with us, Rhonda." Stay with me, darling.

Louise numbly rose as the paramedics shouldered past and took charge of the stricken woman. They all watched as the defibrillator sent its futile jolts through the lifeless body. After several minutes, Ted placed an arm on his old friend's shoulder and turned her toward the door as the last of their hope slipped away.

Chapter 1

LOUISE FOLDED THE Fort Myers *News-Press* into quarters and set it aside. Today's crossword puzzle had a geography theme—not one of her favorite subjects, but it would be a nice challenge for later this afternoon. Yesterday's puzzle was dedicated to golf terms, and it had taken her only twenty minutes to knock it out.

She drained her coffee cup and gazed out at the canal behind her home. Boat traffic had dropped considerably since snook season ended in mid-December. Louise missed the company of the fishing enthusiasts. When the waterway was busy, it gave her a sense of being with other people, even if all she ever did was wave to those motoring past her seawall. Without the occasional boaters, there had been whole days during which she never saw another soul.

This was her first winter in Southwest Florida, where she and Rhonda had planned to live when they retired from teaching high school in Greensburg, Pennsylvania. For almost ten years, they had looked forward to the warm weather, and the free time they would have to engage in their two favorite pastimes—golf and each other. Instead, she had made the move alone early last fall when the old house in Greensburg sold. Were it not for the

Boston terrier at her feet, the loneliness of her new home would be almost unbearable.

"I hadn't planned on doing this by myself, Petie."

Intent on proving to his mistress that she wasn't in this alone, the small dog whimpered until she pushed back from the table to allow him access to her robe-clad lap. Petie seemed to sense she needed an extra dose of affection this morning, and he was more than happy to oblige.

Grateful for the reminder, Louise helped him up and waited as he turned twice, then dropped into a heap. His ears flattened in anticipation of her hands cradling his head. "You're such a good boy, you know that?" she asked, delivering a loving scratch behind his ears.

"Got to get that, Petie," she said, nudging the dog from her lap almost as soon as he got comfortable so she could catch the phone in the kitchen. "Hello."

"Hey, Lou! How are you doing today?"

"I'm good, Shirl." That was technically a lie, and Louise knew it, but she didn't want to inflict her depression on her longtime friend. Shirley and her partner, Linda, had retired to Cape Coral two years earlier, and had bent over backwards to include her in their activities ever since her arrival. "How about you and Linda?"

"We're doing great. We have a tee time at twelve-thirty. If you want to join us, I'll call out to Pine Island and see if they can find us a fourth. Think you're up for a round?"

Louise had been looking forward to playing golf this winter and getting to know some of the women who played in the senior league at the club. Unfortunately, those plans were put on hold when she clumsily fell in the shower and broke her left wrist. That was the week after she had joined Pine Island Golf Club, so she hadn't even had the chance to play. She had gotten her cast off the week before Christmas, but as yet had not tested her strength or coordination.

"I don't know if I'm ready for that yet. I was going to try to hit a bucket of balls this week and see how it felt."

"Maybe you should, Lou. A bucket or two might just get your swing back."

"It's probably going to take more than a bucket or two. But at least it doesn't hurt anymore."

"Well, hurry up and get with it! You're missing out on the best time of the year to be out on the course."

"Okay, you're my inspiration, Shirl. I might just go on out to the driving range today." It would be a great excuse to get out of the house, and it would put a stop to this feeling sorry for herself.

"Atta girl, Lou! You'll be back in the swing before you know it."

"If that was supposed to be a pun, it was awful."

Shirley chuckled as her quick mind lined up a few more. "Bad puns from me are par for the course, right?"

Louise groaned. "You're going to drive a wedge between us."

"Don't be silly, Lou. No one drives with a wedge."

"How does Linda putt up with you?"

Shirley let loose a groan of her own. "She putts up with me because I'm lovable. That reminds me, she's making lasagna on Friday night. You're coming over, aren't you?"

Louise hesitated to answer.

"Don't worry. It'll just be the three of us."

"Okay. You want me to bring anything?"

"Angel wants you to bring Petie," she answered, a reference to their greyhound.

"We'll be there. Thanks for calling." Louise calmed her roiling stomach, relieved that Shirley and Linda weren't scheming again to introduce her to one of their single friends. They tried that last fall, inviting a woman to dinner who, like Louise, was new to the area. When it became clear the newcomer was interested in more than just a dinner with friends, Louise excused herself early and dashed home to the comfort of her canine companion. The thought of dating someone sent her into a panic.

Louise hung up the phone and scribbled a reminder on her calendar for Friday. With a sigh, she noted that the dinner with her friends was practically the only social event on her January schedule. *What a difference a year makes!* This time last year, her calendar had been full of things to do—boys' and girls' basketball games, band concerts, school plays, curriculum meetings—anything she could find to stay busy, to have someplace to go other than the quiet house. It was hard some days not to second-guess her decision to retire.

"I'm feeling sorry for myself again, Petie. You want to go for a walk?"

The dog's ears went up and he began to prance from the front door to the closet where his leash was kept. His mistress had just said his favorite word. He waited impatiently as she changed into a jogging suit and her sneakers.

"Come on, let's go." This was part of her regular exercise regimen, something she did twice a day for both herself and the happy terrier.

An hour later, Petie lay stretched out on the cool kitchen floor while Louise stood at her bedroom dresser in white micro-fiber golf slacks and her bra. Her morning routine was complete: breakfast and the newspaper, a walk through the neighborhood with Petie, a shower, and a check of her email and the weather in Greensburg.

The first part of her day seldom varied. For Louise, the challenge was finding something interesting to do next. Most days, she worked the crossword puzzle after lunch; and she was gradually working her way through the classics in literature, something she had always planned to do when she had more leisure time. In the evenings, she watched television, usually the news, a couple of game shows, then a movie or a ball game.

The one element Louise hadn't incorporated into her Florida routine was people. She craved laughter and friendship, two of the things she had treasured about her life with Rhonda, but she hadn't yet pushed herself to get out. In the four months she had lived in Cape Coral, she had met only a few of her neighbors, mostly young couples with small children. Linda and Shirley had made friends with a number of lesbian couples through their activities at the golf club, but the broken wrist had sidelined Louise. Now that it was healed, it was time for her to take the initiative and get out there to meet people and make friends.

Rhonda Markosky watched from the pewter frame on the dresser, her usual mischievous eyes following the love of her life around the room. The school picture was made in September of 1999, three weeks before she died.

"Turn your head, sweetie. I know how much you hate it when I wear blue and white." Louise drew a long-sleeved blue golf shirt from the drawer and slipped it over her head. Blue and white were the school colors at Westfield, and Rhonda complained that she had seen it enough in the band uniforms to last a lifetime. "Now wish me luck. I'm going to go butcher a bucket of balls."

Passing the full length mirror beside the bedroom door, Louise admired her look. She and Rhonda had loved collecting stylish golf attire.

The closet held two sets of clubs, her own and those of her late partner. Louise had parted with most of Rhonda's personal items, but the woman had so loved golf that she couldn't bring herself to get rid of either the clubs or the dozens of accessories, accumulated over the years as gifts at Christmas, birthdays, even Valentine's Day.

Exiting through the garage, she loaded her clubs into the trunk of her silver Mercury Sable and activated the automatic garage door.

"This will kill a couple of hours. Only about"—she easily did the math in her head—"a quarter of a million to go."

April 2000

"Shhhh ... here she comes!"

Louise halted in the hallway outside her classroom door, trying to catch a clue about what her homeroom was up to. The sophomores were generally well-behaved, but whenever they went completely quiet before she even entered the room, it was cause for concern.

"Good morning," she said, surprised to find her students already seated and facing forward. Darren Ulster, the man who had replaced Rhonda as band director, was standing at the back of the room. A large cardboard box sat atop her desk. "What's this?"

No one answered, but it was obvious by their excited grins that all of the teenagers knew the contents. Louise glanced from the box to their faces and back.

"Open it and see," Michele Sanders said.

Louise approached her desk with suspicion, grabbing a yardstick from the chalk tray as though she intended to poke the box before getting too close. "Is it alive?"

That brought a short burst of giggles, but no one said a word.

Filled with apprehension, she set the yardstick down on her desk and pulled back the cardboard top. The sight inside nearly melted her heart—a black and white puppy, not more than eight weeks old. "Oh, my goodness!"

The students left their seats en masse and started for the front of the room.

"Easy, everybody. You'll scare him," Michele warned as they clustered around their teacher's desk.

Louise finished folding back the flaps on the box. "Oh, my goodness," she said again, reaching inside to pick up the trembling dog. "Who are you, little fellow?"

"He's your new Boston terrier," Michele said, still grinning with excitement. "My neighbor's dog had puppies and everybody chipped in and bought him for you. Mr. Ulster helped too."

Louise was so touched that her eyes immediately filled with tears. She turned the puppy in her hands and held him to her face. "Did you hear that, little fellow? I guess you're coming home with me." He responded with a lick to her nose, which caused everyone to laugh. Louise cradled him to her chest and stroked his neck. "Does he have a name?"

"My neighbor called him Petie, but you can name him again if you want to."

Louise looked him over. "Petie suits him just fine." She scratched the dog underneath his chin and looked up into the smiling faces of the students gathered around her. Her heart swelled with love and gratitude for each of them. "You've managed to render me speechless."

"We hope you like him," a boy said.

"I think I'm in love with him already. Thank you all so much."

"He's in love with you too," Michele said.

The bell rang to announce the start of first period.

"I didn't even get to take roll," Louise said, still clutching her new puppy, but reaching with her free hand for her roll book as the students began filing out the door.

"I took care of it for you," Darren said. "Everyone was present. No one wanted to miss today."

"Thank you." Louise gave the band director a grateful smile, not just for taking care of her administrative duties, but for his hand in the surprise. "So how did they rope you into their conspiracy?"

Darren shrugged. "I heard Michele talking about it one day in band. When I found out what they were doing, I wanted to help."

"How are things going down in the band room these days?"

"I think we've smoothed out all the rough spots. They still miss her, though."

Louise nodded. "We all do." She had little doubt the puppy in her arms was meant to bring her cheer, a sign that her students had noticed her quiet desolation since Rhonda died. "You know, Rhonda would have liked you," she said, delighting in the smile it brought to the young man's face as he walked out the door.

The first wave of algebra students bustled into the classroom. Right away, they huddled around her desk and the new addition, just as her homeroom students had done.

"Something tells me we aren't going to get much math done today." She didn't mind one bit.

Chapter 2

LOUISE GRIMACED AS she watched her drive take a sharp right turn about eighty yards out from the tee. She had never had a problem with a slice before; what's more, she usually got at least a hundred and sixty yards out of her driver. Sure, she hadn't swung a club since last summer, but this was quite an unwelcome discovery. *That has to be the wrist.*

Smack!

She and Rhonda had taken up golf with Linda and Shirley nearly twenty years ago, all four joining a modest country club near their home. Summers off from teaching afforded lots of time to practice, and over the years, the women had become quite adept at guiding the "stupid little ball" into the "stupid little cup." Louise's long game had peaked about ten years ago; these days, her drives were shorter, but her chipping and putting had improved.

Smack!

Again, her shot sliced viciously, this time clearing the fence and falling onto the adjacent fairway on Number Nine.

"I don't know if they told you or not, but there's a fifty-cent surcharge for every ball that leaves the driving range."

Louise looked back to see a short, stocky woman of about sixty with bright blue eyes, and a shock of sun-bleached hair poking every which way from the top of her visor. The darkly tanned face, arms, and legs suggested this woman had spent many, many years on Florida's fairways. She was grinning, apparently amused by Louise's frustration.

Embarrassed that someone was witness to this horrible display, Louise looked away, trying to ignore both the remark and the remarker. Instead, she fished in her bag for a pitching wedge, confident that she wouldn't slice her short irons. Leveling her hips, she positioned her hands slightly in front of the ball that sat on the artificial grass tee.

Smack!

Louise frowned as she watched it fall well short of the 75-yard marker.

Smack!

Smack!

Darn it! Only fifty yards with a pitching wedge!

"You know, this game's got a lot of funny rules, but there isn't one that says you can't use a seven-iron when you need it."

The woman's teasing manner was lost on Louise, who bristled at the comment. She was irritated at her own loss of distance, and further exasperated by this stranger who suddenly found her game so interesting. Turning, she confronted her tormentor, intent on sending her on her way.

"Do you mind?"

"Not at all," the woman answered matter-of-factly, leaning against the ball dispenser as she folded her arms across her chest. "Usually, I get paid to say things like that, but I have the discretion to waive my fee in certain circumstances."

A perfectionist when it came to just about everything, Louise found this stranger's taunting humiliating. She hated making mistakes in front of people and she knew she was a better golfer than what she was showing today.

"Perhaps you should save your expert advice for somebody who's willing to pay for it." Louise regretted her tone as soon as the words left her lips. It wasn't like her to be rude to people ... *but this woman is so arrogant!*

"It's your lead arm, by the way. It's not pulling through, so you're getting the slice from pushing the ball with your trailing arm. And since the strength in the swing comes from the club speed ... which starts with the lead arm, you're not getting the distance."

"I know that! I haven't swung a club in a while. I didn't expect to come out here the first day and hit like Babe Zaharias." Louise couldn't seem to contain her sarcasm.

The woman chuckled. "That's good ... because she's dead."

Louise felt her face go beet red, and was unsure if it was anger or embarrassment. It was probably both and she had most certainly had enough.

"Would you be so kind as to go annoy someone else now? I would like to continue my practice in peace."

"Of course," the woman said, her smile still polite, but now not as warm. "By the way, you have a beautiful ... swing."

"What you have, my dear, is a beautiful behind," Marty Beck grumbled to herself as she headed into the clubhouse. She had no idea who the intriguing newcomer was, but she had definitely played her all wrong. Most people on the driving range at least chuckled at her overtures and eventually, they were charmed into taking a lesson or two. This woman had chewed her up and spit her out.

Marty entered the shop to find not her boss, but one of the boys who hustled tips by cleaning clubs and delivering them to the club drop after a round. "Hey, where's Bennie?"

"He had to go out to Seven. Ben Hogan's wrapped around the pin." In this case, Ben Hogan was not the late golfing great but a six-foot alligator that made his home in the lake between holes Four and Seven.

"I'll get the desk if you want to head on back out." Marty knew the kid made more money helping the members ... just like she made more money when she picked up a new client for lessons.

She walked behind the counter and went straight to the thick black notebook that held the new member applications. With its member rolls full, the Pine Island Golf Club operated as a private course during the busy season, November through May. That meant all of the golfers on the course today—including those on the driving range—were either members or their guests, and a guest wasn't likely to be left alone hitting a bucket of balls.

"So why don't I know you?" Marty asked aloud as she thumbed through the recent applications. The last entry in the book was one she had taken from a man four weeks ago when the club reached capacity. Bennie must have signed up the woman on the driving range; Marty was sure she would have remembered meeting someone like that.

Someone like what? She stood on her tiptoes to see if she could catch another glimpse of the mysterious woman through the window, but the building that housed the golf carts blocked the view of the far end of the driving range where she had been hitting.

Okay, someone so attractive with such a natural swing. And someone who cares enough about her game to practice with intensity. Marty really liked to see the casual players work on their game instead of just coming out on the weekends to hack. Helping people play well was what the job was all about for her. If golfers cared enough to take a lesson now and then and practice on the range, she respected their game, no matter what they scored. Heck, even she and Bennie took turns helping each other work out kinks from time to time. A serious golfer never outgrew the need for coaching and practice.

"Whatcha doing?" Katie Compton breezed through the doorway that separated the pro shop from the lounge and snack bar. Katie managed the food and beverage side of the clubhouse. Though new to Pine Island, the young woman was an old hand at this kind of work and the members had taken to her right away.

"I was just looking at the member books. Did you see a woman come in a little while ago on her way out to the driving range?"

Katie shook her head and came to look out the window.

"You can't see her from here. She's down on the end." Marty closed the book and put it back in place beneath the counter. "I was just wondering who she was. I hadn't seen her before today and our last new member came on a month ago."

"Maybe she joined while you were up in North Carolina."

"Why would she wait all this time to come out to hit?"

"I don't know. Maybe she comes to play on your days off."

Marty doubted that. Though Tuesdays and Wednesdays were her regular days off, she usually ended up at the club anyway, either to give lessons or to join a foursome on the course. "I don't think so. Maybe Bennie just let her hit today on a guest pass or something."

"So how come you're so interested?"

Katie's teasing tone caused Marty to frown. "It's not a big deal or anything. I just didn't recognize her is all."

"Right, I've noticed that you tear through the member book every time you see a new face."

"You're a smart ass. Don't you have dishes to wash or something?" Marty marched behind the grinning woman, swatting her with a towel until she disappeared back into the lounge.

The uncharacteristic lull at the pro shop ended as the afternoon wave of golfers began streaming in. Marty never got another chance to walk back out and take a peek at the stranger.

August 1966

Louise entered the school library filled with anticipation. She was excited about seeing her fellow teachers after the summer break, and eager to get another school year underway. Today was the Thursday before Labor Day, and the first day back for teachers in Westmoreland County. They would have two days to get their classrooms in order before the students returned on Tuesday.

"Louise! Look how much your hair has grown."

"Hi, Betty. It's so good to see you again." Louise gave the home economics teacher a warm hug. They shared cafeteria duty during fourth period, and had gotten to know each other quite well. "I was in Wheeling most of the summer with my dad and I just decided to let it grow." For the past four years at Westfield, she had worn her dark hair short, teased high in the style of the day with bangs that covered her eyebrows. Now it reached just below her ears, and she had it parted on the side and curled under all the way around.

"How is your father?"

"He's fine, but he's lonely now that Mom's gone. He wants me to come back home and get a job there, but I told him how much I like Westfield."

"I'm sure he misses you, but I'm glad you're staying here."

"Me too. I can't imagine ever leaving this place ... and all my friends. It's my home now."

The women made their way through the crowd of teachers to a table in the corner, where their principal and the secretarial staff handed out class rolls and duty rosters. Right away, they picked up their packets and stepped away from the table to compare assignments.

Louise groaned. "I can't believe I drew cafeteria duty again. How about you?"

"Yippee! I'm the Class of '70 sponsor this year. No more food fights."

"Aw, I'm going to miss our talks. You always made lunch so much fun."

"I'm sure we'll still see plenty of each other, though. Look, they finally got us one of those electric percolators for the teachers' lounge. No more running down to the cafeteria for coffee." They stopped to draw two cups from the aluminum pot, both noting the librarian's nervous demeanor at the rare proximity of beverages to her precious books. "I dare you to act like you just spilled yours."

Louise chuckled with mischief and turned, her laughing brown eyes meeting those of a woman she didn't know standing with an unfamiliar group across the room. She was surprised when the stranger shot her a bright smile. "I see we have a few new faces," Louise said, turning back to Betty when the woman looked away.

"Oh, that's right! I meant to tell you that I met the new math teacher. His name is Mitch Lowry and he transferred over from the junior high. I talked to him the other day when I came in to order my supplies."

"I'll be sure to say hello then. I wonder what he teaches." Louise was elated to find that she had inherited the six Algebra II sections from Mrs. Klecknor, who moved with her husband to Philadelphia at the end of the last school year.

"He said he likes geometry. That's why he wanted to teach high school." Betty leaned closer so that Louise could hear her whispered

words. "That's him with his back to us. He's not bad, Louise. And I noticed that he wasn't wearing a wedding ring."

Louise blushed demurely, recognizing her friend's implication. "I'm sure he's very nice, and I look forward to working with him."

"We should go over and say hello."

"Do you know any of the other new teachers?" She was curious about the woman who had looked at her and smiled.

"I think that woman talking with Mitch is Rhonda Markosky. She's the new band director. She was at the junior high too. My friend Pat teaches home ec over there and she says Rhonda just kept them in stitches all the time." As if on cue, the group of new teachers laughed aloud. "And the kids love her."

"Let's just hope she can hear better than Mr. Jones," Louise said, her reference to the former band director, now retired. "Look, she's drinking a Pepsi already and it isn't even nine o'clock."

"Come on. Let's go introduce you to Mitch."

Louise could feel her confidence wane as she walked behind Betty, anxious about what kind of impression she would make on the new math teacher. She hated the awkward feeling that always seemed to descend whenever she was around men who might be interested in her. She hoped Betty wouldn't make her matchmaking efforts obvious, especially in front of the new band director, who might herself be attracted to Mitch Lowry. The two junior high transfers were obviously friends.

"Hi, everyone! Welcome to Westfield." Betty smiled with her usual warmth and enthusiasm. "I'm Betty Carlson, the home economics teacher."

"Hi, Betty. Good to see you again." Mitch stepped forward and offered his hand.

Louise hung back, waiting for Betty to make the introductions. Before that could happen, Ted Meyer, who taught civics and world history, joined the group.

"Sounds like the newcomers are making trouble already. What's so funny over here?" he asked.

"I just told Rhonda what the drummer got on his IQ test," Mitch answered, still grinning at his joke. "Drool. Get it?"

The new teachers laughed again, all looking at the band director for her reaction.

"Are you going to let him get away with making fun of your students, Rhonda?" Ted asked playfully. It was clear she was biting her tongue to suppress what was likely the most delicious comeback.

"I've got one for you, Mitch," the new band director finally said. "What do math teachers use for birth control?"

Louise's face burned at the mention of such a risqué topic in mixed company. For an instant, she contemplated turning away, but as a math teacher herself, she couldn't resist hearing the answer.

"Their personalities!" Rhonda announced, roaring with laughter as her friend from the junior high absorbed the insult with obvious good humor.

Louise, on the other hand, was not amused at being the butt of this woman's joke, even though her inclusion had been inadvertent.

"That was a good one," Ted said, still chuckling at the antics of these newcomers. "Say, have you met everyone?" He held out his arm to invite Louise inside the circle and introduced her to the new teachers one by one.

"And what do you teach?" Rhonda asked, still smiling.

"It so happens I teach math," Louise answered icily.

"Well, I ... uh, I think we have cafeteria duty together."

Chapter 3

LOUISE TURNED IN the shower to allow the pulsating nozzle to massage her knotted shoulders. In retrospect, she should have stuck to her plan to start with only a small bucket of balls. But the kinks in her game—the slice and the loss of distance—had compelled her to keep practicing, and now she was paying a price for being overly ambitious.

She had been stubbornly determined to work out the slump on her own after that golf pro had intruded on her practice. Dismally, she realized the woman was probably a permanent fixture at Pine Island, and sooner or later, they would meet again. Louise hoped to have her game back by then. It was embarrassing to make so many mistakes, especially since the woman was a professional golfer and would probably be watching her.

To her great consternation, Louise had been unable to stop thinking about the arrogant golf pro. She felt bad that they had gotten off to such an inauspicious start, but the woman had just come off as such a know-it-all.

"She's a golf pro, Louise. She's supposed to know it all," she reasoned aloud, turning off the shower as the water began to cool. When she joined the club last fall, she had met Bennie Benfield, but there was no mention in any of her club materials that Pine Island also had a woman pro.

"I wonder if ..." Louise hastily pulled on her robe and returned to the small study, clicking on her computer's Internet icon. She twisted back and forth in the swivel chair as she waited for her ISP to connect. Moments later, her question was answered.

"Seasonal pro, Martha Beck." A picture of the smiling golfer leaning on her driver accompanied a brief biography.

Martha Beck joined the professional staff at Pine Island Country Club in 1986. A native of Holland, Michigan, Marty played on the LPGA tour for three years, ending her career with an eighth place finish in the 1968 U.S. Women's Open at Hazeltine National Golf Club in Minneapolis. In the summer months, you can find her at Elk Ridge Golf and Country Club in Banner Elk, North Carolina. And when she's not on the golf course, you—Never mind, this is one lady you can always find on the golf course!

Louise squinted and peered at the thumbnail photograph, shaking her head. The golf pro appeared much younger and several pounds lighter in the photo than she had the other day on the driving range. "I bet this picture was made the day you started work there." Martha Beck was attractive in a rugged sort of way ... more so now, Louise admitted. She didn't mind a woman with extra weight—Rhonda had put on quite a few pounds as she got older, eventually wearing a size 18 in most clothes. In fact, Louise preferred the older, stockier version of the golf pro to this one of several years ago. The present-day Marty appeared happier and more comfortable with herself.

Louise was startled to realize where her thoughts had wandered. It shouldn't matter to her one whit if Martha Beck was skinny or stout!

Marty sat at the end of the table, shivering in the paper shift. Why in the world they always kept these rooms so cold was a mystery to her. It was bad enough that she had been kept waiting almost forty-five minutes. She was about to get up and put her shirt back on when the door to the examining room finally opened.

"Marty! How are you feeling?"

"Like a popsicle. Are you guys hanging meat somewhere?"

Dr. Lowenstein laughed impassively, ignoring her complaint. "Let's have a look at your incision. Lie back on the table, please." Marty did as instructed and the doctor opened her top to inspect the scar on her belly. "Have you experienced any more difficulties with digestion?"

"No."

He went through his verbal checklist as he prodded her incision. "Well, it seems you're progressing right on schedule. The incision looks fine, but I think it's best if we give it about three more weeks to heal before you start swinging a club again."

Marty sighed. She had hoped to be cleared to play, but hadn't really expected it so soon after the surgery. The emergency gall bladder removal had come following a severe attack a month ago.

"Are you still following that low-fat diet I prescribed?"

"Yes," she answered glumly.

"Good. I'd like to see you drop twenty-five pounds. I think you'll feel better in the long run, and I know it will be healthier for you."

"Twenty-five pounds!"

"At least that much. That will put you at one-forty, which is still a little on the heavy side for someone who's only five-two."

Marty sighed again. The only thing she ever lost on a diet was her sense of humor. "I'll give it a shot."

The doctor departed and Marty began to get dressed. She was glad to have the visit over with, but disappointed he hadn't cleared her to go back out on the course. At least it wasn't cutting into her work too much, she reminded herself.

It was two full days before the soreness finally dissipated enough for Louise to consider returning to the driving range. As she went through her morning routine, she made the decision to take it easy today; and if that golf pro came around again, she would try to be nicer.

The weather forecast called for temperatures in the low eighties, the warmest day since early November. Louise had worn her jacket on her morning walk with Petie, but pulled it off so she could feel the sun on her arms. Though it was a glorious day to play golf, she wasn't yet ready to venture onto the course. Her swing still needed work.

Louise chose dark green slacks with a pale yellow sleeveless golf shirt for her outing. She would be underneath an awning at the driving range, so there wasn't any real danger of getting sunburned. Still, she thought it was a good idea to protect her face, so she put on a bit of foundation. That made the skin around her eyes look pale so she dressed them with a bit of eye shadow, just enough to bring them out. To balance the look, she finished with a touch of lipstick.

Before leaving, she took a moment to appraise her look. *Not bad for sixty-three.* For the most part, she had kept the same figure throughout her adult life; except recent years had deposited an extra ten pounds, nearly all of it on her hips. She hadn't put up a fight at all when her hair began to go gray, and she was pleased now that the silver contrasted nicely to the few dark strands that remained.

"Oh, my hat would look good with this!" she said aloud, returning to her closet for her favorite straw hat, wide-brimmed with a black sash. She studied her appearance once more and her shoulders slumped. "You're just going to the driving range, silly. You probably won't even see a soul."

Fifteen minutes later, Louise pulled the Mercury into a shady spot beneath a pine tree. Her parking spot was adjacent to the awning for the driving range, so she set out her clubs on a vacant tee before checking in at the clubhouse for her token.

"Hello, Bennie." She greeted the pro amiably.

"Hi, there. How'd it go on the range the other day?"

"Not too bad. I just got the cast off my left arm so it's still a little weak, but I hope to start playing again soon."

"That'll be great. Say, we have a drawing here for some accessories ... you know, gloves, ball sleeves, socks. Why don't you fill out one of these slips for me?"

"Of course, thank you. And I'd like to get a couple of tokens for range balls ... a large bucket, I think."

"Sure thing." Bennie took her money and handed over the tokens for the ball machine. "Good luck today."

"Thank you." Louise scanned the crowd of golfers around the pro shop, hopeful that Martha Beck would be among them. She needed to get their uncomfortable first meeting behind them, and the only way to do that was for Louise to apologize for her rudeness on Monday. But the blond woman was nowhere to be seen.

Louise went on out to the range and loosened up a bit by stretching her arms and twisting back and forth. Then she filled her bucket and dumped about a dozen balls into the trough next to the tee. Today she would start with her pitching wedge and work up to her driver. Maybe she could straighten out the wrinkles in her swing before she got to the fairway woods and that worrisome slice would be gone.

Before long, she was lost in the rhythm of her task, swinging smoothly and reclaiming a bit of her lost distance. She was startled by a familiar voice and turned to see Martha Beck coaching a woman of about fifty who wore entirely too much makeup and obviously colored her dark red hair.

"That's it, follow through," the pro encouraged.

"I don't know, Marty. It still doesn't feel right," the woman whined. "Maybe you could show me again … you know, holding the club with me like we did the other day?"

Louise picked that moment to switch from her seven- to her six-iron, unable to resist a peek at the personalized lesson the pro was giving this Tammy Faye Baker look-alike. Marty was settled behind the woman, her muscular arms wrapped around her waist, her hands closed over the woman's hands as they gripped the club. In tandem, they drew the club overhead.

"That's right, parallel to the ground," she coached.

Together they swung through, sweeping the club head in a perfect arc past the trailing shoulder.

"Just like that."

"That felt great," the woman gushed. "Let's do it again!"

"That felt great. Let's do it again," Louise muttered in a low squeaky voice. Both of those women acted like they were up for the Flirt of the Year Award.

Smack!

She hooked her six-iron.

Smack!

Smack!

Still hooking, but better distance. That was because Louise was swinging harder than usual, instead of letting the club do the work. Too much of that, and she would be sore again tomorrow.

Smack!

Smack!

"You know, we're open till dark. You don't have to hurry."

Louise felt her face go red. *Why does this woman always show up when I'm screwing up?* "You again!"

"Now don't get excited. I was giving a lesson and saw you over here. Thought I'd just say hello and properly introduce myself. I'm Martha Beck, Marty to my friends."

"Hello, Martha," Louise answered curtly, emphasizing her choice of names. In only a matter of minutes, she had gone from wanting to apologize to being irrationally irritated.

"Hi." Marty looked over her shoulder at her struggling student, then back at the pretty woman who didn't seem to like her yet. "Uh, nice hat."

Marty shoved open the door to the pro shop and went straight behind the counter to where Bennie sat counting receipts. "Did you get her name this time?"

Without looking up, the head pro held the slip of paper over his shoulder.

Marty snatched it and grabbed her glasses from the drawer. "Louise Stevens. Who is she?"

"She's on the printout. She joined last September."

"Why hasn't she played?"

"Said something about just getting her cast off. She must have broken something right after she signed up."

That would explain why she hadn't come around, Marty thought. But there was no explaining that woman's disposition. "Have you ever heard of anybody here at Pine Island who didn't like me? I'm adorable!"

Bennie chuckled, figuring the newcomer had dressed Marty down again. "What did you say to her?"

"I just introduced myself ... and I told her she was rushing her swing."

"Some people don't like criticism. They only want advice when they ask for it."

"I guess." Marty pulled out the member book again and went back to September, finally locating the information for Louise Stevens. She lived close by, over near West Cape High School. She moved here last fall from Greensburg, Pennsylvania. That sounded familiar ... someone else at the club was from there. She was *never married* and listed her occupation as *schoolteacher, retired.* Her other interests were music and reading; and she had a pet, a Boston terrier named Petie. Marty smiled with satisfaction when she read the emergency contact information: Shirley Petrelli or Linda Druschel.

Louise Stevens was family.

Chapter 4

WHERE'S ANGEL?" LOUISE teased Petie, who stood in the passenger seat with his feet on the dashboard trying to find his friend. "Huh? Where's Angel?"

Petie began to bark and Louise petted him to calm him down. She put the car in park and turned off the engine. When she opened her door, the terrier vaulted her lap, hurrying toward the front door of Shirley and Linda's house.

"Wait for me!" She reached behind her and grabbed the fresh-cut flowers she had picked up at the grocery. On the way over, she was thinking it was time she returned her friends' hospitality, and now that she had her cast off, she would plan a small dinner party of her own.

The front door opened and the greyhound dashed out to meet his friend. "Go see Petie!" Angel's long tail wagged and Petie's twitched in shameless joy. Both dogs stopped suddenly to relieve themselves against a lemon tree in the front yard. Then they switched places and relieved themselves again.

"Those two are so predictable!" Louise exclaimed.

"So are you," Linda answered, spying the flowers. "You were told not to bring a thing."

"I just picked these up at the store today. I thought we could enjoy them together."

"Come on in."

Louise inhaled the savory odor of basil and garlic, both of which were generously used in Linda's tomato sauce. "Dinner smells delicious. I still haven't figured out how it is that the German in this house cooks the best Italian food, while the Italian ..."

"Can't boil water," Linda finished. "Good thing she's handy with power tools."

Louise helped herself to a vase from beneath the cupboard and set the flowers on the counter, pleased to note how they brightened the room.

Shirley handed Louise a glass of Chianti. "So how did it go at the driving range?"

Louise frowned. "Not so good. I've started slicing my driver and fairway woods, and yesterday, I was hooking my long-irons."

"How does your arm feel?"

"It doesn't hurt anymore. It's just not very strong. I was hitting the ball farther yesterday, but it was all over the place."

"You ought to call Marty Beck. She's the pro at Pine Island and I bet she could help you with it," Linda suggested innocently.

"I don't think I ... well, Bennie Benfield is the one I usually deal with out there."

"Bennie's nice," Shirley agreed. "But Marty's a hoot. She really knows her stuff too. And she goes to our church," she added, using her favorite euphemism to describe other lesbians.

"I've seen Marty Beck in action," Louise said, not making eye contact with either of her friends. "She's quite a flirt. It's a little inappropriate if you ask me."

"Marty? No, she's harmless," Linda said. "I don't even think she sees anybody."

"I heard she went through a bad breakup a long time ago," Shirley added.

"Still, if I'm going to take a lesson, I'd just as soon have it with Bennie. He's always been respectful."

Shirley shrugged in defeat, not understanding at all Louise's strange reaction to their friend, the golf pro. "You think you'll be ready to play next week? We're on for Thursday. If you want, I'll call out to the club tomorrow and see if they can get us a fourth."

"Sure. But I warn you, I'm probably going to be hitting the ball everywhere but in the fairway."

With that settled, the women sat down to dinner and their usual friendly banter. Louise appreciated these friends more than she could ever say. They alone knew what she went through in losing Rhonda, and they had been there to help her through it. Like Rhonda, Shirley had been a band director, but at neighboring Greensburg High School, and she had keenly felt the loss of her dearest friend. It was Shirley and Rhonda's chance meeting at a band workshop over twenty years ago that had brought the four friends together.

"Oh, Shirley and I want you to come with us to the Valentine's Dance. It's a fundraiser for the Gay and Lesbian Community House, and we had the best time last year! We met so many nice people."

"A dance?" Louise could feel her stomach knotting. In her whole life, she had been in lesbian bars only three or four times, and that was when she and Rhonda had gone out of town. The last thing on earth she wanted now was to find herself in a place where women might ask her out. "I don't know, Linda. I don't think ..."

"Please say yes. We'll go together, just the three of us. I'll even let you dance with Shirley."

Louise shook her head. "I don't think so. Valentine's Day is a special occasion. You two should be together without having to worry about a third wheel."

"You're not a third wheel to us, Louise. You're our friend and we like being with you. Please think about it," Linda pleaded.

"Okay, but I'm not promising anything."

Louise waited for her computer to come to life, eager to check her email so she could get out to the driving range. She smiled when she saw a note from Spartan02, the screen name for former student Michele Sanders. When Michele had asked upon graduation if she could email her favorite teacher, Louise saw no reason to decline. She would never allow anyone close enough to know about her relationship with Rhonda, especially a former student, but that didn't mean they couldn't stay in touch, perhaps even be friends.

> *Dear Miss Stevens,*
> *Sorry I haven't written for awhile, but my classes this semester are even harder than the ones I took last fall. I couldn't believe that was even possible! I did make the dean's list, though, so I guess all that studying paid off. I wanted to ask you about spring break, which is the third week in March. I'm going with my parents to Sarasota to visit my grandmother and I see on the map that Cape Coral isn't far away. I was hoping it would be okay if I drove down for a quick visit just to say hi, and maybe get some career advice. If it doesn't work out, that's all right. I'll just find another way to keep driving you crazy!*
> *Love, Michele*

Louise laughed at the last line, remembering how Michele had promised at graduation to write her so often that it drove her crazy. It would be nice to see a friendly face from Westfield, she thought, especially Michele's.

Dear Michele,
Congratulations on making the dean's list! I'm very proud of you and it doesn't surprise me at all that you're doing so well. It would be terrific to see you in March. What do you say we put your golf class from last semester to good use and take on the links here at my club? That will give us a nice chance to relax and catch up. Just let me know when you'll be available and I'll make us a tee time. You want career advice? Retire! <g> Study hard!
Love, Louise Stevens

July 1966

"Good morning, ladies and gentlemen," the announcer barked to the crowd, just as he had when he sent the preceding nine groups of three off the first tee at the Hazeltine National Golf Club in Minneapolis. "At the tee is ..." He went on to introduce the first golfer in the group, highlighting the fact that she was last year's Open champion and the leading money-winner for 1965. Her tee shot sailed to the right over the hill out of sight, and the crowd applauded.

"At the tee is ..." The second woman in the group was one of the hottest players on the tour this year, having won the two previous tournaments in Milwaukee and Iowa. Her shot also cleared the hill on the right, and the crowd cheered.

Finally, the third golfer approached the tee, her blond ponytail draping over the back of her visor. Unlike the others in her group, who wore culottes and sleeveless blouses, this one was dressed in shorts and an open-collar golf shirt.

"At the tee is Martha Russell, from Holland, Michigan. Miss Russell has played on the LPGA tour for three years, finishing third at the Peach Blossom Open in Spartanburg, South Carolina, in 1965."

Marty cringed at the meager introduction. Here she was, playing the best golf of her life, teeing off on the last day of the U. S. Women's Open in the next to last group, just one group behind the leaders.

After yesterday's blistering round of seven under, she was tied with these two women for fourth place with a legitimate shot of winning the championship. That round—a course record for tournament play at Hazeltine—had won her the attention of both the sportswriters and the gallery, a first for the struggling pro.

"Remember, it falls left over that hill, so you want to stay high on the right," her caddy advised. Wallace Beck was a longtime friend and golf buddy from her hometown. Realizing his own limitations with the game, he had thrown in with Marty when she decided to try to make it on the ladies' pro tour. For three years, they had traveled the country in an old station wagon on a shoestring budget, finishing out of the money on roughly half her starts.

"You don't think I should try to carry the slope on the left like I did yesterday?" With nothing to lose, Marty had taken one chance after another in the third round, even finishing the day with an eagle on the par five eighteenth hole.

"There's a lot of money at stake here, Marty. If it were me, I'd play it safe all day."

The young golfer considered his advice. If she played a conservative game, she stood to collect over a thousand dollars with a fourth or fifth place finish. But dropping as few as five strokes could mean falling out of the serious money. On the other hand, a repeat of yesterday's round might net her the $4,000 winner's purse, and would likely land her a sponsor.

Marty nodded and addressed the ball.

Smack!

The gallery gasped and applauded excitedly as her hammered drive sailed cleanly over the slope on the left side. For the first time in her brief career, she watched as a good portion of the crowd climbed down from their bleacher seats to follow her group on the course.

Wallace shook his head as she handed him the club. Marty Russell was about the stubbornest woman he knew.

Chapter 5

MARTY BURST THROUGH the doors of the pro shop, spotting Bennie crouched over his desk. "Hey, the guys are here in the truck for Ben Hogan. You want to take them out there, or you want me to?"

Bennie dropped his pencil with a sigh. "I'll go. If I spend another minute looking at these numbers, I'll go blind."

"I told you to let Katie look at those. She's really good with that kind of thing."

"Yeah, maybe I will." He stood up and grabbed his cap. "Oh, your buddy Pat Shapiro called a little while ago. I told her you'd call her back when you got in."

"Did she say what it was about?"

"No, but I'd guess it has to do with Tami, wouldn't you?"

Tami Sparks was the teenage phenom Marty had worked with at Pine Island four years ago. Marty knew early on the girl could be a legend someday if she got the right help.

She dialed the number of her friend and waited, wondering for the tenth time today if the lovely Louise Stevens might show up to hit a bucket of balls.

"Hello."

"Hi, Pat. It's Marty."

"Hey! How have you been?"

Marty sat down on the edge of the desk. "Good. I donated my gall bladder to science a few weeks ago, but the stitches are holding."

"Ouch! You okay?"

"Yeah. What's up?"

"Guess which amateur got a sponsor's invitation to a tournament up in North Carolina two weeks before the Open?"

"The one in Asheville? How'd she manage that?"

"It turns out the sponsor is a University of Florida alum and he's been following Tami's season in the conference."

"Is she still undefeated?"

"Still rolling. But here's the best part. Are you sitting down?"

"Yeah."

"If she does well, she's going to enter the qualifying tournament in September. Jeff thinks she's ready, and he's agreed to caddy for her on the tour."

Marty jumped off the desk and stood ramrod straight. "Wow! What do you think? Is she good enough to go pro?"

"I think so. But more important, she thinks so."

"Wow! Pat, this is fabulous! Does she have any idea how big a decision this is?"

"Are you kidding? She's getting so excited that I'm probably going to have to spend the next five months bringing her back down to earth so she can hit the ball."

"This is just great news." But inside, Marty's stomach was churning. She always knew this day would come, and that the regrets about giving up the chance to guide Tami onto the pro tour would gnaw at her.

"You know, this would never have happened if you hadn't spotted her early on."

"Come on. We both know that's not true. She's too good to stay hidden. And besides, you and Jeff are the ones that turned her into a champion, Pat."

"That's nice of you to say, but Tami and I both know how important it was for her to get the basics from somebody like you. Anyway, I hope you'll make it over there. It'll be good to see you again."

"Count on it. But do me a favor and check with Tami first. I don't want to show up and make her nervous."

"Will do, but I don't think it will be a problem."

"Thanks for calling, and let Tami know that I'm proud of her."

"Sure thing."

Marty hung up and the phone rang again immediately. It was Bennie on his cell phone calling for backup. She stuck her head in the bar to ask Katie to keep an eye on the pro shop; then she took off in a cart toward Seven.

Louise bent over to place another ball onto the tee. She was happier today with her stroke, but she still had problems with her fairway woods and long-irons.

She had spent the last three days cooped up in the house while Southwest Florida got five inches of much-needed rain. She rejoiced in knowing Greensburg got its equivalent in snow, about fifteen inches over the weekend. No matter how homesick she was for her old life, there wasn't a single day Louise missed the snow.

As she had watched the rain fall steadily on Sunday, she wondered what people like Marty Beck were doing. They probably had paperwork and such to tend to, or they rearranged their stock and repaired the broken carts. Louise doubted a golf pro would just take the day off because of rain. Besides, she knew there were lots of fools who played in the rain, especially on weekends, because it was their only chance all week to hit the links.

Louise had been thinking again that she needed to apologize to Marty, especially since it was obvious Shirley and Linda thought a lot of her, but she was nowhere in sight today. Just then, the object of her thoughts suddenly barreled past in a golf cart with Bennie Benfield, headed for the clubhouse. Rather than hit her few remaining balls, Louise scuttled them into the grass in front of the tee and shouldered her bag. Quickly, she marched into the clubhouse just as the golf pro disappeared through the opposite door into the parking lot.

"Hi, Louise. How'd you do?"

"Good, Bennie. I think I'm about ready to play a round." She noted his pants were wet from his ankles to his knees, but didn't even stop to think why.

"Just give us a call. We'll put you down."

"Thanks." Louise emerged into the parking lot just in time to see Marty climb into the passenger seat of a tan and green Subaru wagon. The driver was the woman who had waited on her earlier in the pro shop, a woman much, much younger than Marty Beck, and they were obviously familiar.

As the car drove away, Louise shook her head. "Some people just don't know how to act their age."

March 1995

"Hey, baby! Want to go out for dinner?" Marty pulled off her visor and hung it on the hook by the kitchen door, not missing the fact that the table wasn't set and there was nothing to suggest dinner was imminent.

Angela stormed into the kitchen, her face streaked with tears and her eyes red and angry. "Where have you been, Marty?"

"What do you mean where have I been? I was at work."

"Bennie said you weren't there—that you must have left."

"Yeah, he should have looked out on the driving range. I was giving a lesson." Marty was accustomed to Angela's irrational outbursts and she struggled to remain calm. This time, her girlfriend's tone seemed to hold more venom than usual. Marty couldn't understand why she was getting the third degree. It wasn't even dark yet, and Angela knew the course was open until the last golfer played in.

"He did look on the driving range. You weren't there."

"I was there all afternoon. You can't see all of the tees from the pro shop. If he'd put down the phone and walked out there, he'd have seen me."

"For your information, I didn't talk to him on the phone. I wanted to show you the part I got for the lawn mower and see if it was the

right one, so I stopped by after work. Bennie and I both walked out to the driving range and we didn't see you. Your car was already gone and that was over two hours ago."

Marty felt her stomach drop. She could count on one hand all the times in six years when Angela cared enough about what she was doing at the club to stop by, and of all days, she had chosen today.

"I can explain this, Angela."

"Don't bother, Marty. I'm not going to go through this again. I've put up with your flirting for six years and I even believed your lies about how innocent it all was."

"It was innocent!"

"Then where were you today? And don't insult me with another lie."

Marty slumped into a chair at the kitchen table. "Angela, I'm not like you think I am. I don't go out there every day looking to pick up somebody. I love you, and I want us to be happy together." Marty hadn't been happy in so long she had forgotten what it felt like. But she wanted to be.

"Then answer me. Where were you?"

Tears of guilt began to roll down the golfer's cheeks. "I was with somebody ... a woman I gave a lesson to this afternoon."

Angela slammed her fist on the kitchen table. "I knew it! You've been lying to me all these years and I've bought it, just like a fool."

"No! It was just ... we went for a drink. It wasn't anything more than that. I promise you, and I won't see her again."

"I told you not to insult me, Marty. I want all of your stuff out of here by Friday. And don't even think you're going to stay here tonight. I'm not putting up with you for another minute."

Marty's heart broke as she saw the pain in Angela's face. She had never cheated on anyone until today, and she had never felt worse in her whole life.

Chapter 6

LOUISE SCANNED THE lot for Shirley's station wagon. She was nervous about playing again, even more so after Shirley called to say they had gotten a fourth. Louise knew she was being silly, but she was anxious about the person with whom she would be paired today.

When they left Pennsylvania and their careers in the public schools, Linda and Shirley dropped the pretense of being only friends. Both of their families knew about their relationship, so there wasn't any reason to hide things anymore. Here in Cape Coral, they weren't exactly openly affectionate, but they used endearments that left little doubt to casual observers they were a couple.

That made Louise anxious for a couple of reasons. If they lined up someone for their foursome who was straight, the woman might be offended by their familiarity. Then Louise would be stuck with her in the golf cart for eighteen holes, trying to steer clear of the other two and keep the conversation going without talking about touchy subjects.

But it might be even worse if they lined up another lesbian—especially if she was single! The last thing she wanted was to play golf with somebody acting like they were on a date. That would probably send her into a tailspin not unlike the one after Linda and Shirley's dinner party with that woman last fall.

"Calm down, Louise," she admonished herself before getting out of the car. "At least you get to spend the afternoon playing golf with your two best friends."

Louise got out and retrieved her clubs from the trunk. Shirley and Linda seemed to be running late, but there was no reason to wait in the parking lot. She carried her clubs to the drop and headed into the clubhouse. She could pay her green fee and wait inside for her friends.

Or not.

Louise nearly turned around and walked back out when she realized Marty Beck was the only other person in the pro shop. Instead, she sidled in between the racks near the door and pretended to look at the golf shirts.

"We have some ladies clothing over on this side ... if you're into that sort of thing."

Louise felt her face redden. *Why on earth does this woman have to be so sarcastic about everything?* Shirley said it wasn't like that at all. She said Marty had an easygoing manner, that she didn't take many things seriously. Louise was going to try to give her the benefit of the doubt. Maybe if she laughed and went along with the joke ...

Before she could recover, Linda appeared at the front door. "Hi, Lou. You ready?"

Louise could only nod, her nervousness having caused her to swallow her tongue.

"Hey, Marty. Did you get us a fourth?"

"Sure did. Her name's Pauline Rourke. She's warming up on the driving range." She leaned across the counter and whispered loudly, "Red hair, extra makeup. Can't miss her." She grinned with mischief.

Not that woman! Louise remembered the flirtatious scene on the driving range last week. Not only was she going to be stuck with a single woman, but one who was ga-ga over Marty Beck, of all people!

Shirley joined them after parking the car, and the three women paid their green fees and picked up score cards. Louise needed new socks, but she felt a crushing need to get out of that shop—and out of the golf pro's presence. By the time they walked out to meet their fourth, her stomach was doing flip-flops.

Shirley and Linda took off in the first cart, leaving Louise paired with Pauline. Though apprehensive at first, by the turn on the ninth hole, Louise admitted to herself that she actually liked the flamboyant woman quite a bit. Pauline was new to Cape Coral and eager to make a lot of friends—women friends, she said.

"No more men for me! That's why I told Marty to call me whenever she had some sisters playing."

Louise blushed at the sudden realization that her friendship with Shirley and Linda had led people at the club—including Marty Beck—to conclude that she, too, was a lesbian. Not that it wasn't true … she just hated to think total strangers might be making assumptions that weren't any of their business.

"Do you like to go dancing, Lou?"

"I … well, I don't go out much," she rasped, her throat suddenly dry. She grabbed her Styrofoam cup and sipped a long, steadying drink of ice water through the straw. "I recently lost someone very dear … someone I spent over thirty years with. I don't really feel much like …"

"It's okay, I understand. When my husband left me for his bookkeeper, I thought I'd never go out with anyone again. It takes time."

"I don't know if time will be enough," Louise said quietly, as if to herself more than to Pauline. She pulled the cart up to the tee and got out. "This one's a par five, 470 yards. Better give it all you've got." She was finished talking about personal things, and managed to direct the conversation elsewhere through the back nine.

"I've enjoyed it, ladies," Pauline said as she peeled off her glove on the eighteenth green. "Anyone want to stop in for a cold one?"

The others nodded in agreement and filed into the clubhouse.

The after-golf socializing was something Louise had come to appreciate over the years. Being a member of the club was more than just having access to the facilities; it meant you were part of a community. That sense of belonging was what Louise missed most about Westfield High.

"What can I get for you?" The server perched over their table, familiar-looking blue eyes smiling a welcome.

Louise recognized the woman instantly as the driver of the Subaru—the woman Marty Beck had gotten into the car with. *She can't be more than thirty-five years old!* Louise couldn't imagine what someone so young and attractive would see in an older woman like Marty.

"The first round's on the house, Katie."

Louise's stomach jumped suddenly as Marty swooped into the lounge and pulled up a chair between her and Pauline.

"And could I get a club soda?"

Louise couldn't believe the golf pro's audacity. Here she was sitting down to flirt with one of her protégées and asking her ... whatever that young woman was ... to fetch her drinks.

"So when are you going to get back on the fairways, Marty?"

Shirley's question took Louise by surprise. *Back on the fairways?*

Marty sighed. "The doctor said two more weeks."

Doctor? Louise grew suddenly concerned. Marty appeared to be fine, so what could it be?

As if reading her mind, Shirley continued, directing her comments to Louise. "Marty had that same gall bladder surgery Linda had six years ago."

"Except mine was with a laparoscope," Linda said. "Just a little incision. Poor Marty had to be cut open."

"Aw, you poor baby!" Pauline gushed. "Are you all right?"

"I'm fine," Marty assured. "I think the doctor just wants to make sure I don't pop the stitches."

Louise unconsciously breathed a sigh of relief before returning to her irritated state. She still didn't think Marty Beck had any business going out with a woman half her age. Anybody could see what that was about!

The server returned, passing out the drinks, saving Marty's club soda for last. "Here you go, Mom."

Mom?

"Thanks, hon. Have you guys met my daughter?" Marty made the brief introductions, and Katie returned to her work behind the counter.

Her daughter?

"She and my grandson moved down here last fall from Michigan. It was a good thing, too. I don't know what I would have done if she hadn't been around to help after my surgery."

She has a daughter and a grandson! Louise suddenly felt silly about having jumped to conclusions. After all, Linda had said she wasn't seeing anybody. This was her family.

"So how was the round?"

"Not bad," Shirley answered. "Lou usually kicks our butts, but she's been gimpy with her arm lately, so I managed to beat her today by a couple of strokes."

"Yeah, I've watched her on the range. I can see that she's a natural," Marty said, smiling as she waited for a reaction from the gray-haired woman sitting beside her. "By the way, I'd like to officially welcome you to the Pine Island Golf Club, Miss Stevens. As a new member, you get one free lesson with the pro—that would be me—any time you want."

Louise was shocked at Marty's sincerity and she stammered to think of something witty to say. "You mean I haven't gotten that over with already?"

Marty chuckled and looked at her lap in resignation. "Well, the complimentary lesson isn't mandatory. You do seem to be a very good golfer, and I hope you enjoy playing here at Pine Island." With that gracious remark, Marty picked up her drink and walked back out to the pro shop.

The women sat in uncomfortable silence as they tried to make sense of what had just happened. All three were scowling at Louise as if she had been caught cheating on her score card.

"What?" she asked defensively.

No one answered, but their expressions remained unchanged.

"Fine!" Louise answered, pushing up from the table in pursuit of the golf pro. When she reached the doorway leading to the pro shop, she stopped and took a deep breath. *Try not to say anything else stupid, Louise.*

Marty was in the corner rearranging the sweater display. It was obvious inventory was down, since there was empty space on many of the shelves. Louise watched as the short woman stretched on her tiptoes, trying in vain to reach a folded stack on the top shelf.

"Let me," she said, her voice low and contrite. Long arms stretched over Marty's head and lowered the sweaters into her waiting hands. "Can't have you popping those stitches."

"Thank you," the red-faced woman muttered as she turned toward her benefactor.

"You're welcome." Louise waited, hoping Marty would make just one more attempt at friendship so she could respond in kind.

"Is there something I can do for you, Miss Stevens?"

"My friends call me Lou."

"What should I call you?"

"Touché." Louise looked down, her eyes not hiding her sense of shame. "How about you call me Lou? I'd like for us to be friends."

"Okay." Marty smiled tentatively. "Is there something I can do for you, Lou?"

Louise sighed. It was definitely her turn to make a friendly overture. "I've been having a little trouble with a slice, and I thought maybe you could—"

"Your slice isn't that bad. I think you just need to close your grip a little to keep the club from flaring. If you want to set up a lesson, we can try a few things. I bet we'll have it worked out in no time."

With mild disappointment, Louise noted Marty's professional demeanor, a marked departure from the teasing nature she had shown at the driving range. She chided herself inwardly for being so wishy-washy about how she wanted the golf pro to act. It wasn't fair to complain about one and then turn around and object to the other.

Maybe it wasn't really friendship Marty wanted, but a good working relationship at the club. That was a reasonable expectation, Louise thought. She shouldn't have read so much into it in the first place.

Marty went behind the counter and opened her appointment book. "How's Monday for you?"

Louise followed her and leaned over the counter to peer into the book. She could see Pauline's name etched in at ten. "Monday's good."

"One o'clock?"

"I can make that." It wasn't like her schedule was crammed full.

"I'll put you down, then."

They were spared the awkward search for parting words when a group of men bustled through the doorway, laughing and joking boisterously about their round.

"See you Monday," Louise said as she retreated to the lounge.

"One o'clock," Marty answered with a smile.

Louise stopped again in the doorway and drew another deep breath. She was immensely relieved to have the clumsy start with Marty Beck finally settled. So why was her stomach still in knots?

Marty and Katie climbed into the Subaru, this time with the mother behind the wheel.

"So that's the woman you've been asking everybody about," Katie said smugly.

"What are you talking about?"

"I'm talking about Louise Stevens, the woman who handed you your head when you tried to hustle her out on the driving range last week."

Marty tried to feign innocence. "Yeah, that was her. She finally came in to set up a lesson."

"And did you ask her out?"

"No! She has a slice and she wants some help working it out." Marty shot her grinning daughter an irritated look.

"Why didn't you ask her out? You know you want to."

"Where in the world did you get a crazy idea like that?"

"Well, let's see. Could it be that I keep finding the member book opened to her page? Or that I found her name and address in your pocket when I did the wash? And since when do you come into the lounge for a drink with members during the day?"

Marty looked away to hide her smile. Katie had her six ways from Sunday on this one, but her interest in Louise Stevens was apparently one-sided. "I'll admit that I think she's an attractive woman, but I don't think she's interested in me."

"Then what's wrong with her? You're a catch."

"I know, honey. But some people just can't see the obvious."

"Her hair's beautiful. I hope mine turns silver like that someday."

"Fat chance, kiddo. Your hair's just like mine. It's going to look like a dirty broom in a few years if you don't paint it." Marty was glad for the change of subject. She turned off Pine Island Road and pulled into a gravel lot next to a fenced-in playground. "Do you want me to go?"

"No, I'll get him."

Marty waited with the motor running while Katie collected six-year-old Tyler from day care. Having these two around these last few months sure had eased her loneliness, but Katie and her husband Mike needed to work out their problems. For that, her daughter and grandson might have to return to Michigan.

May 1967

The tardy bell rang for sixth period, the last class of the day. Standing in the hallway, Louise could see Joey Muir dashing toward her classroom, and she teasingly stepped into the room and grasped the doorknob. Ever so slowly, she pushed the door closed, allowing the boy to barely squeeze through the slim opening before it latched.

"That was mighty close, Mr. Muir. Would you go to the board, please?"

The class chuckled as Joey dumped his books on his desk and sheepishly took his place at the chalkboard. Everyone recognized this as Miss Stevens' way of encouraging a timely arrival to her class.

"Copy this expression and then write it as a ratio in its simplest form." She read aloud the number from their textbook and Joey wrote it on the board as instructed. "The rest of you get to try this from your desks, since you were conscientious about getting here on time."

Louise walked over and stood next to the confused student, walking him through the process of reducing both sides of the ratio. As she watched him work, she heard several students whispering at their desks, and distinctly caught the name of her friend, Miss Markosky. Louise planned to call Rhonda right after school to see why she had left before lunch. She hadn't seemed sick at all this morning in the teacher's lounge.

Subtly, she trained her ear on the conversation. If her students had any idea of her keen sense of hearing—

"... and the lady who lived there just barely got out! But some of her stuff got burned up."

"What was that?" Louise hurried to the group of girls who had been whispering. They immediately sat up straight and returned to their schoolwork.

"Sorry, Miss Stevens."

"What were you saying? Something about a fire?"

"Yes, ma'am. I was in the office just before lunch and the fire department called and said Miss Markosky's house had caught on fire."

Louise's heart began to race. Rhonda lived in an efficiency apartment on the top floor of a three-story house. Her landlady was an elderly woman. "Was anyone hurt?"

"No, ma'am. I don't think so."

"Has anyone heard from Miss Markosky since she left?" Louise scanned the room to see if the band members had gotten any news. No one replied. "I'm going to the office and see what's happened. Please continue with the remaining problems on this page."

Louise's attempts to get additional information were futile, and when the final excruciating minutes of the last hour passed, she left school at once en route to her friend's home. She couldn't bear the thought of Rhonda facing this kind of tragedy on her own.

In their first year together at Westfield, the two women had formed a solid friendship through their daily lunch discussions. Louise had even volunteered to ride the band bus with Rhonda to help chaperone the students when they traveled to away football games. Gradually, their time together had grown to also incorporate evenings and weekends. They didn't have all that much in common, but they enjoyed spending time together just the same.

Louise pulled up in front of Rhonda's house, horrified to see one whole side charred from the foundation to the roof. Several pickup trucks sat out front and people she didn't recognize carried salvaged belongings from the front door.

Rhonda had a private entrance, a wooden staircase on the side farthest from the fire. From the street, Louise could see the open door leading into her friend's apartment. She parked and carefully started up the stairs, which were wet and covered with a slushy ash. The stench of smoke was still heavy in the air, though the fire department was no longer on the scene.

"Rhonda?" She called from the stairs to announce her arrival. "Rhonda?"

Louise stepped into the dark apartment and the sight nearly broke her heart. Her friend sat on the floor, sifting through stacks of soggy, blackened sheet music.

"It's all ruined ... everything." Rhonda looked up and broke down into sobs.

Louise rushed to her friend's side and dropped to her knees, taking Rhonda in her arms and hugging her fiercely. "It'll be okay. Thank goodness this didn't happen in the middle of the night."

Rhonda squeezed back, smearing soot on Louise's white blouse. "My pictures of Daddy ..."

"Shhh. I'm so sorry, honey. At least it was only things and nobody was hurt." Louise couldn't bear to think of what might have happened to her dearest friend. She held Rhonda close, rubbing her back in small circles until the tears finally stopped. Louise scanned the room, noting with irony that the piles of sheet music, the clothes closet, and the dresser had taken the worst of it, while the kitchen area and bathroom—neither containing many personal items—had been spared.

"I have such a mess to clean up."

"I'll help you. Just tell me what you want me to do."

"You shouldn't even be in here, Lou. You're still all dressed up."

"So are you."

"That's because I don't have a choice. I'm going to have to wear this dress to school every day for the rest of the year." She managed a feeble smile.

"No you won't. We'll go to the Greengate Mall tonight and get you some new things."

Rhonda nodded in resignation. "At least I still have shoes," she quipped, pointing to the shoe pouches on the back of the bathroom door. As a band director, she was on her feet all day. When she dressed each morning, she always chose her outfit to go with the shoes she wanted to wear.

"Good thing you're such a shoe hound," Louise teased gently.

Rhonda stood and took another sad look around the room. "I didn't have much, Lou. But all of it was important to me." Her eyes filled with tears again.

"The only thing that matters is that you're all right."

"Somebody from the Methodist Church came up here a little while ago and said I could stay in their fellowship hall for a few days."

"You'll do nothing of the sort. You're coming home with me." Louise grew excited thinking about the idea of sharing her apartment with Rhonda. They were already spending most of their free time together. They were certainly compatible, and it would be fun to live together. "In fact, I can take my sewing machine back to Wheeling next weekend and you can have my extra bedroom. I don't sew that much anyway, so I don't really need the room."

"You mean to stay?"

"If you want to! We'll have to get another bed and dresser, but I was going to start looking for something for that room anyway."

"I don't need a whole bed," Rhonda answered, her own excitement building. She walked across the soot-covered room and grasped the brass headboard. "I can still use this. All I need is a new mattress and box springs."

"I have extra sheets," Louise offered. "And towels."

"My towels are okay. They're in here." Rhonda went into the bathroom and came out with a stack of folded towels. "They'll have to be washed to get the smell out but they're still good."

"Then it's settled. You're moving in with me as of right now. Let's get this stuff down to the car."

Rhonda grabbed her friend's arm as she began to gather up the few personal effects that had survived the disaster. "Lou Stevens, I don't think I've ever had a friend that I loved as much as you."

Louise folded Rhonda into her arms for another hug. "I love you too, Rhonda. And you're the best friend I've ever had."

Chapter 7

LOUISE TWISTED FROM side to side in front of the full-length mirror on the back of her bedroom door. She had tried on nearly everything in the house looking for something nice to wear for her golf lesson. Finally, on Sunday, she had made a trip to the country club at Burnt Store so she could find something that wasn't already hanging in the pro shop at Pine Island. Louise didn't like to look like everyone else.

She was satisfied with her choice, a white golf shirt with trim on the collar and cuffs to match her plaid slacks. Her saddle-oxford golf shoes gleamed from a recent polish, and the straw hat lay on the corner of the bed.

Each time she crossed the room, she saw the eyes of her departed lover following her as she primped and preened. Louise usually talked to the picture as she got dressed, but she hadn't done so today. She felt guilty for that, even more so because it made her feel like she had something to hide … which she didn't.

"I have a golf lesson today … a free one, because I'm a new member." It was silly to turn down a free lesson, so with that justification, she relaxed. "Remember the time we went to that golf clinic and that instructor kept putting his hands on your hips while you were swinging? I thought I was going to have to wrap my five-iron around his neck," she said, taking a seat on the corner of the bed. "Then you took a big drink of your Pepsi and burped for him like a frat boy." Louise shook her head and chuckled at the memory. "And when he walked off, you said he was lucky you didn't give him something from the other end. I laughed so hard I couldn't hit the ball to save my life."

Louise sighed heavily. "Golf just isn't as much fun without you, honey. Nothing is. But I'm trying." That settled, she gave Petie some fresh water and a scratch, and left for the club.

Well ahead of schedule, she arrived at the driving range. Marty Beck was nowhere to be seen, but that was okay with Louise. She wanted a chance to warm up a bit before they got down to the business of working out the problems with her swing.

Smack!

There was that wicked slice again. Marty had said something about closing her grip so the club wouldn't flare. She tried it.

Smack!

Her second shot was definitely better, and with more distance.

Smack!

Smack!

Louise hit those last two shots right down the middle, her slice no longer in play.

Smack!

The ball sailed cleanly off the tee, straight ahead for over a hundred and fifty yards. That was, without a doubt, the best drive she had hit in the last three years.

"So was there anything else I could help you with?" The golf pro had slipped up quietly to observe her student unobtrusively. "You appear to be quite the accelerated learner."

"I, uh ... I seem to have come out of my slump."

"I didn't think it was all that big a deal when I saw you hitting the other day. You were doing everything else so well, it didn't make sense for you to be slicing like that."

Louise was inordinately pleased at the compliment on her game, especially coming from a golf pro like Marty.

"But I have to confess that I'm a little disappointed you didn't need my help after all."

"That's not true! You were absolutely right about my grip. I brought my left hand over just like you said and now the club head comes around square."

"Then I'm glad I could be of service," Marty answered, not knowing if she should stick around or head on back to the clubhouse. Louise didn't seem to be in need of a lesson, and she didn't want to risk giving her unsolicited advice about what might make the ball carry another ten or fifteen yards. "I guess I should just—"

"But ... but I have this hook on my long-irons!" Louise exclaimed, sounding almost braggadocios. Quickly, she drew her three-iron from the bag, smacking her first shot over a hundred yards out on the fly, sans hook.

"Hmm ..."

Smack!

Still no hook.

Louise recalled the usual kinetics of a hook. On her next shot, she played the ball off her front foot, executing a neat dog-leg left.

"You should play the ball a little more in the center of your body, hands slightly in front," Marty corrected gently.

"Like this?" she asked, overstepping so that the ball was in fact closer now to her back foot. This time, she shanked it, sending it over the fence into the ninth fairway. "Oops! I know. That'll cost me fifty cents."

Marty chuckled, almost certain she was being played, though why the proud woman would want to do that was a mystery. "Tell you what. You line yourself up the way you think you ought to be, and I'll come over and fine tune your position."

Louise obliged, settling slightly off-center with her hands behind the ball. She knew it wasn't right, but wanted Marty to help her … so Marty would feel good about herself.

Marty stepped up behind her and reached around. "Okay, here's the problem. Let go of the club."

Louise did as she was asked, focusing completely on the muscular leathered arms that encircled her waist.

"To start with, you want the grip to rest against your stomach like this." She held the top of the grip with only her fingertip.

"Uh, my stomach's a little higher than that, Marty."

"Oh, okay." Glad her red face was hidden, the coach continued. "On taller people, it sometimes ... rests ... a little lower. Now on your irons, there's always going to be just a teensy lilt in the shaft. You know, if you let go of it, it would balance for just a second before it fell back. And the ball sits right in front of your nose with your feet spread even. Got it?"

Now acutely aware of the woman who was pushed up behind her, Louise suddenly took stock of what was happening. Here she was, acting juvenile over Marty Beck, just like Pauline Rourke had done the other day. Furthermore, she was making fools of both of them with her put-on girlish ineptitude.

"I think I've got it now," she interjected, stepping forward to escape the seeming embrace. "Why don't I give it a try?"

True to form, Louise proceeded to loft four shots in a row more or less down the middle, all falling over a hundred yards away.

Marty shook her head as she admired the results. "Well, as I said earlier, you're one gifted learner."

"Uh, thanks," Louise stammered. "I guess I should be going." Not making eye contact with the pro, she stuffed her club back into the bag, which she heaved onto her shoulder as she turned quickly toward the parking lot.

Air, I need air!

Click-tunk!

Click-tunk!

Marty slumped in her chair behind the counter, bouncing a golf ball in a ricochet off the tile floor and concrete wall.

Click-tunk!

"You're back early," Bennie said, intercepting the ball at the top of its arc. "Your one o'clock didn't show?"

"No, she showed. She had a couple of little problems, but we worked them out." Marty picked up another ball from the fifty-cent basket.

Click-tunk!

"Pretty fast learner."

"Yeah, she really is. She's got good mechanics." Marty's thoughts wandered back to that brief moment when she had stood behind Louise with her arms wrapped around her waist. When the lanky woman began shifting her hips and arms, she had almost gotten the sensation of dancing.

Click-tunk!

And then all of a sudden, Louise had pulled away, leaving Marty floundering in search of her professional demeanor. The more she thought about that moment, the more embarrassing it was to think her reaction had been so transparent.

November 1967

Louise closed her novel, unable to concentrate on the intricate mystery. She had read the same page three times or more, stopping to listen each time a car went down the street.

It was after midnight and she was waiting up as usual to hear about Rhonda's date, this time with Jackson Hampton, a foreman at the glass plant in Jeannette. The two had gone to a seven o'clock movie and were probably going to grab a bite afterward. But the late hour hinted at more, and Louise was starting to think she should just go to bed and try to forget about it.

It made her uneasy to think about what Rhonda and Jackson might be doing so late. In Louise's mind, Jackson was not a good match for her best friend. She always thought Rhonda deserved someone like a doctor or a company executive, not a factory worker. But Jackson was handsome and he drove a brand new Corvette, two characteristics Rhonda found very appealing.

Louise stood up and stretched, rolling her head to loosen the kinks in her neck. As she set her milk glass in the sink, she finally heard the unmistakable sound of a car door closing. She rushed into her bedroom, suddenly self-conscious about being awake so late. She didn't want Rhonda to think she was being nosy.

"Lou?" Her roommate called out from the living room. A moment later she tapped on the bedroom door and opened it a crack. "Hey, I saw your light on under the door."

Louise had pulled back the covers and was climbing into bed. "Yeah, I was up late reading my book. I was just about to go to sleep." She noticed that Rhonda's lipstick was faded and smeared a bit at the corners. And that her blouse wasn't tucked into her skirt all the way around. "Did you have a good time?"

Rhonda laughed evilly. "Not bad. Ol' Jackson was quite a surprise."

Louise suddenly felt nauseated. She hated knowing that Rhonda had just had sex with her date, but she couldn't tear herself away from the intimate details, which Rhonda usually shared if she showed interest. "A surprise, huh?"

"I'll say. He's hung like a horse!" Rhonda plopped down on the bed beside Louise and clutched her back. "Do you have any idea how hard it is to have sex in a Corvette?"

"I can't say that I do," Louise answered demurely, her face reddening at the image. At twenty-seven years old, Louise didn't know what it was like to have sex at all, except through what Rhonda had shared about the few times she had gone all the way with her date. Rhonda knew she was a virgin, and that she was anxious about making love for the first time. Louise was grateful that Rhonda was willing to share the details of her experiences so she would know what to expect. But this was the first time since the two women had moved in together that Rhonda had been intimate with a man, and it was unsettling for Louise to hear about such a recent escapade rather than an experience that was well in the past.

"Well, I don't recommend it," she said. "But for just a minute there, it was pretty nice."

Though it made her extremely uncomfortable, Louise had to know more, especially what Rhonda had done and how she had felt. "What was nice?"

"I guess the best part was just before he ... you know, went inside me. He was touching me with his fingers and it felt really good. I thought I might even have an orgasm, but he didn't do it long enough."

For the barest instant, Louise felt what might have been the same sensation between her own legs. This happened nearly every time she and Rhonda talked about intimate things. At times, her mind would conjure up visions of Rhonda naked with her legs spread, a man's hand or mouth stroking her most private place. Rhonda had always said the mouth was best.

"So you really like Jackson?"

"Mmm ... he's okay. But to tell you the truth, I don't think we'll go out anymore. He got all mushy after we finished, saying how much he loved me. I think he just thought that's what he was supposed to say ... besides, I don't feel that way about him."

Louise was relieved to hear that Jackson was history, but she was more confused than ever about what Rhonda was looking for in love. How could she give her body to these men without having deeper feelings for them? Louise thought Rhonda should wait for the right man, someone she truly loved who would love her just as much ... someone who deserved her.

Chapter 8

LOUISE ENTERED HER home from the garage, squatting to greet the excited terrier. She had been gone much longer than intended, but Petie was long past making mistakes in the house.

"Hey, sweetie pie. You really missed quite a show, boy." She scratched his head until he dropped to the floor and rolled onto his back. "Your mama was possessed by aliens at the golf course."

Louise didn't know what had come over her all of a sudden at the driving range, but the instant she recognized a long-forgotten feeling, she felt as though she was about to suffocate. The sensation was so overpowering that she had left at once, rolling down the windows on her car as she drove onto the causeway that went out to Sanibel. There, she parked and walked along the beach, breathing in huge gulps of salt air to clear her head.

Little by little, she had put the pieces together, concluding with no small measure of guilt that what had happened this afternoon with Marty had been set in motion long before she got silly on the tee. In fact, Louise traced the start of it all the way back to the day she went looking on the Internet for information on Pine Island's woman golf pro. She asked herself why she had done that, and answered as honestly as she could. She was looking for something not to like about Marty Beck, some way to dismiss her own rude behavior as inconsequential. Instead, she had found the brief bio intriguing; and the picture was quite cute—just like the real thing.

That feeling prompted a new behavior, something Louise hadn't concerned herself with at all since Rhonda died. She actually took pains to make herself attractive, using an extra dab of makeup and lipstick; and then it was the new clothes. All of it was because she wanted Marty Beck to think she was pretty.

"Are you ready for a walk, young man?"

Petie was more than ready to get outside, and he pranced to the closet to wait for his leash. Louise clipped it into place and took him out through the front door. It was dark already and they would have to be careful to watch for cars.

After five hours of dissecting her behavior, Louise was no closer to understanding what she wanted from this new friendship with Marty Beck. She was almost certain the golf pro had been open to some sort of advance, but Louise couldn't imagine herself going down that road and she had never intended to give the impression she would.

Fortunately, she had stopped short of making complete fools of both of them and they would probably be able to pretend nothing had really happened. "That's because nothing did happen," Louise said aloud as she waited for the terrier to finish his business in the vacant lot around the corner from her house.

"Good boy, Petie." She tugged his leash gently and turned him toward home. She froze in her tracks as she watched a Subaru wagon turn slowly onto Southwest 57th Court, speeding up once it passed her house.

If that wasn't Marty Beck, she would eat her straw hat.

March 1971

Three-year-old Katie Beck never seemed to run out of energy. The little girl practically ran from one distraction to the next, as if challenging her mother to keep up.

"Child, you are wearing me out." Marty caught up with her daughter in the kitchen, where Katie had learned that a properly placed chair gave her access to everything on the counter.

Katie giggled and stretched for the cookie jar.

"Oh no, you don't!" Marty swept her up, twirled her around, and they both crumpled to the floor in a heap. Marty wouldn't trade these moments for anything.

"Hungry," the child proclaimed.

"Me too. I'm tired of waiting for Daddy." Again. *"Let's eat."*

Katie jumped up and ran to climb into her high chair as Marty stood and got down their plates and utensils. There wasn't much point in waiting for Wallace, she knew. For the past three months, he had been coming home late more times than not. His late nights started about the time he hired his old girlfriend, Donna, to run the bar at the clubhouse, so Marty didn't doubt where he was.

Marty had grown miserable with her life, especially Wallace, but that didn't have much to do with Donna. She was desperately missing the thing she loved most—outside of this pint-sized dynamo in the high chair. She hadn't played golf more than three or four times since Katie was born.

Before she got pregnant, she was working full-time in the pro shop, managing inventory and keeping the books. It wasn't exactly "golf," but Marty knew she would need that kind of experience if she ever wanted a bigger role in running a club. Every now and then, Wallace would ask her to pick up a lesson. Those lessons were usually with women—unless the women were attractive and flirtatious. Wallace always made room in his busy schedule for them.

Marty found that she enjoyed teaching the game, and that she had a knack for it. Before long, she had developed a fledgling clientele of women and their friends. All that got put on the back burner when she got pregnant with Katie; but now that the child was three, Marty thought more every day about how she could reclaim that part of her life.

When Katie got old enough to stay with a sitter, Marty offered to start picking up a few lessons, but Wallace kept saying there was no demand. The club had hired a new manager and there just wasn't a place for her anymore. Besides, he didn't earn all that much; and a babysitter would cost as much as she could make giving a lesson, so it didn't make sense for her to do it.

Marty figured Wallace's main objection was that he couldn't carry on with other women if she was around the club all the time. So every day was the same for her. He left early to go to work and came home in time to eat and go to bed. She and Katie went to the park, ran errands, and played in the small apartment.

Marty needed to break this cycle before she went insane.

"I hear Daddy."

Katie whirled around in her chair and craned her neck toward the doorway. Her father always came into the kitchen first thing when he got home.

"Hey," Wallace said gruffly, tossing his car keys onto the kitchen counter before grabbing a beer from the refrigerator.

From his red nose, Marty could tell he had already downed a few drinks before leaving the clubhouse. It was a huge nose ... unsightly under normal circumstances, but never more than when it was bright red, like it was tonight. Marty looked back at Katie and said a silent prayer of thanks for the gene dispersion that had spared her daughter that horrific snout.

"Dinner's on the stove."

"I ate."

A cherry in your bourbon? *Marty didn't care. She hated confrontations. It wasn't worth getting worked up about it. Wallace probably couldn't change enough for Marty ever to be glad she married him.*

He pulled out a chair and turned it around, straddling it as he took a seat across from her at the kitchen table. He hadn't even said hello to his daughter, who was staring at him with wide, curious eyes.

"We need to talk," he said, running both of his hands through his thinning red hair.

"Go ahead."

"I've been seeing Donna again." He slapped his hands on the table as if his great confession was all that needed to be said.

"Yeah, I know."

"You know?"

Marty shrugged. "I figured." She leaned over and lifted Katie's hand from her plate. "Use your spoon, sweetie."

Wallace appeared to be confused by the lack of emotional response, but he pressed on. "I've been thinking for a while about asking you ... for a div—"

"Yes."

"A divorce," he finished.

"Yes," she said again, without emotion. "But you're going to pay child support."

Wallace folded his hands meekly. "I won't be able to pay much."

Marty could tell by the look on his face that the other shoe was about to drop. "You knocked her up, didn't you?"

He grimaced and nodded.

"Great. Then I'm going to need to go back to work, Wallace."

"I said something to Jake." Jake Weimer owned the country club where Wallace worked. "He said Bob Seaver was looking for part-time help over in Hudsonville ... a few lessons, maybe a little work in the pro-shop."

"How considerate of you to work everything out." Hudsonville was about fifteen miles away, not far from where Marty's parents now lived. "So how fast can we do this?"

"Probably not fast enough. But I thought I ought to move into her place pretty soon."

"I think you ought to do that tonight." Marty stood abruptly and scraped her plate into the trash. With her back turned, Wallace couldn't see her satisfied smile. She was going back to work and getting rid of Wallace, all at the same time. Who could ask for a better day than that?

Chapter 9

MARTY GRABBED THE worksheet and joined her grandson on the floor of their small living room. "Okay, what's six plus six?"

"Twelve," the boy answered without hesitation. "And twelve plus six is eighteen. And eighteen plus six is twenty-four. And twenty-four plus six—"

"Whoa! That's not on here. Did you learn all that in first grade?"

Tyler shrugged. "I just figured it out."

"He must get that from his father's side of the family," Katie said from the kitchen. "Lord knows he didn't get it from either of us."

Marty chuckled in agreement. She was awful with numbers. "You're good with the books, though. But I think Tyler here's a genius."

"Miss Adams says I'm a wizard."

"That too," Marty agreed.

Katie finished up the last of the dishes and turned off the light in the kitchen. It was after eight, and Tyler's bedtime. She was about to say so when the phone rang and she grabbed it.

Marty listened long enough to determine it was Mike calling from Michigan. She could always tell that when her daughter's voice went low and serious. "Come on, Tyler. Let's get you ready for bed and I'll read you a story."

No matter how hard Marty tried not to hear the conversation, there was no escaping it in the small duplex once Katie's voice began to escalate in anger. Reluctant to intrude, Marty returned to the kitchen and gestured for her daughter to keep her voice down. Tyler had just gone to sleep.

"I don't care. You didn't leave us any choice, Mike. What were we supposed to do? Starve to death?" Katie paced from the kitchen to the living room and back again. "We have to stay here. If there were any jobs up there, you'd have one! Isn't that what you always say?" She finally slumped into a chair at the kitchen table. "I can't talk about this anymore tonight. You know where Tyler is if you want to see him."

The house went quiet and Marty debated about whether to go into the darkened kitchen or to wait until Katie was ready to talk. When she heard the sniffles, she walked in and took a seat across from her daughter.

"He's still mad at me for taking Tyler."

"You can't really blame him for that, honey. You know he loves his son. And I think he loves you too."

Katie snorted. "If he loved us, he'd be out looking for a job instead of drinking with his buddies." Jobs were scarce in the Midwest these days, especially for carpenters like Mike. There wasn't much new construction, and no one wanted to pay a living wage when there was a glut of available labor.

"It's hard on a man's pride to see his family doing without." Marty watched as Katie's face hardened and she quickly continued. "I'm not taking his side, honey. I'm just saying that I understand, even if he's wrong."

"I can deal with him being out of work. What I can't handle is that he isn't man enough to stand there with us when they're hauling our furniture out or towing our car away." Katie grabbed a tissue from a box on the counter. "Times were hard for us when I was little, but you always worked and made sure we had enough, even if it wasn't fancy."

"Don't forget that I had a lot of help from my family." Wallace quit supporting their daughter when he remarried and started his new family, telling Marty there just wasn't any way he could swing it with the new house. She moved back in with her folks when she went back to work, so at least they had a roof over their heads, and Marty was free to work long hours knowing Katie was taken care of at home.

"And I have a lot of help from you ... which I couldn't do without."

"I'm happy that I'm in a position to help, Katie, and I'm really glad to have you and Tyler here. But being here isn't going to solve your problems with Mike unless you've decided to call it quits."

The younger woman shook her head vehemently. "I know he loves us, Mom. He just needs to grow up."

"I agree. And you're both welcome to stay here as long as you need to." She laid her hand on her daughter's forearm. "But you need to start looking for a way to work things out with Mike before you both wake up someday and realize that you aren't a part of each other anymore. And that means talking instead of arguing."

Katie nodded tearfully. "I know."

"Do you want to fly back to Michigan with Tyler for a few days? I'll get your plane tickets."

Katie shook her head. "I don't want to miss work. I need to show Mike that I can make it on my own."

If there was one thing Marty understood, it was the need for self-sufficiency. Never again would she put herself in a position to depend on someone else. She had learned that lesson once from Wallace, but Angela was the one who had driven it home.

Louise scooped the pasta salad onto the chilled plates and garnished them with mint leaves and orange slices. Linda sat waiting in one of the high-back wicker chairs on the lanai. "Do you need another soda?"

"No, I'm fine. Don't you love this weather, Lou? I can't believe it's February."

Louise chuckled with satisfaction as she carried their plates to the table. "The high in Greensburg today is supposed to be twenty-nine."

"I don't even check it anymore. I used to, but this is home now."

"I'm sure I'll quit looking come June."

"Sooner than that, I bet. It starts heating up in March," Linda said.

"When do the snowbirds start going back north?"

"Usually around April or May. The difference is amazing. It'll feel like we have the whole place to ourselves until after Thanksgiving."

"That quiet, huh?"

"It really is. You can go out to eat without having to wait for a table; and the trip over to Sanibel only takes about forty-five minutes. But the best part is they drop the green fees out at Pine Island and you can get on the course practically any time you want."

"Wow! That is quite a change." Louise recalled reading on the website that Marty Beck worked at a club in North Carolina during the summer months. "But won't it be awfully hot out there on the golf course in the summer?"

"Yeah, but if you have to live in one place year round, wouldn't you rather have hot summers here than cold winters in Greensburg?"

"Absolutely! Rhonda used to say when we moved down here for good she wasn't even going to stand in the shade." Funny recollections of Rhonda almost always made Louise smile, even if the memory was bittersweet; but the reminder that her lover never got the chance to live out her dream of moving to Cape Coral in her golden years brought an unexpected rush of tears. Without another word, Louise got up and retreated to the kitchen for a tissue, taking a moment to compose herself.

Linda sat in awkward silence until Louise returned. "You okay?"

"Yes, thank you. I'm sorry about that. Sometimes things just hit me right out of the blue."

"It's all right, Lou. Anytime you want to talk about how you're feeling, I'm here to listen."

Louise had long considered Linda her best friend. They bonded right away over their shared status as "band widows," since Rhonda and Shirley were always talking shop about their music selections, marching formations, or teaching methods. Over the years, she and Linda had grown very close, leaving the band directors to fend for themselves as they carved out time to do things on their own.

"I don't know what's left to say, Linda. Some days I think I've turned the corner, and then just like that, it all comes back."

"I think you've done great, Lou. You're so much stronger than you give yourself credit for." Linda scooted closer and put her hand on her friend's arm. "Look how far you've come ... and you had to get through most of it by yourself."

"No, I had you and Shirley." But what Linda said was true. Most of her friends and coworkers had been sensitive to the loss of Rhonda as Louise's close companion, but she had never gotten the chance to openly grieve losing the love of her life.

"And you still do, so don't be afraid to be sad."

"I appreciate that." Louise gave Linda's hand an affectionate squeeze. "I think it's just going to take a little more time."

"You know, it was good to have you back on the golf course last week. I looked over at you and Pauline a couple of times and you seemed to be having fun."

"It felt good to be out there again."

"What did you think of Pauline? Is she somebody you'd like to be friends with?"

"I liked her. I didn't think I would, but she turned out to be pretty interesting." The implications of Linda's question suddenly dawned on Louise. "I like playing golf with her, I mean. But I don't think we have much else in common socially."

"Sorry, I didn't mean to suggest anything like that, Lou." Linda knew she was walking on thin ice. "I just wondered if maybe she was somebody you'd like to invite to the symphony or something ... just as a friend. Remember, we got four tickets for the season."

"I don't think so. Not because I don't like her ... I just don't think she'd be interested in that sort of thing. She likes country music and line dancing and all that."

Linda was surprised and relieved at her friend's mild reaction. Emboldened, she decided to press her luck. "How about coming with Shirley and me to the Valentine's dance on Friday night?"

"I've been thinking about it," Louise said tentatively. "I know I need to start getting out. Believe me, Petie and I have talked about it quite a bit."

Linda laughed. "What does Petie think?"

"Petie thinks he ought to get chicken gravy on his dinner every night." Louise smiled down at the black and white terrier that had come to sit beside her when he heard his name.

"So does this mean you'll come?" Linda prodded.

"I might stop in for a little while and see how it is."

"Why don't you ride with us?" Linda worried that Louise would lose her nerve if left to come on her own. "We'll go have a nice dinner first. Then you won't have to walk in by yourself."

Louise sighed in resignation. "Okay. I just thought I should have my own car is all."

"Look, if you get there and you want to leave, we'll run you home. I promise. But I think you'll have a good time."

"Do you think ... I wonder if ..."

"What, Lou?"

"Does Marty Beck ever go out to things like that?"

Linda hesitated, not quite knowing how to answer. She didn't want Louise to change her mind about coming to the dance. But after seeing her reaction to Marty at the club, she couldn't figure out if Marty being at the dance was a good thing or a bad thing. "I don't remember if I saw her there last year or not."

Louise nodded and picked a little at her barely-touched plate. She had been looking forward to talking with Linda about seeing Marty drive by the house. But if she did that, she would have to reveal her complicity—the fact that she had more or less invited the golf pro into a flirtatious situation during the golf lesson.

Louise had spent the last couple of days trying to make sense of her conflicting emotions regarding Marty Beck. After the head-clearing walk on Monday, she had come home certain she and Marty could be pretty good friends if they stuck to what they had in common, which was golf. She admitted to herself that she was flattered by the golf pro's remarks about her game; the silly part was, she had responded by worrying about how she looked and what she said instead of how she hit the ball. No wonder Marty had gotten so confused.

But Marty wasn't the only one confused, Louise realized. She had clearly been hoping to hear Marty would be at the dance.

"You're dropping your shoulder," Marty stated bluntly, poking the grip of her driver into Shirley's upper arm. "You get the club back all right, but instead of whipping it through, you lunge forward like a nose tackle. I'm surprised you're hitting the ball at all."

Shirley frowned at the harsh assessment. She had just wanted a quick lesson to help her get more height on her drives. She thought it would be a simple grip adjustment or something.

"Oh, I'm sorry," Marty corrected. "What I meant to say was 'You have a beautiful swing, Miss Petrelli. I'm really surprised you're not on the tour. If we could make just one minor adjustment ...'"

"You're so full of shit, Marty."

The golf pro grinned. "I know. But you really are dropping your shoulder and it's cutting into your club speed."

"Is one forty-dollar lesson going to fix it, or will I need to take out a loan?"

"I've already done the hard part. The rest is up to you." Marty took advantage of Shirley's divided attention to casually fish for information on her schoolteacher friend, the enigmatic Louise Stevens. "Your friend Louise has a nice swing."

"Yeah, she's got a good game." Shirley hit one ball after another under Marty's watchful eye. "I feel like I'm chopping down on the ball."

"You need to sweep the ground behind the ball ... just like a plane coming in for a landing." Marty bent down and guided the club head through its path in slow motion. "Have you and Louise played a lot together?"

"Yeah, we joined a club up in Pennsylvania about twenty years ago. All four of us were schoolteachers, so we got to play in the summer a lot." Shirley continued to hit as she talked. "This feels really awkward."

"That's because you've been hitting it wrong for a long time. Once you get used to doing it right, everything else will feel funny." Marty's brain was stuck on what Shirley had just said. "All four of you?"

"Yeah, Rhonda, Lou, Linda and me." Shirley finally took mercy on the golf pro, laughing to herself that Linda had guessed right about Marty being interested in Louise. "Rhonda was Lou's partner and my best friend. She died three years ago. Had a heart attack in her classroom."

"That's terrible." Marty felt a rush of compassion for the widowed woman. "I'm really sorry to hear that."

"Yeah, we all miss her. But Lou's doing better these days, trying to get out more. Linda and I talked her into coming with us to the Valentine's dance at the Elks Lodge. Are you going this year?"

Marty vaguely remembered seeing a community announcement about the dance in the newspaper. "I meant to get a ticket but I never got around to it," she lied.

"Oh, they sell tickets at the door. You should come."

"Yeah, I might do that."

Shirley began stowing her clubs.

"We've got fifteen minutes left. You want to work on something else?" Marty asked.

"No, I better knock off or I'll be sore. You'll see what I mean when you get to be my age."

"I can't wait. They've already started taking out things on me that don't work anymore."

June 1968

Rhonda stretched out on the sofa, her bare feet in Louise's lap. "I'll give you three days to stop that. After that, I'll ... I'll give you three more days."

The band director stood all day at the front of her classroom, and it had become routine for Louise to rub her feet as they watched television together. Over time, the massages grew to include the calves and knees, and occasionally, the neck and shoulders. Louise enjoyed this, and was content to continue for as long as Rhonda wanted. She liked the physical contact; it was familiar in a way that was soothing to both of them, it seemed.

Today had been the last day of work for teachers in Westmoreland County. Louise was looking forward to a fun-filled summer, which would include a two-week vacation to Daytona Beach in Rhonda's brand new Buick Special. Since Rhonda moved in a year ago, the two women had become almost inseparable.

Louise had never had a friend like Rhonda. The band director was funny and outgoing, but she had a serious side she shared only with Louise in their private time at home. Louise had come to realize that she loved her more than anyone she'd ever known, so much that she preferred being alone at home with Rhonda to dating or going out with others.

Even Rhonda had stopped dating after her night with Jackson Hampton, seemingly content to spend her time only with Louise.

"Just think. These poor feet get to rest now for two whole months," Louise said.

"Don't yours ever get tired, Lou?"

"Sometimes, but I get a lot more chances to sit down during the day than you do." Louise dug her thumbs into the soles of Rhonda's feet, smiling with satisfaction as Rhonda moaned. "Did you get everything put away for the summer?"

"Yeah, but I had to pull all the instruments out and repack them so they'd fit in the cabinets. My back and shoulders are what's killing me tonight."

"You want me to rub your back?" Backrubs were especially nice, Louise thought. She liked that she could get Rhonda to relax so completely.

"You don't have to do that, Lou. You've been rubbing my feet for over an hour."

"I know I don't have to do it."

"I'll probably fall asleep on you."

Louise picked up Rhonda's feet and swung them to the floor. "Tell you what. Let's go get ready for bed, and I'll come in when you get settled and rub your back. Then you won't have to worry if you fall asleep."

"I'd be crazy to turn down a backrub."

"I knew you were smarter than you looked." Louise jumped off the couch and dashed to her room, closing and locking the door before Rhonda could catch her to pay her back for that remark with her usual playful pinch.

Louise took out her favorite summer pajamas, soft cotton shorts with a puffy top in a lavender floral print. When she heard Rhonda finish in the bathroom, she followed and brushed her teeth. A few minutes later, she knocked on her roommate's bedroom door. The bedside lamp was on and Rhonda was already lying face down in bed. "You ready?"

"Sure."

Louise pulled the sheet to Rhonda's waist and sat on the edge of the double bed. When she laid her hands on Rhonda's back she could feel the warmth of her body through the nylon gown. She started with a fingertip massage and gradually increased the pressure.

"That's wonderful."

"Do you want me to use some lotion?" Rhonda would have to take off her gown for that, and Louise knew she could give a more thorough massage on just the bare skin. She wanted this to be best backrub Rhonda had ever had.

"That would be great. There's a bottle on the dresser."

Louise warmed the lotion in her hands, glancing over her shoulder as Rhonda pulled the gown up over her head and gathered it in her forearms. Her face was turned away and Louise could see the side of her bare breast as it lay against the sheet. She had always thought Rhonda was beautiful.

Despite their familiarity in most aspects of their friendship, the two women had never seen each other naked. Louise had always been extremely modest, and she assumed Rhonda guarded her own modesty out of respect for her.

She returned to the bed and pushed her palms across Rhonda's back, smearing the lotion generously from her shoulders to the base of her spine. She kneaded the stiff muscles of her upper back, and dug her thumbs into the cords along the spine to loosen them up. For twenty minutes, her hands wandered the bare skin.

"Does this feel good?"

"It's heavenly," Rhonda murmured. "I always love the way your hands feel, Lou. You would have been a great musician."

"I don't know about that. But I like doing this ... it's relaxing." To Louise, it was like a continuing caress.

But she was far from relaxed this time. As she worked the muscles in Rhonda's lower back, she began to suspect her friend was completely naked beneath the sheet. With each downward motion, she edged the cover lower. Her suspicions were confirmed when the top of Rhonda's buttocks became visible. She watched in anticipation as more was revealed with each stroke, barely aware that her fingertips were also brushing the round softness of Rhonda's breasts as she ran her hands up her sides.

"Lou ..." Rhonda drew in a breath and sighed deeply. "I need to tell you something."

Louise froze, mortified to realize what she had been doing.

"I'm so scared to say this"—Rhonda's voice quivered and her eyes remained closed—"but I can't keep it inside anymore."

Louise pulled her hands away and stiffened. "You can always tell me anything," she said as calmly as she could, terrified that she had gone too far.

With calculated daring, Rhonda rolled over until she lay on her back, her large breasts bare and her pink nipples hardened with excitement. Her dark red pubic hair was visible at the edge of the sheet.

"I really hope you mean that."

Louise's heart hammered in her chest as she met Rhonda's intense gaze. She swallowed hard and answered, "I do."

"I love you so much, Lou ... and I want ..."

"I'll give you anything, Rhonda." Louise was shaking. She had never been so frightened in her life—or so aroused.

"Then give me everything ... love me."

Louise boldly feasted her eyes upon the sight before her, hungry for it all, but paralyzed with uncertainty. "I don't ... know ..." She hesitantly trailed her fingertips along the smooth skin just above the sheet.

"I need you here." Rhonda took Louise's hand and led it to the wet heat between her legs. At the first gentle stroke, she closed her eyes and moaned.

Louise had never felt anything so delicate in her life. Emboldened by Rhonda's plea, she allowed her fingers to explore the folds, dipping into the hot center until they were covered with slickness. Rhonda's clitoris was hard and swollen, and every time Louise circled it with her fingers, Rhonda thrust her hips upward. Louise tore her eyes from what her hand was doing, shuddering to see Rhonda's heaving breasts and the look of rapture on her face. Scarcely able to breathe, she pressed harder with her fingertips and slid her other hand up to cover a beautiful breast. If this was wrong, she didn't care.

"Oh God, Lou!"

Louise could barely hold onto her prize as Rhonda began to rise from the bed in a stiffened arch. "I love you, Rhonda," she almost screamed as the woman exploded in ecstasy.

"Hold me, Lou," Rhonda whimpered. "I love you so much."

Louise took the trembling woman in her arms and held her tightly until she stilled. "I've wanted to do that for so long."

"Why didn't you?"

Louise just shook her head. "I didn't know how to tell you. I was afraid ... just like you were."

"I'm so glad you love me."

"Rhonda, I've never loved anyone at all until you."

Rhonda shifted on the bed until they faced each other on their sides. She grasped the pajama top and tugged it upward. "Let me see you."

Nervously, Louise removed her top, blushing furiously as Rhonda looked for the first time at her small breasts. "I didn't get much in that department."

"These are beautiful, Lou." Rhonda reached out and stroked a breast with her fingertips. Then she scooted closer and lowered her mouth to take the pebbled brown nipple between her lips.

"Oh, Rhonda!" Louise felt the warm liquid gather between her legs as Rhonda sucked her hypersensitive breast. Then the lips traveled up her neck and she opened her mouth to meet Rhonda's as their tongues swirled together in their first kiss. Rhonda's hands swarmed all over her body and Louise squirmed instinctively to get closer, needing more contact.

"I want to show you something wonderful," Rhonda said breathlessly when their lips finally broke apart. Her hand was already on Louise's shorts, pushing them to her knees.

Louise raised her hips and finished removing her pajamas. She didn't know what to expect from the touch but she needed it like she had never needed anything before. Her body felt like it was on fire as Rhonda's tongue tracked across her navel.

Rhonda slid lower, kissing the tops of the bare thighs as she positioned herself half on and half off the bed. Then she gently reached beneath Louise's thighs and gave them a slight nudge. "Open your legs for me."

Louise lifted her knees, her head back against the pillow and her eyes closed to concentrate on the glorious sensations that filled her. When she felt Rhonda's flattened tongue slide against her tingling center, she thought she might burst from excitement. With each stroke, a jolting impulse grew stronger at the base of her clitoris.

"I want to be the first one inside you, Lou ... please!"

"Yes!" Louise could feel the soft fingertips probing her vagina and she clenched her teeth in anticipation of pain that never came. Instead, the sensation of being filled was exquisite, like nothing she had ever known, and she quickly matched the rhythm of Rhonda's strokes. When she felt the lips close again over her clitoris, she cried out, the jolting now a steady burst of heat erupting from her core. She had never imagined a feeling so sublime.

As the pulsing finally slowed, Louise was enveloped with a wondrous sense of release. Rhonda crawled up to rest beside her, pulling the sheet up to their chins as Louise rolled onto her side and scooted her naked body close. There was no turning back from this new awareness. No matter what else they said or did after tonight, nothing between them would ever be the same.

Chapter 10

"I SURE WISH you were here to go with me tonight, sweetheart." Louise smiled wistfully at the photograph of her late partner. "I miss you all the time, but never more than when I picture you in that sexy green outfit."

Louise was remembering the last occasion they had gotten decked out, when they had driven into Pittsburgh for dinner to celebrate their thirty-first anniversary the summer before Rhonda died. She had worn the same black dress she had on tonight; Rhonda's deep emerald pantsuit had looked stunning with her auburn hair and green eyes.

Louise's eyes stung with tears as she remembered that night. She quickly brushed them away and tried to smile. "We never got to dance enough, did we?"

An evening out with other women was a rare event for Louise and Rhonda. Only when they traveled would they venture out to a lesbian club; not that they enjoyed the bar environment, but it was a place they could go to dance together. The long-awaited freedom to be openly in love had come too late for Louise and Rhonda.

The doorbell rang, signaling the arrival of Linda and Shirley, her companions for the evening. Louise kissed her fingertips and gently touched the smiling face of her partner. "Happy Valentine's Day, sweetheart."

"What's this for?" Louise asked, holding up the pink heart-shaped sticker she had just been handed at the door to the Elks Lodge.

"That's to let everyone know you're single so they'll ask you to dance," the woman answered as she cheerfully rolled her red ink stamp on the back of Louise's hand.

Shirley snorted and walked away quickly. Linda waited for Louise, not even turning around as she held her open palm behind her back to receive the crumpled sticker she knew her friend would never wear.

The threesome entered the hall, which was decorated tonight in Valentine themes. There were hundreds of red, pink, and white balloons, and each of the red-papered tables held a vase of roses, with glitter hearts and ribbons scattered about. The lights were down, but not so low that Louise couldn't see the makeup of the crowd. More than half were men, and they stood in clusters near the bar, many dressed in tuxedos. Most of the women were positioned at tables near the dance floor. They were women of all ages; everyone was in festive attire, some in dresses, but most in slacks or pantsuits.

Louise scanned the crowd looking for a familiar face ... Marty Beck's face, to be precise. She had wondered all week if the golf pro would come to an event like this. It was a possibility, she concluded, since Marty had such an outgoing personality.

"There's Pauline," Shirley said.

Louise spotted their golf buddy and followed her friends to a large round table near the wall. It was a perfect place from which to people-watch, though Pauline and the woman who appeared to be her date already had snagged the seats offering a view of the entire room. Louise grabbed a chair that at least would let her watch the dance floor.

Pauline stumbled a bit with the introductions, not knowing the other woman's last name, and Louise then saw that both women were wearing the pink Valentine stickers. It was nice, she thought, that they had found each other so quickly at the dance. She wanted Pauline to have a good time, and the woman had made it clear she was interested in meeting lots of single women.

After a few minutes, the new woman got up to leave, and Pauline turned her attention to Louise. "Where's your sticker, Lou?" She flashed a teasing grin, knowing very well her new friend was probably terrified about being seen as available.

"I must have lost it ... when I gave it to Linda to throw in the trash."

All of the women laughed, glad to see Louise keep her sense of humor. "That's too bad. I bet they have extras. I'll go get you one."

Louise glared evilly. "Just be careful not to trip over my foot as you walk by my chair."

"You're such a stick in the mud. Come dance with me."

Louise hesitated.

"Come on. I promise not to marry you or anything." Pauline stood and held out her hand.

Louise smirked, her irritation exaggerated and by now, completely for show. Taking the dance floor, she was determined to have a good time.

They grappled for just a moment with the position of their hands, before Pauline suggested, "Why don't you lead? You're taller."

At five-seven, Louise had stood two inches taller than Rhonda; but she had never been the one to lead. "You'd better watch your toes, then. Rhonda was always in charge whenever music was involved." The tune was slow and they stood close, but their bodies didn't touch.

"You look fantastic tonight, Lou."

"Thank you. You look very nice too." The woman's simple blue dress was understated, given the redhead's usual flamboyant style.

"Is it your first time out like this since you lost your partner?" Pauline asked, her voice gentle and sincere.

Louise nodded. "Pretty much. I've been to a couple of dinner parties with Linda and Shirley and things like that."

"But no dates?"

"No," she said, shaking her head.

"So what are you looking for tonight?"

Louise shrugged. "I just want to make a new friend or two ... get out of the house for a change and watch people have a good time, I guess."

"That's all? You're not looking for anybody special?"

"No! I just wanted to come out and dance with some of my friends ... and hope everyone else leaves me alone."

"So if you wanted to be left alone, how come you wore that dress?"

"What's wrong with this dress?" The dress in question was black silk, and clung to her body in all the right places. But its most distinguishing feature was its plunging neckline, a V that dipped low enough to show the hollow between her breasts.

"Nothing's wrong with it at all. You look fabulous. I just wondered if you were hoping someone in particular would notice."

"I'm going to start stepping on your feet now," Louise responded with playful sharpness, hoping to deflect the conversation. She was saved instead when the song ended.

Pauline led her back to the table and said seriously, "Okay, have it your way. But if you get tired of sitting here by yourself looking like a million dollars, let me know and we'll take another spin."

Louise answered by planting a quick kiss on her cheek. "Thank you. Now get your pink-stickered self out there and have fun."

Pauline grinned and looked around, spotting her next target sitting alone a few tables away. "See you later."

Louise sat down at the table, smiling to see Linda and Shirley laughing and dancing out on the floor. No sooner had she settled into her seat than a strange woman appeared at her side. She was a large woman with very short hair, about sixty years old, and she wore black trousers with what looked to be a vintage red and black paisley smoking jacket. She wore several pink stickers on her lapel, presumably to emphasize her availability.

"Would you give me the honor of this dance?"

"Uh," she fumbled for a way to graciously decline. "I was just out there. I thought I'd sit for a few minutes."

Bad idea, Louise.

The woman pulled out a chair and plopped down at the table. "I'm Kit. I don't believe I've had the pleasure of making your delightful acquaintance."

"I'm Louise," she said, tentatively offering her hand, which the newcomer gallantly kissed. "On second thought, I believe I would like to have another dance." *It would take you away from my table.*

When the music concluded, Louise excused herself as politely as possible, explaining that she was looking "for someone in particular" and wished a disappointed Kit a wonderful evening. Linda and Shirley were already waiting when she returned to her chair.

"You're a regular social butterfly, Lou," Shirley teased.

"I can't believe I let you two talk me out of bringing my car."

"You aren't ready to leave already, are you," Linda asked.

Louise shook her head. "No, I just haven't had to handle that sort of thing since I quit dating men thirty-five years ago. And I didn't want to hurt her feelings. She was nice."

"I'm sure you did just fine," Linda said. "I'll make Shirley stop picking at you."

"If you can make Shirley do things, make her go get us a glass of wine."

"Your wish is my command." Shirley squeezed the shoulders of both of her companions and headed toward the bar.

"Do you need us to run interference?"

Louise shook her head. "No, I want you to have fun without worrying about me. But I'll be disappointed if I don't get to dance tonight with my best friend." She took Linda's hand and led her onto the floor, where they danced together close for two songs in a row. When they returned, Shirley was waiting with their drinks.

"Here's your drink. Louise. You sit here and behave yourself now while I go dance with my woman."

Louise raised her glass in a toast as she watched her friends disappear into the crowd. She looked around again, still wondering if she would see a familiar blond head. It would be nice to see someone else she knew.

The next hour brought a steady stream of women asking Louise to dance. Not once did she decline; neither did she accept a second request to dance or an invitation to sit and chat, citing her desire to spend more time with her friends. To prove that point, she danced again with Linda and once with Shirley. When her friends took to the floor together again, she looked at her watch. *I could stand this ... for another hour or two.*

"Are you having a nice time?"

The question startled Louise, but not as much as the sight of Marty Beck standing at her table.

Chapter 11

"I ... MY FRIENDS ... we ..." Louise stammered. "Won't you please sit down?"

Marty was dressed in pleated black gabardine slacks with flat black shoes, her red silk shirt opened at the top to reveal a full cleavage. Louise had never seen the woman without her golfing visor, and was pleasantly surprised to find a rather flattering hairstyle, layer upon layer of the sun-bleached strands.

Marty grinned and pulled out a chair. "You look very nice tonight."

"Thank you."

"Actually, that isn't quite true."

Louise felt her defenses go up, bracing herself for the kind of teasing remark that Marty used so regularly in her interactions at work. *Does she always have to do this?*

"What you are is beautiful. I saw you dancing earlier with Linda, and I doubt anyone else in this room could do justice to that dress."

Louise couldn't believe her ears. That was probably the nicest compliment she had received in years. "Why, thank you, Marty. You look very nice too." She really did, Louise thought, unable to stop herself from appreciating the billowy silk against the tanned skin. Red was a good color with that bright blond hair and Marty's blue eyes were prominent even in the dim light.

"Thank you."

Both women smiled nervously.

"So," Marty said hesitantly. "I think you and I may have gotten off on the wrong foot or something when we first met. Do you think we could just start over?"

"You mean ... like a Mulligan?"

"Yeah," Marty nodded, smiling. "That's it. We'll take a Mulligan."

"Good! I'd like for us to be friends." Without even thinking about it, Louise reached over and put her hand on Marty's forearm. "So where's your pink sticker?"

"Probably in the same place as yours."

Louise chuckled. "It doesn't matter, you know. If you're sitting by yourself, you might as well be flashing a 'blue light special.'"

Marty started to laugh then caught herself. "Do you want me to go?"

"No! I want you to stay." Louise realized the implications of what she had said. "Unless you have other people you'd like to see."

"No, I already said hi to some friends on my way over here. I wanted to talk to you, but if you want to be by yourself, I'll—"

"Please stay. I really need to apologize for the way I've acted, especially that first day we met. I was just embarrassed about hitting the ball so badly, and I knew I could do better."

"I'm the one who should apologize, Lou. I have a problem sometimes knowing when to shut up."

"No, I'm the one who made such a big deal out of it. I shouldn't have—"

"Whoa! Stop. We agreed to take a Mulligan, so none of that other stuff even happened. And we get to start brand new." Marty held out her hand. "My name is Marty Beck, and I'm very pleased to meet you for the first time."

Louise smiled and shook Marty's hand. "I'm Lou Stevens, and I'm pleased to meet you for the first time too."

"So tell me all about Lou Stevens. How did a nice girl like you end up in a place like this?"

"You mean how did I end up in Cape Coral or how did I end up at the Elks Lodge?"

"Tell you what. I'll start. I'm sixty-one years old and I grew up in a little town called Holland, Michigan. It's right on the lake, straight across from Chicago. And I've been playing golf practically all my life."

"Okay, I can do that. I'm sixty-three and was raised in Wheeling, West Virginia, where my father worked in the mines. I moved to Greensburg, Pennsylvania when I was twenty-two and taught high school math for forty years."

"All right, it's your turn to go first. What else should I know about you?"

Louise drummed her fingers on the table, thinking more about what she wanted to know about Marty than what she wanted to reveal about herself. "You should know that I love music, especially the symphony. I'm a hockey fan—Go Pittsburgh Penguins!—and I started playing golf in 1981."

"Wow, that's a long time ago. No wonder you're so good."

"Your turn."

Marty thought about what Louise had said and answered, "My favorite music is probably bluegrass, but I don't listen to it very often. I'm a hockey fan too—Go Tampa Bay Lightning!—and I'm terrible at numbers. My six-year-old grandson's a genius, though."

"Most people who think they're terrible with numbers just didn't have the right math teacher."

"Well, if you had been my teacher, Miss Stevens, I'd have worked my tail off."

She's such a flirt! "And if you had been my student, Miss Beck, I'd have seen to it."

"Oh, I bet you were tough." Marty folded her hands and leaned forward across the table. "I like this game. Whose turn is it?"

"It's yours."

"Okay, I was married for five years back when I had Katie. My last relationship ended about eight years ago"—Marty looked down at her hands—"when I did something very foolish. I live with my daughter and grandson for the time being, but usually I live by myself."

When she met Katie at the club, Louise had assumed that Marty was married before, and she knew the part about the last relationship ending several years ago from Shirley and Linda. The bit that was new was that Marty had done "something foolish" to bring about the breakup.

"It's your turn, Lou." Marty seemed nervous, as though perhaps she had revealed too much.

Louise shifted her thoughts from Marty to Rhonda, and her voice lowered. "I spent thirty-one years with a woman who died much too soon. This was where we intended to retire. Instead, I've come here by myself. And sometimes, I'm so lonely I can hardly bear it."

This time, Marty reached out and clasped Lou's hand. "I'm really sorry. I can't even imagine what it must have been like to lose somebody like that."

"Thank you." Louise worked to compose herself. Things had been going much better than she had expected tonight and she didn't want to cry now and turn the evening into something sad.

"But there's no reason you should ever be lonely. Look around at all these people."

Louise scanned the room, daunted by the idea of pushing herself into the social circles of these strangers. Most were couples, and the single women she had encountered seemed to be on the make.

"I bet you could find somebody here who would enjoy going to the symphony, or just for a walk on the beach ... which happens to be one of my favorite things to do."

Before Louise could decide if that was an invitation, Linda and Shirley returned from the dance floor.

"Hey, Marty!" Shirley said with enthusiasm. "You sure clean up well!"

"Look who's talking. Hi, Linda. Nice dress."

"Thank you. Good to see you here."

"You two looked like you were having a good time," Louise said.

"We were, until my hip went out on me. I think I overdid it," Shirley said, rubbing her upper thigh. "It's hell getting old."

"I've been trying to get her to see a doctor about it," Linda explained. "She's worried they'll want to replace it and she won't be able to play golf any more."

"Don't let that stop you," Marty said. "I bet every foursome on the course this winter has at least one artificial hip ... or maybe a knee."

"I just think I need to soak in a hot tub. That always helps."

"Shirley and I were thinking we should probably go."

Louise started to pull her wrap from the back of her chair.

"Wait!" Marty turned to Louise. "Why don't I take you home?"

Louise was caught completely off guard and looked to Linda and Shirley for an answer as to what she should do.

"I think that's a great idea," Linda said. "I'd feel awful if you had to leave early on account of us."

"I don't know. It has been a long day."

"But we haven't even danced yet," Marty pleaded. "What if you stayed just a little while longer and had a couple of dances with me. There's one now." A timeless Righteous Brothers tune began and couples from all over the room headed to the dance floor.

Louise looked at Marty then back to Shirley and Linda. Seeing their smiles of encouragement, she acquiesced. "Okay, I guess I could stay a little while longer."

Taking Marty's calloused hand, she followed her to the dance floor where they squeezed in among the other couples. Automatically, she placed one hand on the shorter woman's shoulder as Marty's hand went to the center of her back. Marty's thigh brushed against hers every time they swayed to the right.

Gradually, Louise relaxed, moving comfortably to the music and enjoying the feel of the soft silk of Marty's blouse beneath her fingertips. Her nervousness about being left on her own was dissipating. She felt secure with Marty, much as she had with Pauline. And if Marty was thinking about something other than friendship, she would deal with it when it came up. But there was no reason not to enjoy a dance with a friend. Louise imagined a lot of single women would love to be in her shoes right now. Marty was quite cute and there was something intriguing about the way she—

"So how do you like it in Cape Coral?" Marty asked, interrupting her thoughts.

"What's not to like about weather like this in February?"

Marty nodded. "We hear that a lot, especially when people first get here. It's pretty miserable in the summertime, though. I always leave around the first of May for the mountains and stay there through October."

Louise didn't give away that she knew this from her exploration of the website. "So you're a snowbird."

"More like a migrant worker," Marty chuckled. "There really aren't enough people playing down here in the summer to support two pros, and I've built up a pretty good client base at a club in North Carolina."

The song ended but another one started right away, and the two women remained in their embrace.

"I bet it's beautiful there."

"It is. How about you? Are you going to head back up north for the summer?"

Louise shook her head. "Maybe for a quick visit. I'll probably go see my brother and his family in Wheeling. But this is home now. I sold the house up there."

"How do you like being retired?"

"I miss teaching ... but everything changed when Rhonda died. I needed a new start."

Louise was sure she felt Marty pull her closer when she mentioned Rhonda. Their thighs were now in constant contact, and the fingertips at the base of her back were moving up and down in a slight caress. It was reassuring in a way, and Louise welcomed it.

They finished the dance without talking and when the music ended, Marty escorted Louise back to the table. "I know I only asked for a couple of dances, but I'll stay as long as you like."

The crowd had started to thin and Louise noted by her watch that it was nearly midnight. "We should probably call it a night. Don't you have to work tomorrow?" She figured that weekends were busy on the golf course.

"I do. In fact, tomorrow's my day to open up at six-thirty, so heading out probably isn't a bad idea."

Marty held Louise's coat for her, then offered her arm as an escort. Louise went along, all the while thinking she was acting now as though Marty was her date ... like they were "a couple" rather than just a couple of friends. If it turned out she was sending Marty the wrong signals again, she would have to set her straight.

They walked quietly through the dark parking lot until they reached the familiar two-toned Subaru. Marty's gallant demeanor seemed natural for her, Louise rationalized as she waited for her to unlock the passenger side and open the door. Marty would probably be like this with any of her friends, so it was silly to think it was more than just a friendly gesture.

"I live on Southwest 57th Court."

Marty nodded noncommittally. "By the new high school."

"That's right."

"Is it a new house?"

"Brand new. Rhonda and I picked out the floor plan about five years ago when we bought the lot. I had them start construction last spring when I made the decision to retire and I moved down here back in September when my other house sold."

"There are some nice houses over there."

"You know the neighborhood?" Louise was questioning now if Marty had been the one who cruised by her house that night. Surely, there was more than one green and tan Subaru wagon in Cape Coral.

"Sort of. I looked at a couple of places over there a few years ago before I bought my duplex." Marty turned onto one of the parkways that cut across the commercial area of Cape Coral.

"So you have a duplex. I bet that's handy with your daughter and grandson."

Marty chuckled. "Not really. I have the other side rented to a retired couple from Ohio. Katie and Tyler live with me on my side. I've only got two bedrooms, so we're on top of each other right now."

"That sounds pretty crowded."

"I hate to move my renters out because I don't know what's going to happen with Katie. She and her husband need to figure out what they want, and he's in Michigan out of work."

Louise found this domestic side of Marty quite interesting. She wondered what kind of mother Marty had been, and what kind of grandmother she was now. With her playful side, she seemed like somebody a little boy would adore. "You haven't said much about your grandson. Most grandparents don't want to talk about anything else."

"Tyler's great. He's really smart. I didn't get to see much of him when he was a baby because they lived in Michigan, but I'm enjoying him now. And no, I haven't taught him to play golf—yet."

"But I'm sure you will." They turned onto Louise's street and Marty slowed down. "It's the last one on the left."

"This is a very nice house."

"Thank you." The polite thing to do would be to offer a tour. "The next time you're here, if it isn't too late, I'll show you the inside." *Friends do visit each other's homes, Louise.*

"I'd like that." Marty turned off the engine and opened her door as Louise opened hers. The golf pro hurried around and offered her hand. "You can't possibly think I was going to just drop you in the driveway. I have a reputation to worry about, you know."

"I'm not surprised to hear that you have a reputation," Louise said with a smile. She liked the way that Marty was keeping things light. Sure, Louise knew she was capable of walking herself to the door, but it felt nice to get such special treatment ... even from a friend.

As soon as they stepped onto the porch, Petie began to yap excitedly from the other side of the door.

"Who's that?"

"That's Petie. He's the man of the house. And he thinks he's huge."

"Don't they all?"

Louise laughed, surprised a little at the off-color remark. It struck her as something Rhonda might have said.

"Why, Louise Stevens! I had no idea you had such a dirty mind. I was talking about dogs."

"Of course you were."

Louise fished her keys from her clutch bag and Marty snatched them from her hand and held them up to the light from the lamppost.

"Let's see ... this one is definitely a car key. So this must be the house key." She slid it into the lock and gave it a turn. "Thanks for staying to dance with me and for allowing me to bring you home. It was the best part of the whole night."

Louise was taken aback by the sudden seriousness in Marty's tone. "I'm glad I stayed."

"So ... I'm off on Tuesdays and Wednesdays. How would you like to take a ride out to Sanibel? We could have lunch and maybe walk on the beach a little."

This was the invitation Louise had thought she heard earlier. She wanted to go. It would give them a chance to clear the air and talk about things they might enjoy together. "I'd like that."

"What if I pick you up at eleven o'clock on Tuesday?"

"I think that would be fine." There was nothing else at all on her February calendar.

Both women smiled, their feet frozen to the porch as though the night were as yet unfinished. Only one thing finished a moment like this and Marty took the initiative, reaching up to touch Louise's cheek with her fingertips.

"May I?"

Louise answered by leaning forward to place a gentle kiss on Marty's lips.

Marty smiled again and then reached over to push the door open so Louise could enter her home. "Happy Valentine's Day, Lou. I'll see you Tuesday at eleven. Goodnight."

Louise entered her house and closed the door, leaning against it as she listened to Marty leave. Petie's claws clicked excitedly on the tile floor in the entryway, but Louise was numb to everything but the tingling sensation still on her lips.

"Petie, I just kissed Marty Beck right on the mouth!"

August 1968

Rhonda kissed the bare heel and trailed her tongue along the smooth skin of Louise's calf, stopping to nibble on the soft flesh at the back of her knee. Once unleashed on that night two months ago, the love they had held inside exploded into a wondrous new realm of sexual adventure; and they were filled with curiosity and free of inhibition. Ravenous for one another, they had made love practically all summer.

"God, Lou ... you've got the most gorgeous ass." Higher she climbed, cupping the curves of Louise's bottom as she kissed the length of the downy cleft.

Louise climbed higher too, her body in tune with Rhonda's practiced hands and mouth. There wasn't an inch of her Rhonda didn't know, nor an inch she hadn't mastered. After waiting twenty-eight years to discover sex, Louise was insatiable.

Her need growing with every touch of Rhonda's lips, she drew her knees up to open herself. "Please ..."

"I know what you need, baby." Rhonda filled her from behind, scooting up to slide her stiffened nipples across Louise's back as she gently drove her fingers in and out.

"... so good," Louise panted, loving the feel of the heavy breasts stroking her skin. "Make me come."

"Fight it, Lou ... make it last."

Louise groaned with frustration, knowing that if only Rhonda's fingers would touch her throbbing clitoris ...

But Rhonda had other ideas. She continued her gentle strokes, steadily increasing the pace before finally adding a digit and thrusting her hand deep inside, causing Louise's whole body to rock with the sudden force.

Caught by surprise, Louise's gut tightened in a powerful grip as though to pull Rhonda completely inside her. She lost her battle for self-control, burying her face in the pillow as she gritted her teeth and screamed.

"Oh, my God," she gasped as they both collapsed. Rhonda held her tightly and stroked her head as her body shuddered with aftershocks. "Oh, my God."

"Is that all you can say, hon?"

"Let's quit our jobs and stay right here forever."

Rhonda chuckled as she wiggled to prop up on her elbow. "Teachers' meetings won't ever be the same, Lou. And how will I be able to pass you in the hall knowing how it feels to do what we just did?"

"No problem. We'll hide behind the trophy case like the kids do." Louise casually ran the backs of her knuckles across Rhonda's nipple, satisfied to see it stiffen to a peak.

"It'll get crowded back there. That's where I meet Artie Skodak." Rhonda squirmed to get away from Louise's vengeful pinch.

"You tell Artie that he'll be a sorry boy if I catch him with my woman." Artie was a rising junior at Westfield, first-chair trumpet, and he had a powerful crush on the band director.

"You know, Lou?" Rhonda's voice turned serious. "We're going to have to be very careful at school. Not just when we're with people, but all the time. The walls have ears, and we'd both lose our jobs if anybody ever found out about us."

"I know that."

"I know you do. I'm just thinking there might be some times that we have to do things that hurt each other's feelings, just so people won't see the truth."

"You mean like be rude to each other?"

"No, not that. Gosh, we'd better never have a fight in front of anybody or they'll all know."

Louise laughed. "That's for sure. One of us would end up crying and the other one would be so sorry."

"Then we'd probably have to run off and make love." Rhonda scooted closer again so that her large breasts rested against Louise's side. "I was just thinking that you probably shouldn't come to the band room as much as you did last year. And I have no business being up on the second floor at all, so I can't just wander into your classroom anymore like I used to."

Louise was already feeling a twinge of the hurt that Rhonda had predicted. "I'm going to be the Class of '72 sponsor next year, so I won't have cafeteria duty anymore. That means we won't see each other very much at school."

"I still want you to ride the band bus to the games. I really need your help with that, and it's not like anyone else wants the job. We just have to be careful around the band parents."

Louise nodded, her mood spoiled by her understanding that these restrictions were necessary.

Rhonda leaned over, bringing her face close to Louise's. "We can hold back for a few hours a day, Lou. We're still going to have this." She laid her hand over Louise's heart. "I'm not ever going to let this go—never—but I don't want us to do anything that might cause us to lose each other, or to lose the jobs we both love."

Louise clasped the hand on her chest and brought it to her lips. "I love you so much, Rhonda. I intend to make my whole life with you, so we'll do whatever we have to do."

Chapter 12

LOUISE STARED BACK at the computer screen, the lump in her throat so hard it hurt.

Dear Miss Stevens,
I'm really nervous about writing this. It has to do with my trip to Florida. I was going to wait and tell you everything when I got there, but the more I thought about it, the more I thought I should tell you ahead of time in case you changed your mind about wanting to see me. The good news is that I have decided to major in math and be a teacher, just like you. But the bad news—at least some people think it's bad news—is that I realized for sure when I got to Slippery Rock that I am gay. I guess I always knew, but it was hard to accept it back at Westfield. I hope it doesn't make you think less of me, but I know that homosexuality goes against what some people believe. If you want to change your mind about seeing me over spring break, I understand.
Love, Michele

Louise had long suspected Michele would one day discover this part of herself, and she wasn't surprised to see her main concern was how others would react. It broke her heart to imagine the young woman's fear that the people in her life would change their feelings overnight in light of this revelation.

She understood Michele's apprehension more than she could say—that is, more than she *would* say. Her former student's courage at coming forward made her ashamed of her silence, as she struggled with her need to offer reassurance and her reluctance to undo the secrecy that had defined her life with Rhonda. All she could do was voice her support, downplaying the importance of the girl's concerns in hopes Michele wouldn't press her for more.

Dear Michele,
There is no need for you to worry or be nervous. You're still the same thoughtful and sweet young woman you always were. Besides, you can't change your mind about coming to see me now—I've already told Petie! That's great news that you've decided to become a math teacher. I promise not to scare you off with too many horror stories. Can't wait to see you.
Love, Louise Stevens

"Why do I have to go to daycare on a Tuesday?" Tyler liked Tuesdays and Wednesdays because his grandma always picked him up from school.

"Because Grandma has a date this afternoon to go to the beach with her new girlfriend," the boy's mother answered.

Marty smirked. "I'm never telling you anything else as long as I live." She pulled in behind the long line of cars at the elementary school. "We'll do something fun tomorrow, Tyler. I promise."

"Can we go to the beach, too?"

"Maybe we'll go out to Pine Island and see the fishing boats." Marty knew that was one of her grandson's favorite things to do.

"Cool!" The excited boy unhooked his seatbelt and leaned forward for two kisses before leaping out of the car.

Katie continued to grin as they left the school parking lot, now en route to the club where her mom would drop her off at work. "You won't lose track of time and forget to come pick us up, will you?"

"I'm seriously thinking about it."

"So what is it you like about Louise Stevens? She's not anything like Angela, or Gretchen, or ... who was that woman back in Holland?"

"You mean Sue?"

Katie nodded. She had effectively put her memories of that woman out of her head.

"I guess what I like about Louise is that she isn't anything like them. She's a lot more independent and she doesn't seem so ... bossy, I guess. I think she's somebody I could have fun going out with without any strings attached."

"What if she's looking for more than that?"

"I doubt it. You can usually tell when somebody's got something more serious in mind and I just don't get that from Louise."

"Hmm ... maybe not, but ..."

"What?"

"I just think it would be hard for somebody like her to have just a casual relationship when she's used to being with one person for a really long time."

"We'll probably talk about it today and get clear on what we're looking for. But I really doubt she's got more in mind than just having some fun."

Louise leaned forward to apply her makeup, careful to see that her foundation was evenly spread. It contained a high grade sunscreen, something she needed whenever she went near the water. With her fair skin, a hat wasn't enough to protect against the reflection, and nothing aged you like too much sun.

For the thousandth time today, Louise's thoughts went to Marty Beck. The golf pro's skin was softer than she had expected, at least that was the impression she got when she had put her hand on Marty's deeply tanned forearm.

Marty was due at her door in less than an hour. And as soon as she arrived, Louise would spell out the parameters of their friendship. She hadn't actually meant for that kiss to land on the lips the other night. It just happened. It was supposed to be a friendly kiss on the cheek, just like the one she had given Pauline.

Her makeup in place, she reached behind the door to retrieve her top, a striped pullover with a boat-neck collar that coordinated with her light green pedal-pushers. Capri pants, they were now called, for whatever reason. Louise had gotten dressed in the bathroom today, mindful to avoid the watchful eyes from the pewter frame. All weekend, she had been consumed with guilt, not knowing where to even start her usual conversation with the photograph.

Louise knew rationally that she didn't owe any explanations to her departed lover. In fact, in the three years since Rhonda had been gone, Louise had more than once vowed to find a new girlfriend, someone who wouldn't leave her with all these plans for her life unfulfilled. What really mattered to Louise was that she didn't want another partner. No one could ever take Rhonda's place in her heart, and the idea of starting over with somebody new seemed like too much work.

What she needed here in Cape Coral was a good friend.

She stood back to check her appearance, swiping her lips one last time with the pale pink lipstick. Satisfied, she went into the living room to talk with Petie about her plans for the day. Over and over, she practiced what she would say to Marty, nervously watching the clock as she anticipated the woman's arrival. The moment of reckoning finally arrived, and she heard the car pull into the drive.

"Okay, Petie. Wish me luck."

Louise took a deep breath and opened the front door to find Marty smiling behind mirrored sunglasses. She was wearing baggy shorts with a loose-fitting tropical shirt, and her white feet peeked through her sport sandals. Louise thought she looked adorable.

"Hi, come on in." Louise held the door open for her to enter. Petie danced animatedly at their feet. Fortunately for both women, dogs that demanded attention were great icebreakers. "Petie thinks you've come to visit him."

"I have." Marty pushed her glasses up on her head and dropped to her knees to pet the terrier, whose tail twitched as he sniffed her for traces of other dogs. Finding none, he allowed a few pets before running behind his mistress's legs.

"He's a little bashful at first."

"He's a cutie. How old is he?"

"Three. He was a gift from the students in my homeroom."

"I bet he's a lot of company."

"He is. I think he likes sharing his house with me."

Marty stood up and looked around. "This really is a nice house."

"Thank you. I promised you a tour. You want that now?"

"Sure. Lead the way."

The open floor plan with skylights gave the modern home a spacious feel. Most of the furniture was wicker or rattan and everything was decorated in tropical pastels. The living room melded with the dining area, which was separated from the kitchen on the right by a bar with two tall stools. On the left side of the house was an alcove hallway leading to a study, a bathroom, and a guest bedroom. To the right of the living room was a door to the garage, a closet, and another short hallway beside the kitchen that led to a master suite. Both the dining area and master bedroom opened onto a screened-in lanai.

"This is very nice, Lou." The tour ended in Louise's bedroom, where Marty's eyes were drawn to the photograph on the dresser. "This must be that special woman you told me about the other night."

"That's right. Rhonda Markosky was her name. She was the band director at Westfield, where I taught math. That was her last school picture."

"She's got a beautiful smile. She looks like somebody who liked to have a good time."

"That pretty much describes Rhonda to a T." Louise traced her fingertips around the frame wistfully, catching herself before she drifted off with her memories. "Can I get you something to drink?"

"Are you ready to go? I thought we'd have lunch at South Seas Plantation over on Captiva."

"I love that place!"

"Great! Shall we?"

Captiva Island was connected to Sanibel by a small bridge. The trip to the resort and restaurant at the very end of the island took an hour and twenty minutes from Cape Coral and by the time the women were seated, both were hungry.

"The seafood pasta looks good," Louise said.

"Sure does. Unfortunately, I'll have to get my seafood on a bed of lettuce instead of linguine. My doctor wants me to lose twenty-five pounds."

"Twenty-five pounds? You'll disappear!" Marty was a little overweight, but that seemed like a lot to Louise.

Marty chuckled. "I think there will still be plenty of me left, but I haven't been having much luck with my diet. When you have a six-year-old in the house, you eat a lot of hotdogs and pizza. I'll be lucky if I lose ten."

"Well, I think that's enough. Any more than that and there won't be anything to hold onto." *I did not just say that!* Louise stopped short as her mortifying words hung there between them.

Marty flashed a lascivious grin. "I guess one could always tie me down."

Louise brought her hands up to cover her reddening face. "I don't know where on earth that came from. Sometimes I think aliens just come in and take over my mouth."

"It's no big deal, Lou. For what it's worth, I thought it was pretty funny."

The still-blushing woman peeked over her hands, afraid to speak at all because being around Marty Beck made her say the strangest things. The waitress saved her when she appeared to take their order.

"So what can we talk about besides my weight? Why don't you tell me what it was like to teach high school for forty years?"

Grateful for the change in topic, Louise began to talk about her teaching years. Marty listened intently all through lunch, amazed at the perspective one developed through the portal of teenage lives. "So what part of teaching gave you the most satisfaction?"

"I liked knowing I was teaching them something they'd use forever. And it was fun to see them get excited about things like pep rallies and homecoming … stuff like that. I usually got caught up in all of it with them. But the best part for me was that I really cared for them, and I think the feeling was mutual."

"I bet they liked you."

"I got a note from one of my favorite students this morning, in fact. She's coming to visit her grandmother in Sarasota over spring break and wants to get together."

"That's really something. They must have really liked you a lot to stay in touch."

Louise nodded. "I liked them too ... so many of them were special. I don't know how I would have gotten through losing Rhonda if it hadn't been for those kids."

"So why did you leave? Why didn't you just stay until they kicked you out?"

Louise smiled, but her sorrow shone through. "I ask myself that sometimes when I'm feeling sorry for myself. I guess I just didn't want to break in a new homeroom of freshman when my favorite class graduated."

"Special kids, huh?"

"They really were. And I have to admit, being there without Rhonda was hard. I just didn't think I could face it another year. I needed a change."

"I'm sure it was tough."

Louise pushed her half-eaten plate away, unaccustomed to such a heavy midday meal. Determined to brighten their mood, she changed the subject. "So what about you, Marty? It must be a dream job to play golf for a living."

"Most of the time it is. Why don't we head out to the beach and I'll tell you about it?"

Marty paid the check, refusing Louise's offer to share the bill, but not her offer to compute the tip. Then they drove back over the bridge to Sanibel and parked beneath the pines at Bowman Beach.

"I'm warning you, Lou. There is to be no laughing at my feet," Marty said as she tugged her sandals off. Her feet appeared bright white in contrast to her tanned legs.

"I'm not laughing." Louise covered her mouth to suppress a smile. "But do they glow in the dark?"

"They do. So there." Marty tossed her shoes back into the car and closed the door, holding out her arm to escort Louise over the footbridge that crossed the dunes. Louise let go when they encountered others as they started down the beach.

"You promised to tell me all about how you ended up a golf pro," Louise said as she slid her hands into her pockets.

"It's not very exciting."

"I imagine most things would be more exciting than teaching math."

Marty chuckled. "Well, I guess that would depend on your point of view. At least I understand golf. I can't say the same about math."

"Shirley said you used to play on the tour."

"Yeah, that was a long time ago. I wasn't very good, at least not good enough to make a living at it."

"Start before then. How old were you when you first started playing?"

"Seven. We lived next door to a golf course and I used to watch people tee off at the hole near our house. I had a bucket of stray balls that I found in the woods, and one day I fished a broken club out of the trash and got my dad to cut it down and put a new grip on it so it was just the right size. That I was all I needed to get hooked. I'd take my bucket of balls out to the vacant lot and hit them all and go pick them up, over and over."

"Aw, I bet you were so cute."

Marty laughed. "Yeah, my mom didn't always think so, because I never wanted to do anything else. The pro let me hit from the driving range every now and then, and one day he gave me an old set of clubs that he was about to throw away. I thought I'd died and gone to heaven! I kept practicing and just got better and better. Wallace was playing a lot then too."

"Who's Wallace?"

"Katie's dad … or as I like to call him, Loser. We were friends back then, and he agreed to caddy for me if I could make the tour."

"Didn't you think about playing on a college team?"

"I wasn't exactly the best student ... poor math skills, you know." Marty grinned. "Besides, I got my tour card and the time was right. We headed out, one tournament after another it seemed like ... for three years."

"How did you do?"

"Pretty lousy most of the time. My best finish was third place at a tournament in South Carolina that most of the top players skipped so they could have a break. And there wasn't much money to be made back then, even if you were good."

"So you couldn't make a living at it?"

"Some nights, I couldn't even buy dinner. My last event was the U. S. Open at Hazeltine National in Minneapolis."

When Marty started to wade in the gentle lapping waves, Louise stopped and leaned on her shoulder so she could take her sandals off. Her bare feet welcomed the cool water. "What made you stop after that?"

"I was on top of the world that last day. I was playing so well—I even had a shot at winning—and then the wheels came off." Marty sighed at the memory. "When it was over, Wallace just threw the clubs in the station wagon and we headed back to Holland. I bet we didn't say five words to each other all the way back."

"That was it?"

"That was my last tournament on the pro tour. We both hired on at the club where we played growing up. They made Wallace the full-time pro and I gave lessons part-time and worked the rest of the time in the pro shop."

"Wait a minute! They made him the full-time pro? He was your caddy!"

"That's right. And everybody in Holland knew I could beat him from the blue tees, even Wallace, but that's the way it was back then. 'Course, it didn't matter much in the long run, because we got married eventually, and I got pregnant with Katie … not necessarily in that order."

A revelation like that might have shocked Louise years ago, but now, she found it an interesting facet of Marty's life. "I don't know why, but I have a hard time picturing you married and pregnant."

Marty chuckled. "I have a hard time with the married part myself. Every now and then, I come across that marriage license and it's like it happened to somebody else."

"And Katie?"

"Now that's a different story. I was so mad at Wallace about that because he didn't ... well, let's just say we weren't exactly trying to have a baby at the time. But I fell in love the second I saw her."

Marty took Louise's wrist to check the time. She never wore a watch because it interfered with her golf glove. "Speaking of Katie, I guess we should head back. I have to pick her up so we can go get Tyler from daycare."

"It's been a nice walk." *And a nice afternoon.*

"We'll do it again."

When they reached Louise's home, Marty once again jumped out of the car and walked around to escort Louise to the door. Petie barked from the other side.

"I had a wonderful time. Thank you." Louise really had enjoyed her day, and even wished it didn't have to end so soon. Marty was easy to talk to and they both seemed to have much more to say. Except they hadn't talked about the one thing Louise had meant to discuss—her interest in being only friends. But that didn't seem to matter as much right now. Whatever this was she and Marty had enjoyed today was exactly what she wanted.

"I did too. We'll definitely do it again."

"Okay, but it's my treat next time."

"You've got yourself a deal." Marty snatched the key ring from Louise's hand and opened the door, allowing the excited terrier to join them on the porch. "I brought your mommy home, Petie."

Louise shook her head in amazement. "Look at him. He's just as happy to see you as he is me."

"Yeah, that's because I brought you back." Marty smiled, her blue eyes sparkling in the waning sunlight. "He might not like it when I keep coming to take you away."

Louise liked the idea of making days like this a regular thing. "He'll just have to get used to it."

Marty hesitated for a moment before closing the distance between them. Just as she had on Friday night, Louise leaned in and touched her lips to Marty's, this time holding the contact a little too long for either one to dismiss it as mere friendly intent.

Chapter 13

LOUISE HAULED HER clubs out of the trunk and leaned them against the stand at the club drop, where one of the attendants would pick them up and place them on a cart. Her playing partners were nowhere in sight, but they usually didn't appear until almost tee time. She had come to the club early today, hoping to have a chance to talk to Marty privately.

Hours of pacing and talking aloud to both Petie and Rhonda since Tuesday had led Louise to conclude there was absolutely nothing wrong with having a close friend like Marty. It wasn't like they were going to sit around on the couch and neck. But Louise had never had a "friendly" friend that she could really share things with, at least not since she and Rhonda became lovers. Of course, Rhonda had always been a friend, but a friend who was a lover and a partner was different from a friend who was just a friend. Linda had actually been just a friend ... but Linda had Shirley, so she couldn't be a really close friend. Marty could be a different kind of friend because Marty didn't have a girlfriend.

It all made perfect sense to Louise, and if she wanted to kiss her friend on the mouth once in awhile, she could do that. She had talked that part over with Petie, not with Rhonda.

She parked the Sable and entered the pro shop, disappointed to see Bennie behind the counter instead of Marty. She picked up a sleeve of Calloway balls and laid them by the register. "Hi, Bennie."

"Louise! Three balls for you." He rang up the purchase.

"That's right. One for the God of the Lake, one for the God of the Rough, and one to putt in on Eighteen."

He laughed in agreement. "We ought to get that printed on the side. You're playing with ... Petrelli." He found their reservation. "They haven't checked in yet, but Pauline's out on the range with Marty."

Louise flinched, recalling the first time she had seen Pauline almost three weeks ago. The redhead was practically throwing herself at the golf pro that day.

"I think I'll warm up on the putting green until the others get here." No way did Louise want to see a repeat of that ... *flirt-fest.* Heck, Pauline had admitted she was only interested in one thing!

Louise retrieved her putter from her bag and dropped the three new balls onto the green. Four small pins were set at various positions on the green so a player could practice a range of distances. She sent all three putts to the farthest hole, her closest attempt stopping more than five feet from the target. She walked to the other end, gathered them, and putted again, this time for the closest pin. Sinking two of three, she collected them again and aimed next for a mid-range pin.

"You know, it's bad luck not to putt out."

Louise whirled toward the familiar voice and broke into a grin. "Marty!"

The golf pro stood smiling as she leaned on her driver at the edge of the green. She was wearing dark brown golf shorts with a white short-sleeve shirt—and the ever-present khaki visor boasting the club's logo.

"The last person that didn't putt out on this green lost his ball and his three-wood to Ben Hogan."

"Ben Hogan?"

"Yeah, Ben was the alligator we had in the lake on the front nine. He's making his new home in a swamp near Immokalee these days."

Louise picked up her balls and dropped two into the pocket of her slacks. "I was hoping I'd see you today. I wanted to say thanks again for the other day."

"It was my pleasure. Shall we do it again next week?"

Louise liked that idea. As far as she was concerned, they could have a standing date ... er, meeting. *Oh, what the heck!* "It's a date then. But we agreed next time would be my treat, and I was hoping you might come to my house for dinner this weekend."

Marty tucked her driver under her arm and walked closer. "I'm on a very strict diet, you know."

"I can work with that." Louise smiled at Marty's seeming acceptance of her invitation. "Tomorrow night? Seven?"

"I shall be there, Miss Stevens."

"That Marty Beck's just the cutest thing, isn't she Lou?" Pauline was driving the cart off to the rough on the right, where both she and Louise had hit their tee shots on the eighth hole.

"Mmm ... Marty's very nice." *And cute.*

"That's not what I said. I said she was cute. Don't you think she's cute?"

Louise leaned out of the slow-moving cart to search for her ball. "She's cute."

"So what's up with you and Marty? You two going out?"

Louise could feel her pulse quicken. The last thing she wanted was to get into a cat fight over a woman. "There's my ball!" She got out and selected a club—a seven-iron since her ball had practically burrowed into the high grass.

"It's no big deal, Lou. I saw you leave the dance with her the other night. I was just wondering. You two looked like you were getting along very well."

"Marty and I are just friends."

"So you're not going out?"

"We went for lunch together the other day." Louise lined up her shot. "And we're having dinner this weekend."

"But you're just friends."

"Yes," Louise answered through gritted teeth. With all the concentration she could muster, she chopped down on the grass and sent the ball into the fairway. Her shot didn't carry far, but her next one would be much easier. She got back into the cart for the short ride to Pauline's ball, also in the high grass.

Pauline chose a club and studied her lie. "I was thinking about asking Marty out."

Louise bit down on her lip.

"I was worried about stepping on your toes, though." The redhead never once looked up from her ball as she talked. "But if you're just friends, I guess it doesn't matter." She whacked the ball and it carried ahead, still in the rough. Her next shot would be difficult as well. "Does it?"

Pauline proceeded with her third stroke then drove the cart behind a tree while Linda and Shirley hit their second shots. Louise then walked to the center of the fairway with her six-iron, the pin straight ahead about a hundred yards. She caught the ball solidly and her third shot sailed over the green to the other side. *Right into the sand trap.*

She stomped back to the cart in disgust and slammed her club into the bag. "You know, Pauline, if it's all the same to you, I'd rather you didn't ask Marty out."

The redhead grinned. "I doubt she'd go out with me anyway. I think she's got her eye on somebody else."

"You shouldn't go out with your hair wet, Mom. I swear you're as bad as Tyler sometimes."

"It'll dry by itself in no time." Marty tucked her short-sleeved blue shirt into her khaki chinos. "And it'll look the same either way."

"But it won't be dry when you get there. Do you want to walk in with wet hair and have Louise think you don't care what you look like when you're with her?"

Marty sneered. "Why are you always so mean to me?" Nonetheless, she pulled the hair dryer from the drawer and began to dry her sodden locks.

"I want you to make a good impression. Tyler and I might have to head back to Michigan someday, and I want to leave you in good hands."

"You don't have to worry about me, Katie. I've been taking care of myself for a long time."

"Yeah, and going out with wet hair, I bet." Katie sat down on her mom's bed to watch her finish in the bathroom.

"So you think you're going to head back to Michigan?"

"Mike called me at the club this afternoon. I might take you up on your offer to fly up there and talk with him ... just for a couple of days."

"If he's ready to talk, I think you should go, sweetheart. You can't work things out twelve hundred miles apart."

"I know. But I don't want to take Tyler out of school unless it's to move back up there for good. I was thinking I'd fly to Chicago on Monday and have Mike come get me." Katie had weekends off to be with her son. "Could you cover for me at the club if I stayed until Wednesday night? I hate to miss work, but I either have to go when Tyler's in school or get a sitter."

"Sure." Marty turned off the dryer and fluffed her hair. It actually did look nicer, she grudgingly admitted. "Have you decided what you want to accomplish?"

Katie shook her head. "Not really, but I'm not going back to a bunch of promises. We can't live on that."

Marty sat down beside her on the bed. "I know, honey. I also know you can be pretty stubborn. You get that from me. All the other bad stuff you get from your father, but I'll own up to the stubborn part."

"What do you want me to do, Mom? Just pull Tyler out of a school where he's doing good for a change and go back to living on peanut butter and stale bread again?"

"No! I'm not suggesting that at all. If I had my way, you and Tyler would stay right here. Mike doesn't deserve to have you with him until he gets his act together. I think leaving him the way you did took a lot of guts, and I'm really proud of how you came down here and went right to work at the club."

"Then what?"

"I'm just worried that you'll forget how nice it was to be in love with Mike. That can't be gone forever and I hope you don't go up there and back him into a corner with ultimatums."

"There has to be some kind of ultimatum. He has to get a job or we're staying here."

"I agree. It's just that I know how you can be about not giving in—not that I think you're wrong this time—but it might take some compromise. And maybe you and Mike have to ask yourselves if you're still in love enough to work through this."

Katie sighed. "I feel like I am, but then I get mad at him when I think about him just sitting back and letting them repossess everything we owned."

"That's why you have to watch yourself about being stubborn. You can't go forward if you keep letting yourself go back to things like that."

"I know." Katie pushed the bangs from her mother's brow. "This means I get to advise you on your love life too, you know."

"I dried my hair, didn't I?"

“Do you take cream and sugar?” Louise asked from the kitchen.

“Yes, both.”

“Why don’t I let you fix your own?” Louise brought a tray bearing two steaming mugs of coffee and the condiments to the dining table. The dinner dishes were stacked in the sink.

“Dinner was delicious,” Marty said. Roasted chicken with winter vegetables and steamed asparagus. “Who knew something could taste so good and not be bad for you?”

“Let’s move into the living room where we can be more comfortable.” Louise picked up the tray and led them to the sofa, where they settled on opposite ends. “I take it you don’t cook much.”

“I’m pretty dangerous around open flames. I can usually follow directions on a box, but the rest of it is beyond me.”

They kept up their conversation, which was practically a seamless continuation of what they had talked about on Sanibel—stories about life on the golf course and in front of the classroom. Louise decided she really liked Marty’s playful side and the way she built up her stories to a punch line. No wonder everyone who knew the golf pro seemed to like her so much.

“You want more coffee?” Louise asked, eyeing the empty cup.

“Sure. It’s decaf, right? Otherwise I’m going to be calling you in the middle of the night wanting to talk because I can’t sleep.”

Louise chuckled. “It’s decaf. Believe me, I’d be the same way.” She poured more coffee and returned to the sofa. “Rhonda used to drink a Pepsi first thing in the morning. Some days I swear I can still hear that top popping off.”

Marty picked up her mug and settled back. “Why don’t you tell me more about Rhonda?”

Louise shifted uncomfortably, feeling as though she had breached some sort of social etiquette by bringing up her late partner's name again. Marty didn't seem to be put off by it, though. "What do you want to know?"

"I don't know ... whatever you want to tell me. I just think anyone who wants to really know you has to know her too."

"That's so sweet of you. I think a lot of people are uncomfortable talking with me about her, even Linda and Shirley sometimes. They're afraid it's just going to make me sad—and it usually does—but it hurts more to feel like people are trying to pretend like she doesn't exist anymore."

"Of course she still exists."

Louise related the story of how she and Rhonda met, and how they had come to be best friends. She told of Rhonda's fun-loving personality, and her love of music, travel, and golf. She described their closeted lifestyle, her voice giving away some of the bitterness she felt for not being able to share with others the fact that Rhonda had been deeply loved.

"At her funeral—which her family took over because neither of us had gotten around to making any plans of our own—one of her sisters said something about how sad it was that Rhonda had never found someone special to spend her life with. It was like nobody in the family even noticed that Rhonda and I had lived together for thirty-one years. We owned a house together and neither of us ever went anywhere without the other one. I don't know which bothered me most—the fact that they believed she was alone all her life, or the fact that they knew better but wouldn't own up to it."

"That must have hurt so much."

"It did. So did sitting in the sixth row behind relatives who didn't really know her at all ... and a bunch of giggling girls that had never seen a dead person before." Louise's eyes clouded with tears at the awful memory. "I'm sorry. This is why nobody ever wants to talk about her."

"It's okay." Marty scooted closer and put her arm around Louise's shoulders. "You guys were so lucky to have each other."

"Thank you." Marty's strong arm felt good. It seemed to Louise as though Marty understood she still needed to draw comfort and strength from those around her. "I appreciate you asking about her. I know it isn't fun to hear all of that."

"I don't mind. I feel like I know you better already, and that was worth it to me. I hope it was to you too."

Louise nodded and pulled herself together. "Turn about is fair play, though. You have to bare your soul now."

Marty fell back against the couch and groaned.

"And it doesn't count if you're not bawling your eyes out when you finish."

"Oh," Marty grimaced. "I don't know if I have any stories that make me cry. I've never had anything close to the kind of loss you had to go through. I just made a whole lot of miserable choices."

"I bet you broke a dozen hearts."

Marty chuckled. "Hardly. My sordid past is more along the lines of Wallace. Not that there were any more men—his sorry ass was enough—but my relationships usually ended right on time, if not a little late."

"That's too cryptic for me to figure out." Without even thinking, Louise leaned back into Marty's arm and reached up to pat the hand that came to rest on her shoulder.

"I just spent too much time and energy on the wrong people. Sue was the first person I got involved with after Wallace. She was nice enough and we had a good time together, but she didn't really like being with Katie and that was a deal-breaker."

"How old was Katie then?"

"About ten. But that was my fault as much as it was Sue's because I didn't deal with it like I should have. A couple years later, I met Gretchen, and she had two teenagers of her own, so at least that wasn't a problem." Marty then shuddered, prompting Louise to laugh.

"Something tells me I have to hear the Gretchen story."

"Gretchen had a restaurant—nothing fancy, just a family place. She kept trying to get me to quit golf and come to work with her. Can you imagine me working in a restaurant?"

Louise laughed again and shook her head.

"I'd rather teach math … and I think I'd be better at it."

"I can't picture you at all in a classroom … or a kitchen. In fact, I can't picture you anywhere but on a golf course."

"Gretchen didn't see it that way. About that time Bob Seaver—he was the manager at the club where I worked—he put together a group of investors to buy a course in the North Carolina mountains. He asked me to come down and work the season, and not just for the pro shop and the youth clinics, but as the full-time assistant pro from May to October. I had to choose between Gretchen and golf. It took me about half a second."

"No contest, huh?"

"Not with her. My problem was with Katie, because she wanted to stay with my mom in Michigan and finish high school. It was hard to leave her, but we all talked about it, and it was only for six months. It was too good an opportunity to pass up."

Louise leaned forward and freshened their coffee cups. "So how did you end up at Pine Island?"

"I answered an ad in a trade magazine. Turned out Bennie was from Grand Rapids and we knew a lot of the same people." Marty took a sip of her coffee and added a spoonful of sugar. "And then I met Angela."

"And you were with her for … how long?"

"About six years. We split up eight years ago. I made a mistake, a pretty big one," Marty confessed. "I sort of cheated on her and hurt her bad. I'd never done anything like that before, and I couldn't believe how awful I felt about myself."

"Sort of cheated?"

Marty cocked her head sideways as she thought about it. "I went out with somebody. We didn't really do anything, but I probably would have if the opportunity had presented itself."

"That doesn't sound like much. Couldn't you work through it?"

Marty shook her head. "No, she threw me out the same day. She never even spoke to me again."

"After six years together? You didn't even get to apologize?"

"No. To be honest, our relationship was never really all that good to begin with. We had a lot of differences, and sometimes I think we only stayed together because we were both tired of things not ever working out with anybody. Looking back on it now, I'd say we wasted six years of our lives ... five, anyway. The first one wasn't so bad. I didn't mind so much that we weren't together anymore but I hated ending it that way."

"And there hasn't been anyone since then?" Louise recalled what Shirley and Linda had said.

Again, Marty shook her head. "It's pretty jarring to wake up one day and realize that you don't like yourself very much. It takes a long time to come back from something like that."

Louise reached over and snaked her fingers through Marty's. "And how do you feel about yourself now?"

"I like who I am now, even if it took me sixty-one years to get there."

Louise squeezed her hand. "I'm glad to hear that, Marty. I think there's a lot about you to like." She enjoyed the unexpected blush that crept up the golf pro's neck.

"I think I've dumped enough on you for one day, Lou. I should probably be going. I have to be at work early tomorrow."

The women stood up and moved toward the door where Marty donned her lightweight jacket.

"Thanks for dinner. Oh, that reminds me about lunch next week. Katie's heading up to Michigan for a few days to talk things out with her husband. I'm going to have to cover for her in the clubhouse, and then I've got to pick up Tyler."

"Maybe another time then?" It wasn't the nice restaurant or the walk along the beach that Louise was looking forward to. It was being with Marty again.

"How would you feel about joining us for pizza on Tuesday night?"

"You sure Tyler won't mind sharing his grandmother?"

"Are you kidding? Wait till he finds out you're a math teacher."

Louise thought ahead to what it would be like to see Marty with the little boy and found herself looking forward to it already. "All right, then. Call me and let me know what time."

"Great!" Marty opened the front door and turned back to her hostess. "I really enjoyed tonight."

"Me too." The seconds passed as Louise nervously waited for the kiss she knew would come. Marty finally leaned toward her and she closed the distance, bringing her face lower as their mouths met. As their lips slid slowly against each other, Marty brought an arm to the center of her back and pulled her closer.

Before their lips ever parted, Louise knew it was going to be pretty difficult to call that one a simple kiss between two friends.

November 1978

Louise sighed in frustration as she worked the clasp on her pearl necklace.

"Relax, honey. Let me get that." Rhonda came up behind her at the vanity, where she looked over her shoulder into the mirror. "Why are you so anxious about tonight?"

"We don't know a thing about these women, Rhonda. How do we know they can be discreet?"

"We do know about them. Shirley is a high school band director, just like me. We've gotten to be friends. And Linda teaches elementary school. They'll be discreet because they have just as much to lose as we do." Rhonda fastened the necklace and traced her fingers around to the hollow of Louise's throat. "Are you still mad at me?"

Louise had fumed quietly for three days after Rhonda first told her about the plans to go to the Pittsburgh Symphony with the two women. Then she finally blew up, angry that Rhonda had shared their most closely-guarded secret with people she didn't even know, and without talking to her first. They had never told anyone but her brother Hiram's family about their relationship and only then because they needed his legal advice on two women buying a house together.

"Did it ever occur to you that other people might not be as careful as we are? What if somebody finds out they're lovers and people put two and two together because they see us out with them?"

"Lou, other people don't sit at home on a Saturday night saying 'Gee, I wonder if Rhonda and Louise are out with other women tonight.'"

"I know that! But people can't help but notice things." Louise's anger was escalating and she stalked out of their bedroom with Rhonda on her heels.

"Come on, Lou! Don't you ever wish we could have some friends that we can be ourselves with? Even when we're with your brother, you won't hold my hand or sit close to me."

"Not everybody wants to see people fawning over each other in public."

"We are not the only lesbians in the world."

Louise visibly shuddered. She hated that word.

"There are lots of others out there that we could be friends with. I would love it if somebody else could see how much I love you. I'm not saying we have to make out in front of anyone, but wouldn't it be nice for once not to have to worry about how to act all the time?"

Louise didn't answer and turned her back again to walk away.

"Louise Stevens, turn around and look at me! What's really bothering you? That Shirley and Linda might not be discreet, or that I didn't talk to you before asking them to come along?"

"Our relationship is not only your secret to tell, Rhonda."

"So it's me you're mad at. That's good. But save it for when we get back home, because I don't want you being rude to Shirley and Linda tonight. I happen to think we're all going to end up being good friends. They're both dying for the chance to get out with other women, and so am I."

"Do you not understand what's at stake here?"

"I do. And I'm telling you again—we have nothing to worry about with Shirley and Linda. And I don't blame you for being angry at me. It was wrong for me to tell them without talking to you first."

"Yes, it was."

"I'm sorry, Lou. Please forgive me. I know you want to, but you think I haven't suffered enough yet." Rhonda batted her eyelashes innocently.

"You are impossible, Rhonda Markosky."

"I know, but I'm worth it." She walked over and put her arms around Louise. "And I love you more than ... chocolate."

"You expect me to believe that?" Louise pulled her into a sudden kiss that told her she was forgiven.

"If we didn't have friends to meet tonight, we might just skip the symphony."

Chapter 14

MARTY STOOD BY her bed in her slacks and bra, ironing her best white blouse. When she heard her daughter hang up the phone, she began counting off the seconds before Katie would appear in her bedroom. The visit back to Michigan had gone well, but she and Mike still had things to work out.

"That was Mike."

"I figured. What'd he say?"

"He's still thinking about it. He said he'd talk to one of his buddies and maybe they'd both come down. I told him not to even think he was just going to move down here and keep hanging out with his friends." Katie nudged her mother aside. "Let me do that. You're creasing the sleeves in the wrong place."

Marty gladly gave up her task and sat on the bed. "You know, you guys can have the place to yourself all summer. I'll be leaving in about five weeks."

Katie had taken the newspaper classifieds with her when she went to visit her husband. They both agreed that while construction jobs didn't pay very well compared to Michigan wages, they were plentiful in Southwest Florida. And it was cheaper to live in Florida—plus Katie already had a job—so it was clear Mike was the one who needed to relocate if they were going to be together again.

"We can't just take over your house, Mom."

"Why not? It's just going to sit here empty until October."

"Because Mike needs to be the one providing for his family, not you."

"And there you have it, folks! Katie Compton is too stubborn for her own good. You don't have to think of staying here as Mike's failure. Think of it as an opportunity to get a few dollars in the bank. It isn't going to matter that you're here instead of paying rent somewhere else."

Katie nodded her head. "I'll admit I'm being stubborn about it. If you want to know the truth, I think Mike is afraid to come down while you're still here."

"Well, he ought to be! He's getting a brand new asshole when I get hold of him."

The daughter giggled, relishing the dressing down her mom would give her husband for neglecting his responsibilities. She finished ironing the blouse. "Here you go. Isn't this better?"

"You do good work. Can't imagine where you learned it, though." Marty carefully put on the blouse and fumbled with her cufflinks.

"Where are you going tonight?"

"To the symphony in Sarasota." Marty tilted her chin upward and puffed out her chest to convey her high-brow airs.

"Since when do you like the symphony?"

"You make it sound like I have no class." She tucked in her shirttail and checked her appearance. "Louise likes it, and I'm sure I'll enjoy it too."

"I think it's time you brought Louise home to formally meet your daughter."

Marty snorted. "You met her at the club."

"But she was just another golfer then. Now she's your girlfriend."

"She isn't my girlfriend."

"That's not what Tyler said."

"That little snitch! What did he tell you?"

"He said you smooched her on the mouth after you three ate pizza together."

"You know you can't believe everything a six-year-old says."

"He also said she was pretty."

"He did?"

Katie nodded. "But you're right. Little children don't always tell the truth."

Marty took a blue silk jacket from her closet and pulled it on. "Who raised you to be so mean?"

"So when were you planning on telling us that you and Marty Beck were dating?" Shirley and Linda were surprised to learn Louise had invited Marty along to the symphony.

"We are not dating! We're just spending some time together and getting to know each other a little better," Louise answered, the defensiveness evident in her tone.

"And they aren't calling that dating anymore? Boy, I've been out of the game a long time." Shirley was almost indignant that their friend had left them out of the loop on this important development.

Linda scowled at her partner. She was ecstatic that Louise had invited Marty to join them, and she didn't want Shirley's teasing remarks to cause their friend to have second thoughts. "Does Marty enjoy the symphony?"

"I'm sure it isn't her favorite. But she's looking forward to it."

"I bet she has a good time," Linda said. "I'll never forget the first time Shirley took me."

"Do you remember what it was?" Shirley asked.

"Handel's *Messiah*. How could I ever forget? You practically yanked me out of my seat for the *Hallelujah Chorus*."

"It's tradition to stand for that part."

"You could have just said that instead of pulling my arm out of the socket."

Louise shook her head and laughed at her friends. Her first trip to the symphony with Rhonda had been similar to the one they described. "I remember how Rhonda would whisper to me through the whole concert, telling me all the instruments and movements. Then we'd go home and she'd put on an album and quiz me about every one."

Linda nodded vigorously. "Shirley was the same way. And she used to bring the instruments home one at a time and make me try to play them. I'll never forget the day she introduced me to the 'spit valve.' I'd never heard of anything so disgusting in my whole life."

"Yeah, Rhonda had me come in with her once over the summer to help her clean all the spit valves. It was very disgusting."

Just then, Marty pulled into the driveway.

"Here she is."

"She looks awfully cute in that blue jacket, Lou," Shirley offered.

"Behave!"

The three women gathered their purses and coats and Louise looked back at Shirley one more time.

"Shirley, please don't ..." *Please don't what?*

"I won't," her friend assured. "Let's go have fun."

Marty listened in near-misery as her three companions raved in the car on the way home about the musical selections and the orchestral performance. The last time she felt this out-of-place was when her daughter got married and she had to sit with the wedding planner for six hours going over minutiae.

Each time she had glanced at Louise tonight, the woman had been smiling dreamily at the music, bobbing her head slightly in places at the rhythm. Marty couldn't believe people actually knew this music. How could they remember it without any lyrics or a catchy melody?

"Besides Bach, I think the French composers are my favorites," Louise said. The Sarasota Symphony program had included classic selections from Ravel, Debussy and Bertrand.

"And the bassoon was splendid," Linda exclaimed, the others agreeing at once.

"What part was your favorite, Marty?" Louise turned in the back seat to face her companion.

Marty cringed inwardly. Her ignorance about the symphony was about to rear its ugly head. "I, uh ... I guess my favorite was ... the drums in that first one." She was pretty sure that one was called something like *Bolero*, but she wasn't positive so she decided not to mention it by name.

"Did you say the drums?" Shirley asked from the driver's seat.

"Yeah." Marty felt ridiculous. Her untrained ear couldn't tell the difference between a bassoon and a saxophone; for her, the percussion section was the only sound she recognized. "I liked how they kept getting louder as the song went along."

"That's amazing!" Louise said, reaching over to cover Marty's hand on the seat. "For somebody who's never really listened to this kind of music, you just picked out the single most distinguishing characteristic of that piece."

Relieved she hadn't made a total fool of herself, Marty smiled at Louise and turned her palm upward to intertwine their fingers.

"I always considered the flute to be the center of *Bolero*," Shirley said.

"Maybe," Linda conceded. "But Marty's right about how it starts out softly and gets louder."

"And nothing emphasizes that more than the percussion," Louise added, squeezing Marty's fingers. "So do we have a tee time for next week?"

The conversation moved to golf, and Marty relaxed. She figured Louise had sensed her uncertainty and changed the subject. For that she was grateful, but it left an opening for doubts to creep in—the ones that said she had probably said something idiotic and that all three of them thought she was stupid.

"Goodnight," Louise and Marty stood in the driveway waving to their friends. "You want to come in for coffee?"

"Hmmm ... yes, but I shouldn't. Tomorrow's one of my early days." Marty walked Louise to the door and took her keys as Petie began to bark. "But I'll stick my head in the door and say hi to my buddy if it's okay."

"Are you kidding? He'll be disappointed if you don't."

They entered the foyer and Petie got so excited Louise thought it best to clip on his leash and take him outside right away. Marty took over and led the dog to the tall grass, pointing out to Louise that the lawn was wet from the sprinklers and she should avoid it in her high heels.

"You're spoiling him, you know. I would have taken him to the edge of the driveway, but you're letting him go to his favorite spot."

"He's been here by himself all night. He deserves a treat," Marty argued. "I'm going to bring him something special next time I come over here."

"How about Monday after work?" *Yes, Louise. That's called dating.*

"Monday?"

"The Penguins play the Lightning and it's on TV at seven. I'll fix dinner and we can eat in the living room."

"You're on!" Marty handed over the leash and followed Louise back inside. "But I have to go home and shower first."

"Just bring a change of clothes and shower here. If you have to go all the way home, you'll miss the whole first period."

"You're right. And by that time, the Lightning will be up four-zip and you won't let me watch it anymore."

"More likely the Penguins will be in the lead and you'll be the one who doesn't care to watch."

Marty smiled. "I really had a good time tonight. Thanks for asking me along."

"Did you really enjoy it?"

"I did. I'll admit I didn't know one piece from the other, and if you played them all for me again right now, I probably wouldn't recognize any of them. Well, maybe that first one ... *Bolero.* But no matter what kind of music it is, I like hearing it performed live."

"That really is what makes it so special."

"No, what made it special tonight was being there with you."

"I liked being there with you too." She reached to pull Marty closer and their lips met in a soft kiss ... and another kiss ... and another. Louise's heart began to pound as she realized what they were doing. She heard a low moan—Marty's, she thought, but she wouldn't swear to it. She pulled away and straightened up.

"You okay?"

Louise nodded, unable to speak.

"Then I guess I'll ... see you Monday."

She nodded again. "Monday."

Louise watched as Marty returned to her car. When it left the driveway, she turned out the light and gathered her nerve to walk into the bedroom, where she would have to face that picture in the pewter frame.

Marty blew out a long, deep breath.

"Louise Stevens, you're going to drive me crazy."

There certainly were sparks between them when they had kissed tonight. It was more than just a friendly kiss, but it wasn't full-throttle romance either ... because it seemed to Marty that Louise wasn't comfortable just letting go.

The symphony was their fourth date, not counting the Valentine's dance. With any other woman, Marty figured they might have been sleeping together by now. That's the way it had always been with her back before Angela. Of course, that was over fifteen years ago and none of those women was anything like Louise Stevens.

Her physical attraction to the retired schoolteacher was definitely there. Marty hadn't even realized its extent until their kiss tonight. If things had escalated at the door, she knew she would have gladly stayed. But Louise didn't seem like the kind of woman who would ever let things get out of control. She had spent practically her whole life with one woman; it was probably the only kind of relationship she had ever known. And why would somebody like that want someone with Marty's track record?

Louise turned on her bedroom light, her eyes nervously catching those of Rhonda in the photo on the dresser.

"We had fun tonight, baby. You would have loved it, especially the bassoon. You always said it was one of the most difficult instruments to play."

She began to get undressed and was surprised at the tremor in her hands.

"We were talking tonight about the first time you and I went to the symphony with Shirley and Linda. I remembered we had such a big fight before they got there because you told them about us without asking me. And you said you were sure we could trust them." She walked over and picked up the frame. "Did I ever tell you that you were right about that? They sure have been good friends over the years. I don't know what I'd have done without them when I lost you."

She went into the closet, hung up her dress, and tossed her underthings into the hamper. She returned to the bedroom naked and pulled on a pair of silk pajamas from the drawer beneath her late lover's photo.

"We missed you tonight." She really needed to say that.

As she settled into bed, Louise pondered the truth of her statement. Before Marty had joined them, she and her two best friends had talked a little about the old days, about how the two band directors had spread their love of music to their respective partners. But from the moment Marty had arrived, she hadn't thought about Rhonda again until she returned home.

"There's something I need to talk to you about. I don't think I've figured it all out yet, though ... so it may be a few days." She leaned over and turned out the light. "I love you."

Chapter 15

LOUISE PUSHED THE front door open and hurried to the kitchen to grab the ringing phone. "Hello." She stooped to unfasten Petie's leash, and the terrier made a beeline for his water bowl.

It was Linda. "Hey, Lou! I was just calling to see how you enjoyed last night."

"I had a great time. How about you and Shirley?"

"We enjoyed it. It was nice to be out. Did Marty have a good time too?"

"Yes ... she had fun." Louise hesitated. "I'm glad you called. I was going to call you later on."

"Something on your mind?"

Louise sighed heavily. "You could say that."

"Does it have anything to do with a certain golf pro we all know?"

"Yes and no. I think it has more to do with a certain band director who's no longer with us."

"Why don't I come over for a little while and we can talk about it?"

"I'd appreciate that."

Twenty minutes later, Linda sat on a swivel stool at the kitchen bar watching Louise fill her coffee cup.

"Thanks for coming over."

"You're welcome. Would I be off-base if I guessed that Marty Beck has gotten you thinking about Rhonda these last few days?"

Louise shook her head. "I'd say you'd be hitting the nail on the head."

"How do you feel about it? Do you like Marty?"

Louise sighed, opened her mouth to speak, and then closed it.

"Never mind my questions. Why don't you just talk to me about what's going on?"

"Okay ... you guys already figured out that I sort of like Marty. That silliness about not dating was just me in denial."

"We figured that," Linda said, her eyes full of mischief. "We sort of like Marty too."

Louise rolled her eyes. "That's not what I meant."

"I know, Lou. But Shirley and I both think it's great you're going out with somebody as nice as Marty Beck."

Louise shook her head. "I don't know, Linda." She hated the way she was making her friend fish for every little thing, but Louise just hadn't found a way to articulate what she was feeling without having Linda think she was being ridiculous.

"You don't know what?"

"I don't know if I'm ready for this ... or if I ever will be. I never imagined there would be somebody else in my life besides Rhonda."

"Are you thinking about Marty being in your life, or are you just going out together for fun?"

"I don't know how to go out just for fun! The last time I went out on a date, LBJ was President."

"Maybe you should just enjoy it."

"I don't think it's been long enough. Maybe I should wait a while and just concentrate on making friends before I think about going out with somebody." Even as she said it, Louise didn't like that idea.

"If it's not right for you, let it go. Stop seeing her. Then you won't have to worry about it."

Louise recognized she was being goaded but she didn't mind. Linda wanted her to admit her feelings for Marty. "I don't want to stop seeing her but it feels ..."

"Like a betrayal?"

Louise nodded. "If I was really ready for this right now, I wouldn't feel so anxious about it. Does that make sense?"

"I don't know, Lou. I think it's perfectly natural for somebody in your shoes to be uneasy, but that doesn't have to mean there's something wrong with it. Why not listen to the part that says you want to keep going out with Marty and just ignore all the doubts?"

"How can I ignore Rhonda? She was my whole life for thirty-one years."

"What does Rhonda have to say about it now, Lou?"

Louise set her jaw firmly. "I'm not ... crazy enough to imagine that Rhonda talks to me, Linda. At least I'm not crazy enough to admit it. The feelings I have are mine, but they're the ones she gave me. I'm never going to have that with anybody ever again, so what am I doing with Marty Beck?"

"Having fun? Easing your loneliness? Making a good friend?"

Louise sighed. "That's what I wanted. What I wasn't counting on was that I would feel ... attracted to her." She looked down at her hands, uncomfortable at her admission.

Linda smiled softly and put her hand on Louise's arm. "Maybe you're falling in love again."

Louise shifted nervously in her seat, her expression telling Linda her words were on the mark. "How can I do that?"

"There's nothing wrong with it, Lou. If Marty is someone you enjoy being with—someone who makes you laugh, someone who makes you feel good—it's understandable you might fall in love with her." She stood up and tugged Louise toward the bedroom. "You still keep that photo of Rhonda in here?"

"Yes." Louise followed until they were standing before Rhonda's picture on the dresser.

"She sure was a pretty lady, Lou."

"She was beautiful." Even at sixty-three and sixty pounds overweight, Rhonda had a pretty face and dazzling smile.

"I know exactly what Rhonda thinks about you seeing Marty." Linda wrapped her arm around Louise's waist to soften her words. "She doesn't think anything at all, because she's gone from us."

Louise's eyes filled with tears.

"I know you still feel her spirit with you, hon, and I'm sure talking with her makes it feel like she's still here ... but she isn't. You are, though, and you still have a lot of living left to do. We both know if Rhonda could tell you what she wanted for you, it would be for you to try as hard as you can to be happy. Isn't that what you'd want for her?"

Louise wiped her eyes and nodded. "Yes."

"Of course you would. And it isn't like you have to choose between them, Lou. Marty is the only one you can choose now. You enjoy being with her and you have feelings for her. Why not see where it goes?"

Louise hugged Linda hard as the words sank in. That was what she wanted; she just needed someone to give her permission.

After a few quiet moments, she led the way from the bedroom and the picture of Rhonda. Back in the kitchen, she poured more coffee for the two of them, ready to talk about her new resolve. "What do you really think of Marty? You've known her longer than I have."

"She's always been friendly to everybody. People like her."

"So ... what do you think of me with Marty?"

"You're the best person to answer that. But it's hard not to notice that you two are pretty cute together."

Louise smiled, unable to hide her blush. "Cute?"

"Yeah, the way she always runs around to open your door and the way you take her arm to stand up. Shirley and I were talking about that. You were the one who always did those things when you were with Rhonda."

Louise shrugged. "That was just how we went together, I guess. I never thought about it much. But I know what you mean about Marty. She wants to do those things and it seems more natural for both of us."

"And I saw you two holding hands in the back seat. That was cute too."

Louise rolled her eyes like a teenager who was spied on by her little sister. "I can't believe I'm putting up with this."

"I want to know what happened when we left you two alone," Linda teased.

"We made another date for tomorrow night—dinner here to watch the hockey game."

"That's all?"

"And we kissed goodnight."

"That's what I was after."

"I knew what you were after. And you're probably itching to get out of here now so you can run home and tell Shirley."

"We both care about you, Lou. We want you to be happy."

"I appreciate that. But I really don't know where all of this is going to go."

"Nobody expects you to know already. You and Marty should have fun together and not worry about what's going to happen. Just enjoy this part."

"You're right."

"Besides, Marty leaves soon for North Carolina, so you have a built-in break from each other."

Louise nodded pensively. "I hadn't thought about it that way. That'll sure keep things from moving too fast."

"And by the time she comes back in the fall, you'll have a better idea of what you want."

Louise leaned back on her stool. Linda was right. She didn't have to make any big decisions. All she had to do was keep things on an even keel for another few weeks, and Marty would be gone for the summer.

Louise bit her lip to keep from yelling out when the Penguins scored to take a 4-3 lead late in the third period. All her team had to do was hold on for another three minutes and they would have the win.

Marty slumped at the other end of the couch, sound asleep. She had looked tired all night, Louise thought. The seconds wound down on the hockey game and Louise grabbed the remote to mute the television before the horn sounded. She closed the distance between herself and Marty and placed a hand on the slumbering woman's shoulder.

"Marty?" she called gently.

Marty opened one eye and looked skeptically at her host. "I wasn't asleep." She rolled her head around her shoulders and blinked her eyes a few times. "Okay, maybe I was. Sorry."

"It's okay. You must have been tired." It was after ten and Louise knew Marty's days usually started early.

"Yeah, it's been a long couple of weeks."

"You poor thing. You haven't had a day off in two weeks."

"At least I'm off tomorrow. Please tell me the Lightning won."

"The Lightning won ... not."

"You lie."

"Sorry. The Penguins were just too much for them."

Marty scrunched her face in resignation. "At least dinner was good."

"And the company?"

"The company was the best part." Marty smiled and stood. "I better go before I conk out again. Do you want to do something this weekend? A movie maybe?"

"Sure—an early one so you can get to bed on time." Louise walked her guest to the door. "I'll be at the club tomorrow. That student from Westfield I told you about is coming to visit and we're going to play a round."

"What kind of playing around?" Marty teased.

"Golf, silly! But this girl used to have a crush on me, and she's quite cute, so you never know."

"Hey, I better not catch her flirting with you. I'll have you know I can be very territorial."

Louise knew Marty was only kidding, but she actually enjoyed this small glimmer of possessiveness. "She isn't going to flirt with me! She got over it—they all do eventually."

"I find it pretty hard to believe anybody could get over you, Lou."

"You're the flirt, Marty Beck!"

"Only when it comes to you." Marty stretched her arms out to wrap them around Louise's neck. "Thanks again for dinner."

"You're welcome anytime." She hugged Marty's waist and pulled her closer. Their lips found one another and they got lost in their deepest kiss yet. Louise felt gentle fingers massaging the back of her neck as she slightly opened her mouth to feel the flick of Marty's tongue.

"I'm really starting to like that, Lou," Marty said as their kiss broke.

Louise planted a small peck on Marty's nose, changing the moment from serious to playful. "You be careful going home."

"I will."

Louise watched as the Subaru disappeared. *That was some kiss, Marty Beck.*

"Do you like Florida, Petie?" Michele was on her knees petting the excited terrier.

"I think his motto is 'Home is where my bowl is.' It looks like he remembers you."

"I think so too."

The attention proved too much for Petie and he suddenly ran to the front door and began to whimper.

"I guess he wants to go out," Louise said, grabbing his leash from the hook.

"I'll take him." They walked outside together with Petie leading the way. "Are you sure I look okay to go to your club?"

"You look great!" Michele was wearing brand new shorts and a golf shirt, but she had never seemed confident about her appearance. It was a blustery day, and Louise was dressed in long black pants and a colorful shirt with a blue vest. "I think you've finally filled out a little."

"Yeah, that's the 'freshman fifteen' they always talk about. It's true."

"I remember. There's no one around to make you eat vegetables, so you eat burgers and fries instead."

Michele laughed and nodded. "You have to promise not to laugh at what a terrible golfer I am."

"We're just out for fun, you know. I was only kidding about that dollar-a-hole thing."

"Oh, sure you were. But I brought cash just in case."

"No, you're my guest today, Michele. So tell me some more about your friends. Who all do you keep up with from Westfield?"

As they walked through the neighborhood, Michele filled her former teacher in on all the gossip about her classmates. Louise, in turn, talked a little about her life in Florida—golf, the beaches, her few friends—but without revealing the personal details she had become so adept at avoiding.

"Let's take my car. I've already put the clubs in the trunk."

On the way, Louise described the series of canals, and how they made it a challenge to drive from one point to another.

"Here we are. Welcome to Pine Island Country Club."

"Wow! This is nice. Are you sure I look all right?"

"You look fine. Stop worrying. Besides, we're probably going to play in the water, in the sand, and in the woods today, so you wouldn't want to be wearing your Sunday best."

The pair got out and opened the trunk. Inside were two sets of clubs, one belonging to Louise, the other to Rhonda. Michele realized it right away when she spotted the monogrammed bag.

"These were Miss Markosky's clubs!"

"That's right. And you have the honor of being the first person to use them in over four years." It was a very sentimental moment for Louise when she had taken her late partner's clubs from the closet, but she had no misgivings at all about letting Michele use them. Rhonda wouldn't have minded one bit.

"I don't know if I should."

"Of course you should. Maybe some of her luck will rub off on you."

"Miss Markosky was lucky?"

"Like a red-headed Leprechaun." They set the bags at the club drop and Louise parked the car. When they entered the clubhouse, Louise was surprised to see Marty behind the counter, busy with another customer. If she killed a little time browsing the racks, she could introduce her to Michele as they were signing in. "I think you need a visor, Michele."

"Good morning, ladies." Marty finally sauntered over to where they were looking at the caps, eyeing the lanky youth with Louise.

"Hi, there. I thought it was your day off."

"Bennie had to run up to Tampa to pick up some sprinkler heads and he asked me to come in. Can I help you with something?"

"I don't need anything, but I think my friend here could use a visor."

"I think we can fix her right up."

"That's a good idea," Michele agreed readily, reaching into her back pocket for her wallet. "It'll be a nice souvenir."

Louise put her hand on the girl's wallet and pushed it away, fishing her own billfold from her pocket. "Michele, this is my very dear friend, Marty Beck. She's one of the first people I met when I moved down here. Marty, I'd like you to meet one of my favorite students from all my years at Westfield High School, Michele Sanders."

Marty smiled. "Hi, Michele. Welcome to Pine Island. Any friend of Lou Stevens is a friend of mine."

"Pleased to meet you, Miss Beck."

"Miss Beck!" Marty wailed. "Here, you can have this visor with my compliments if you promise never to call me that again!"

All three women laughed together, and Louise couldn't resist ruffling Michele's short hair. "You ready to hit the course?"

"I guess."

Marty led them to the sign-in sheet. "The greens were cut this morning, so they're pretty quick. The pin placement is Number 3."

"Back center?"

"That's right. You two have fun. And stop by later and let me know how you did." Marty smiled broadly when she caught Louise's wink.

"She's really nice," Michele remarked as they walked out to the cart.

"She sure is. And she's quite a golfer, too. She used to play on the women's tour."

"Wow! If you're used to playing with people like that, you're going to laugh at me."

"No, I won't. We were all beginners once," Louise said, tugging on the bill of the brand new visor. "Now let's play some golf!"

As expected, the novice golfer was all over the course, in the water, in the woods, and in the sand. By mutual agreement, they stopped counting strokes after eight, and Michele beat that only three times on the front nine.

"Tell me more about school. What math classes are you taking this semester?" Louise asked as they stopped to clean their balls on Number 10.

"Just calculus for now." Michele described her course load, and her plans to pick up education classes in the fall. "By the way, if I didn't say it before, I really appreciated what you said about the other thing I told you ... about being gay."

Louise picked up on Michele's nervousness, and hoped she wouldn't sound the same way. "Like I said, you had no reason to worry. It's just a small part of who you are. It doesn't define you."

"I just hope it doesn't keep me from getting a good job. One of my friends at school said she had a history teacher in Philadelphia who was gay. He even sponsored a club for kids that were coming out."

"It's nice some of the schools can have that sort of thing."

"I wish Westfield had had one. It would have been nice not to feel like I was such a freak all those years."

Despite her own anxiety, Louise was overcome with compassion. "You weren't a freak, you know." She put her arm around Michele's shoulder as they walked back to the cart. The serious turn of their conversation had taken her focus from the game and she waved a foursome through as they sat down in the cart. "But I can imagine how hard it must have been to feel like you were all by yourself."

"At least I didn't get picked on like some of my friends, but that's because I was smart enough to keep everything to myself."

"I think a lot of gay people do that ... hide who they are so it won't be an issue."

Michele nodded. "It sure would be a lot easier if people could just be who they are."

Though it hadn't been said as a rebuke, Louise looked away and bit her lip, feeling guilty not only for her silence back at Westfield, but for her continued inability to tell Michele that she understood her fears perfectly. "I think your generation is going to have to lead the way on that one." Michele looked up at her and she smiled. "But I think you're up for it."

Louise saw a familiar face heading their way in a cart.

"Have you two lost all your balls?" Marty quipped, coming to a stop in front of them.

"No," Louise answered. "We're just solving the world's problems."

Marty grinned. "I'm glad to know somebody's hard at work on that. That means I can take the rest of the day off."

"You do that. We'll see you later."

Marty waved goodbye and drove on to the next hole.

"That was really nice of her to stop," Michele remarked.

"Yeah, that's the way Marty is. She's a good friend to have." Louise got out of the cart and drew her driver from the bag. "How about you take honors this hole? Step up there and give it a rip."

June 1981

Louise and Rhonda hauled their respective crates into the house, dumping the folders and texts in the back hallway of their two-story home. They had bought the house together ten years earlier, Rhonda finally convincing Louise it was stupid to continue to live as roommates in an apartment. Everyone already knew they were living together; they might as well be building equity.

"I can't believe this school year is finally over. It seemed like the longest of all my twenty-three years," Rhonda said. "How about you?"

"It has seemed a little longer than usual. Maybe it was all the snow days we had to make up."

"Maybe. I think it was because this year wasn't as much fun."

"Why would you say that?" Louise kicked off her shoes and plopped down on the couch. "It was just like every other year."

"No it wasn't." Rhonda took a chair facing her. "Nothing is as much fun as it used to be, Lou."

Louise stiffened and looked down at her feet. She knew where this conversation was headed.

"We need to talk. We have to settle this once and for all, because it isn't going away." Rhonda's words were calm and somber. "I think with school out, we can use the summer to figure out where we go from here."

"What do you mean where we go?"

"We have to talk about what happened last year."

"I've already said all I want to say about it, and I've heard all I want to hear. Why can't we just leave it at that?"

"Because you haven't left it at that. You're still carrying it around—after a whole year, you're still thinking about it every day."

"I am not." Louise pushed herself off the couch looking for the quickest exit from a conversation she didn't want to have.

"Please sit down and talk to me."

"What more do you want me to say, Rhonda? It hurts me to talk about it. Why do you want to put me through all that again?"

"Because we haven't gone through it at all, honey. You've never really told me how it made you feel, or what you want from me now." Tears filled Rhonda's eyes and Louise returned to the couch. "And every day, we get further and further apart. It won't be long before we can't talk to each other at all."

"It hurts."

"I know it does. And I hurt for you. Sweetheart, I would give anything to be able to undo what I did. But I can't. And we're never going to get past it if you won't even talk to me."

"I am past it. I don't see what good it will do to rehash it."

"You're not past it, Lou. You know that as well as I do." Rhonda wiped her eyes. "We hardly ever make love, and even when we do, we're like a couple of ... robots. We don't laugh anymore. And we don't talk about our future together like we used to. We haven't even planned a vacation together for this summer ... but why should we? A vacation would be fun and we don't have fun anymore."

"You had your fun last year!" Louise answered sharply. "And it's been nothing but miserable for me ever since. I see you talking with this man ... or that one. And every single time I ask myself 'Is that the one?'"

"Does it really make a difference who it was, Lou? I'll tell you everything if it means we can get on with our lives."

"I don't want to know any more about it. It's bad enough that I know you were sleeping with somebody while my father was dying. I don't want a name or a face to put on it."

"Lou, please listen to me." Rhonda came to kneel in front of her and placed her hands in Louise's lap. "I did something awful and I'm so ashamed I can hardly stand myself. I can't believe I hurt you like that and that I put this wonderful life we have at risk. I've never felt so horrible about anything in my whole life."

Louise met her gaze, her own eyes brimming with tears she fought not to shed.

"And the worst part is that there is nothing I can do to fix it. You're the only one who can save us now, Lou. I can't keep living like this ... wondering if you're going to leave me because you don't love me anymore. Or if I'll have to leave because I can't stop feeling guilty about what I did. You're going to have to reach down inside yourself and forgive me. Not because I deserve it—we both know that I don't. Do it because you want what we used to have together." She placed both of her hands on top of Louise's. "I promise you that you will never have reason to doubt me again for as long as we live."

"I do still love you, Rhonda." The tears spilled freely now. "It just hurts so bad."

"I know, honey. And I'm so sorry." Both women were sobbing now. "Please forgive me. Please."

Louise nodded and held her arms open for Rhonda to crawl into the embrace. "I don't ever want to lose you, sweetheart."

"You won't, Lou. I'm always going to be here, and I promise I'll never hurt you again."

Chapter 16

LOUISE DROPPED HER clubs near the driving range and parked the Sable in the shade next to Marty's wagon. They had firmed up their plans for a movie on Saturday night, but she didn't want to wait that long to see Marty again.

Bennie was working the clubhouse when she picked up her tokens for a large bucket of balls.

"I think Marty's giving a short game lesson," he said.

Bennie's casual statement caught Louise off-guard. *How did he know I was looking for Marty?* Even though Louise no longer faced a risk of losing her job, she didn't like people knowing her private business. Thirty-five years of paranoia didn't go away overnight. "Mmmm, thanks. Maybe I'll see her and say hello."

As she walked toward the driving range, Louise took a sidelong look in the direction of the practice green. Sure enough, Marty was standing between a man and a woman, giving instruction as they hit chip shots in tandem. Louise smiled to herself, noting that Marty looked very cute in that dark blue scooped-neck shirt. Even from thirty yards away, she could make out just a hint of cleavage. For such a petite woman, Marty had rather large—

Good lord, Louise! She shook her head in surprise at where her thoughts had gone. She had only just given herself permission to consider them dating.

Louise reached the driving range and selected the tee at the far end because it was shaded. She emptied some of the range balls into the trough, selecting a nine-iron to start.

Smack!

That one felt pretty good, she thought.

Smack!

The ball dropped softly only a few feet from the 75-yard marker.

She smiled at the difference between her game now and when she first met Marty. She hadn't been able to hit the ball more than sixty-yards then. Deciding not to press her luck today, she tucked her iron away and extracted a fairway wood. These shots had been giving her a little trouble lately, and it would be good to work out the kinks in how she was following through.

Smack!

Topped it.

Smack!

That one didn't go straight at all.

"You know, there's a fifty-cent surcharge for every ball that leaves the driving range."

Louise smiled at the familiar line, turning at once to see ... to see Marty approach a woman she had noticed earlier having a good deal of trouble making solid contact with the ball. The woman was quite attractive, but appeared to have had only minimal instruction in the game of golf.

"Oh my! I'm so embarrassed. I can't seem to get in any sort of rhythm. I'm just terrible at this," the woman gushed with obvious discomfiture.

"No, you're not terrible at all. You just need a few pointers and some time to practice," Marty said with encouragement. "Here, let me show you a couple of things. It's Charlene, right?"

The woman nodded. "I don't think anyone can help this lousy swing, Martha."

"I told you. My friends call me Marty," the golf pro said, smiling as she moved toward the golfer.

At the other end of the mats, Louise grew steamed at the exchange. *"My friends call me Marty. Won't you be my friend?"* she muttered angrily.

The golf pro stepped behind the woman to help her find the right position for addressing the ball. Louise watched as Marty wrapped her arms around the woman's waist. It was more than she could stand. Angrily, she kicked the balls from her trough and slammed her club back into her bag.

The commotion caused Marty and Charlene to look up.

"Hi, Lou!" Marty smiled tentatively, obviously surprised at seeing Louise at the range.

Without a word, Louise heaved the bag onto her shoulder and stomped off toward her car.

"Excuse me," Marty said to a baffled Charlene. "Lou, wait up!"

"Louise Stevens, you are such a fool," she chastised herself.

"Lou," Marty panted breathlessly, finally catching Louise at the trunk of her car. "What is it? What's wrong?"

"What's wrong? I'll tell you what's wrong, Martha Beck. What's wrong is that I fell for that silly little 'fifty-cent surcharge' line just like apparently everyone else. I didn't know you had flirting down to such a routine."

"Flirting? Lou, I wasn't flirting with that woman!"

"Then what do you call it?" Louise slammed her trunk emphatically, causing Marty to jump back.

"Lou, come on! I give golf lessons for a living. It's important for me to be friendly, especially when I see people who could really use the help. I wasn't flirting."

Louise wanted to believe she was overreacting, wanted to think she had just imagined something that wasn't there. But Marty had a history of fooling around—she had said so herself. And Louise wasn't going to just ignore this when there was a chance she would get her heart broken.

"Marty, I think we'd better step back and see what's going on here. I don't want to find myself wearing Angela's shoes."

Marty's jaw dropped at the last remark. Angrily, she reached for the car door as Louise moved to pull it shut. "Now you wait a minute! How the hell did this get to be about that?"

Louise jutted her chin out defiantly.

"Let me tell you something," Marty started, her face growing redder by the second. "In the first place, that was eight years ago. In the second place, I did that to Angela—not to you—so I don't have to answer to you for it. And in the third place"—her blue eyes were like lasers pinning Louise to her seat—"I didn't tell you about it so you could throw it in my face!"

With that last retort, Marty spun around and stormed off toward the pool of golf carts. Within moments, she commandeered one and took off recklessly toward the first tee.

Louise sat frozen in her car, stupefied at what had just transpired. *Okay, so what exactly did transpire?* All she knew was that she had been feeling on top of the world only fifteen minutes ago, and now she felt like throwing up.

Katie wiped off the kitchen counters, surprised to see her mother sticking around after dinner on Saturday night to help clean the kitchen. She was willing to bet that being home tonight had something to do with her sour mood since Thursday. "I thought you had a date tonight."

"Canceled," Marty answered gruffly, clanging the saucepans loudly as she put them away.

"Which one of you canceled?"

"Does it matter?" Marty banged the cabinet door.

"Probably not." Katie intercepted her mother and took the Pyrex bowl from her hands. "But whatever happened, you need to stop taking it out on the kitchen."

"Fine. I'll go watch TV."

"Okay, but ..."

"What?" Marty practically barked.

Katie hemmed and hawed, finally blurting out what she wanted to say. "You're scaring Tyler. He hasn't been around you before when you were like this, so he's kind of nervous about it."

Marty sighed dismally. "Like you used to be when you were little."

"Yeah, but I've gotten used to you. I know your bark is worse than your bite."

"I guess I should go talk to him."

"Why don't you talk to me first? What's going on?"

Marty slumped in her chair at the kitchen table and told the story of what had happened with Louise on the driving range two days ago.

"Can't you just talk to her and explain that it's your job to be friendly to people?"

"I was trying to do that, and she said that bit about ending up like Angela. That's when I lost it."

"I can see why that would have set you off."

"Yeah. I embarrassed even myself."

"Maybe you should call her."

"Nah, she doesn't want to hear from me. Besides, I don't need to invest any more in somebody who can't trust me just to go to work every day."

Katie couldn't hide her disappointment at her mother's resolve. "I wish you'd think about it awhile before you give up on her. It's been nice to see you happy lately, and I know Louise is the reason. I bet if you just talked to her, she'd understand."

"I don't know, Katie. Maybe I'm just not cut out for this kind of stuff."

"I doubt that. You like her a lot, don't you?"

Marty nodded. She more than liked her. Louise Stevens was just about all she ever thought about.

"I bet if you called her and apologized for losing your temper, she'd apologize too." Katie handed her mother the cordless phone.

Marty stared at the phone as her daughter turned to walk out of the room. "Tell Tyler I'll be in there to play with him in just a minute."

Marty couldn't understand why Louise had gotten so upset in the first place. She needed to be outgoing and friendly in her job; and besides, she enjoyed it. And she was shocked when Louise had mentioned Angela. She hadn't expected something so below the belt.

But maybe Katie was right. Surely Louise realized once she had time to think about it that there was nothing flirtatious at all about her behavior at the driving range. Louise probably would have called by now if only Marty hadn't gotten so angry. Maybe she should call.

On the other hand, Marty didn't want to make matters any worse. Louise would be coming to the club to play golf even if they couldn't patch this up, and they would see each other again. Maybe she should just try to forget about it for now and smooth things over down the road. Then maybe they could try again.

But she didn't want to just give up on what they already had going. Louise was the first woman in years to spark an interest, and despite the differences in their past relationships, Marty had actually believed they might be able to forge something deeper than just a casual romance. They certainly had seemed to be on that path.

Nervously, she dialed the number and waited while it rang. On the fourth ring, it went to voicemail. She hung up without leaving a message.

"Hmmm," Marty muttered to herself. "We were supposed to have a date tonight. It sure didn't take you long to make other plans."

"Hurry up, Petie! I'm not going to stand out here all night waiting for you to smell every little spot." She gently yanked the terrier's leash and turned toward the house.

Reluctantly, the dog gave up his pursuits and fell into step with his mistress.

Louise had been beyond miserable for the last two days. On Thursday, she had been angry at Marty, for both her flirting and her angry outburst. Rhonda used to get angry sometimes, but she never lost her temper the way Marty had.

But after tossing and turning half the night, Louise awakened on Friday with a new perspective. Marty was right that she had thrown that bit about Angela in her face. Louise realized she needed to apologize ... but when she remembered Marty's red face, she thought it best just to let sleeping dogs lie. Marty wouldn't want to hear from her.

Now it was Saturday night, and what she felt was empty. Without her new companion to look forward to, she was back to days of solitude and melancholy. But it was worse now than before because Marty Beck wasn't just someone to fill her time—Marty had really stirred her heart. And despite all of the reservations she had voiced with Linda, Louise didn't want to let that feeling go.

They were supposed to have gone to a movie tonight. Louise had even gotten dressed on the outside chance that Marty would show up at six-thirty as planned. Of course she hadn't.

Why would she?

"I've been so mean to her, Petie. I don't know why I've acted this way."

Deep down, Louise understood why the green-eyed monster lived inside her, even after all these years, but Marty hadn't deserved to see it. No matter how difficult it was, she needed to apologize.

"I wouldn't blame her if she just wrote me off as a nutcase."

"Why don't you go beat the daylights out of a bucket of balls, Marty?" Bennie was full up to his ears with Marty's surly disposition, now going on three days. Yesterday afternoon, she had rearranged every single rack in the pro shop and he couldn't find a thing. Now she was starting on the files and catalogs under the counter, counting every little item in the display case so she could compile an order list.

"I don't know, Bennie. The way I'm feeling right now, that might not be such a good idea."

"Maybe you ought to just take the day off then. I can manage," he offered. There had been a rush this morning around eight and another before two, but things were slowing down now. That was the usual routine for early spring.

"Thanks, but I think I'd go nuts at home. I'll try not to drive you crazy here, though." Marty knew her irritability was wearing on those around her. She felt especially guilty that her grandson was walking on eggshells at home.

She was embarrassed about the scene with Louise in the parking lot, and knew she needed to apologize for losing her temper. It didn't matter if her anger was justified or not; it was over the top and she had shown a side of herself she thought she had left behind long ago. In short, Marty had overreacted. No matter how angry people got, adults needed to be able to talk, and she had behaved childishly.

The bell over the main entrance jingled to announce a new arrival into the pro shop. From the corner of her eye, Marty caught the image of a head of gray hair, but when she looked up, the figure had ducked behind the racks of menswear near the door.

Great. Now I'm hallucinating. She calmed her jumbled stomach and went back to poring over her order list.

"Hi, Marty."

Marty's heart raced at the sound of the familiar voice. Looking up, she met Louise's tired brown eyes in a quiet gaze. From the look of things, Marty wasn't the only one who had been feeling badly these last few days.

"Hey, Lou."

"Could we go somewhere and talk ... in private?" Louise asked, obviously nervous.

Marty gestured toward the fitting room. "That closet in there is about the only place that's private. Or we could take a walk or something." She didn't care where they talked, as long as she got a chance to apologize. Even if Louise had come to tell her they couldn't date anymore, Marty needed to say she was sorry for how she had behaved. "I'm really glad you came by."

Louise looked toward the fitting room. "In there is okay with me ... if it's okay with you."

Quietly, the two women walked into the small room and closed the louvered door. Marty turned to face Louise, her stomach now in knots with anxiety. "Okay?"

Louise nodded solemnly and leaned against the wall, wringing her hands nervously. "I'm sorry ... especially for what I said about Angela. I'm so ashamed of myself."

"I'm the one who's sorry, Lou. I lost my temper. I don't usually do that ... I haven't in years. I guess that part about Angela just pushed a button or something. We used to argue about the same kind of thing, just like that." She could see from the look on Louise's face that she was making her feel worse than she obviously already did. "But that's no excuse for me going off on you like I did. I'm really sorry."

"It was my fault, Marty. Really, what I said was just plain mean. It was the aliens again. I don't handle being jealous very well ... and that's exactly what it was."

"You had no reason to be jealous, Lou."

"I know. Being nice to people is a big part of your job. It's just that I thought your 'fifty-cent surcharge' line was kind of cute, and I wanted it to be just for me," she admitted sheepishly.

Marty reached for Louise's hand and rubbed her thumb along the back of the palm. "I hate to disappoint you, but I bet I've used that line five hundred times. And I've probably complimented a thousand women, maybe two thousand. I always try to find something I like in everybody. But I don't kiss everybody, Lou." She stepped closer as Louise dropped her arms and bent down. "I save that just for you."

The women looked at each other for a few seconds, both letting go of the anxiety they had been feeling earlier. Marty then tilted her head to meet the approaching lips. As soon as they touched, she felt Louise's arms encircle her tightly and pull her close. She answered with a strong hug of her own. Their lips slid together with escalating passion, and Marty opened her mouth to take in Louise's searching tongue.

Louise moaned and it startled them both so much they suddenly broke the kiss and hugged fiercely.

"Wow," Marty finally said. "We should fight more often if that's what it's like to make up."

Louise laughed softly, her relief evident as she nuzzled Marty's ear with her cheek. "This is so much nicer than fighting. I guess we're going to need another Mulligan."

Marty loosened the embrace and leaned back to look Louise in the eye. "Not this time, Lou. I think we should play this one."

"What do you mean?"

"I just don't think we're ever going to get anywhere if we keep starting over. Don't you see? We had a misunderstanding and we worked through it. That's good."

Louise nodded. "You're right, we did. No more Mulligans. From now on, we play the lie." She pulled Marty close again. "But you better get used to hearing me say I'm sorry, because I screw up a lot."

Marty returned the hug and laid her head on Louise's shoulder. "Me too, Lou. Maybe we can muddle through together."

"It's a deal."

They clung to one another as the tension of the last few days drained. It was Marty who finally broke the spell.

"I guess we should get back out there in case there's a line of people waiting to try on clothes."

The women walked out, both looking sheepish when they realized someone actually was waiting to use the fitting room. They murmured soft goodbyes and made plans for Monday night to catch that movie they had missed.

Marty went back behind the counter, smiling and feeling more chipper than she had in days.

"I'm glad that's over with," Bennie said.

"You and me both, buddy."

"Come on up here, boy." Marty patted her lap, but the Boston terrier remained standing on his hind legs, insisting that he be lifted onto the couch. Marty obliged and he repaid her gesture with licks to the face.

"I can't believe how you spoil my dog!"

"Yeah, right! I've noticed he has his own blanket at the foot of your bed."

It was Tuesday, Marty's day off. Their plans to search for shark teeth on the beach in Venice were scuttled by intermittent thunderstorms. Instead, they were drinking coffee and watching the rain from Louise's living room. The cozy atmosphere invited intimate conversation.

"Marty, I want to tell you about something ... something I've never told anyone before." Louise's voice took on a serious tone and she wouldn't meet Marty's eye.

"Okay." Marty settled the dog in her lap and turned on the couch to face Louise, surprised to see her deeply unsettled by whatever was on her mind.

"It's about how I reacted the other day."

"I thought we'd settled all that."

"We did ... at least the part that had to do with us. But I think you deserve to know why I acted that way." Louise paused and took a deep breath. "Rhonda had an affair with someone a long time ago and it almost killed me."

That was probably the last thing Marty expected to hear and she worked hard to conceal her shock. "No wonder you got so upset."

Louise nodded. "I realized after thinking about it that I really wasn't upset with you. It was more like I was feeling all of those old memories again and I let it hurt me more than it should have."

"Some things are hard to forget," she said. "And even harder to forgive."

"I did, though—forgive her, I mean. It was hard, but that was the only way we could save our relationship. I punished her for it for over a year before she made me see that I was letting it destroy us."

"That wasn't fair of her. She was the one who did it." Either because she was dead or because Louise had loved her so, Marty had a saintly impression of Rhonda. To know now that she had cheated and that she had blamed Louise for letting it break them up made Marty glad she hadn't known her after all.

"No, she was right. She made a mistake—people do that—but I was the one who nearly tore us apart." Louise took a sip of coffee and set her cup on the end table. "It was back in 1980. I'll never forget the date because it was when my father died. He was in a nursing home and they called to say he was going down. I had arranged with my brothers to take turns sitting with him and I was supposed to go on Friday. Hiram—that's my youngest brother—was going to do it on Saturday, but he called me and asked me to switch with him."

From the sad look on Louise's face, Marty could see that the story was bringing back painful memories.

"I had already taken that Friday off school, so I decided to surprise Rhonda with a nice romantic dinner. But she didn't come home. I pitched everything in the trash and cleaned up so she wouldn't know. The next morning I went on down to Wheeling. I called her later in the day to say that I was going to stay Saturday, and she said something about how lonely she was all night in the empty house. I couldn't believe she'd lie, but it was all the proof I needed. And my father died that night, so I didn't want to deal with Rhonda right then. I tried to just push it out of my mind."

"You never confronted her?"

Louise shook her head. "Not then, but it came out a couple of months later. We were at Hiram's house sitting on his front porch. He said something about how he regretted switching nights with me, because he wished he'd been there when Daddy died."

"And Rhonda realized she'd been caught."

"Yeah ... then when Hiram went inside, she asked me why I hadn't told her. I said I didn't want to know anymore than I already knew ... that the details weren't important."

"So you never even talked about it?"

"Not really. But a year or so later, it was clear that I hadn't put it behind us, and I had to if we were going to survive it. So I finally forgave her—really forgave her—and I never doubted her again. To be honest, the years after that were a lot richer than the ones before because we had beaten it together."

"So you were able to love her again after that?"

Louise nodded. "I think I loved her even more when I realized I almost gave up on her."

Marty thought about how miserable she had been during the days they weren't talking. That's when she discovered her feelings for Louise ran deep. And now, her heart went out to know Louise had been hurt so badly by the very thing Marty had done to Angela.

"I think I understand why you reacted the way you did, Lou. For what it's worth, I learned my lesson about that and I won't ever do it to anyone again." She held out her arms and Louise leaned into the embrace, squeezing poor Petie out of his space.

July 1992

"Thanks for coming, and thanks for the book." Marty stood in the doorway seeing the last of their guests out.

"We had a good time. Happy birthday."

"Thanks."

Marty shut the door and turned to see her partner picking up the two remaining cups in the living room. Angela had collected the others throughout the evening as soon as they were emptied, so there wasn't much left to do to erase the remnants of the party.

"Leave that. I'll get it in the morning," Marty offered.

"I won't be able to sleep knowing there's such a mess out here."

After four years together, Marty easily accepted the truth of those words. She had witnessed first-hand the nights Angela had risen from their bed, unable to totally relax when the house was in disarray. She was meticulous about the house—her house. She kept it spotless, and every single knick-knack had a place.

"Let me help then."

Marty retrieved the vacuum cleaner from the closet and began her sweep of the living room carpet. Piece by piece, Angela moved the furniture for her so no stray crumb would escape to mildew and possibly leave a stain. An hour after the last guest departed, the house was in order, the dishwasher humming, and the two women finally retreated to their bedroom.

"It was a great party," Marty said, wrapping her arms around Angela from behind as they got ready for bed. "I can't believe you put all of that together without me finding out about it."

"Yeah, that's because I didn't ask the Pine Island crowd. I figured they'd tip you off." Angela was referring to a small group of lesbians who played golf at Marty's club. They were friends of Marty's, but Angela found them too rowdy for her tastes.

"I'm still impressed that you were able to keep it quiet ... and I really appreciate all the trouble you went to." Marty would have preferred something more casual—and with a few of her friends—but since Angela made all the preparations, she deserved to have the kind of party she wanted. In this case, it had been hors d'oeuvres and birthday cake with champagne. "And the cake was really pretty."

"I knew you'd like it. You didn't mind that it wasn't chocolate, did you?" Chocolate was Marty's favorite, but Angela feared someone would drop a crumb and it would stain the carpet.

"No, it was fine. I liked everything." They got dressed for bed, Angela in her gown and Marty in her panties and T-shirt. Marty snuggled close beneath the sheet, wrapping an arm around Angela's waist. "And I love you." She nuzzled her partner's neck and gently trailed her fingers over the curve of Angela's hip.

Angela turned her face and delivered a quick peck on Marty's lips. "I love you too. Happy birthday, sweetheart." Then she rolled away and scooted her hips backward into Marty's belly.

Marty lay there quietly, absorbing the brush-off she had come to know so well. They used to talk about it—why Angela never wanted to make love—but there wasn't anything else to say. Angela always professed her love, always assured Marty she had done nothing wrong, and always apologized for her lack of interest in sexual expression. Over the last couple of years, Marty had learned to simply pack away her hurt feelings. Sex wasn't all that important, as long as you had someone to love.

Chapter 17

MARTY LEANED BACK on the soft pastel pillows of Louise's couch, stirred at the desire she could see in the brown eyes. She had been waiting for this moment, the moment she and Louise would finally share an intimate pleasure Marty hadn't known in almost twelve years.

Louise peeled off her top to reveal small, firm breasts that looked as though they were made to fit perfectly inside a mouth. Then she ran her long, beautiful hands through Marty's hair before they came to rest on her shoulders.

"Marty."

I love the way she says my name.

"Marty ... wake up, hon."

The slumbering woman opened one eye, realizing immediately the interlude she had been dreaming of was still just that—a dream. Louise was fully dressed and gently shaking her shoulders.

"I fell asleep again. What's that? Three times now? I'm sorry, Lou."

"It's okay. I feel like it's my fault for keeping you out so late. You should be home in bed by now."

Marty sat up and fell forward at once into Louise's lap, resting her head on a soft thigh. It was only a little after ten, but she had been up since five-thirty and on the go all day long. "At least I'm off tomorrow. I can go back to bed after I take Tyler and Katie where they need to be."

Louise stroked her head and helped her to her feet. "I worry about you driving like this. Maybe you should stay here tonight and go home early in the morning."

"I'll be okay." The prospect of spending the night with Louise was definitely bringing her around a bit. But she was tired, and if the time came for them to really be together, she didn't want to have to wrestle with the sandman.

Louise walked her to the door where they turned to kiss goodnight. This was where Marty had noticed the most significant change in their relationship since the argument at the driving range. Their kisses were much more intense now, just as that one in the fitting room had been. They had seen each other nearly every day since then, and Louise seemed to have dropped some of the other guards she had about physical things. They had held hands on the beach this afternoon for a few moments and they sat intertwined on the couch while they watched a movie on television—that is, while Louise watched a movie and Marty slept.

Marty waved goodnight from the car and backed out of the driveway. Louise was still standing in the doorway, her silhouette a far more relaxed figure than it had been on their first few nights out together. Something had definitely changed for them in the last couple of weeks ... just in time for Marty to head north to the mountains.

Three more weeks was all the time they would have here in Florida to see where they were headed. Sure, Louise had said she would come to North Carolina for a visit on her way up to West Virginia and back. That's what Angela had done for seven years—a week in July and another in September. That had been enough for both of them, Marty thought; the time apart was a break they seemed to need.

But Marty hated the idea of leaving Louise behind for six whole months. So much could change during that time. A break like that for a relationship so young would only put distance between them. The realization that Louise might even meet someone else was enough to make her stomach hurt.

As she approached her duplex, she was startled to see a pickup truck sitting in her driveway. When she pulled in behind it, she saw the Michigan plates and smiled to herself. *Mike.*

Marty composed herself in the car. No way would she go in there acting happy to see her son-in-law after the way he had let his family down. But Marty couldn't help but be glad her daughter's marriage had just taken a turn for the better. And there was no denying it would be good for Tyler to have his father around again.

Katie met her at the front door. "Surprise."

"So I see. Where is he?"

"He's out back having a smoke. I told him he'd better not light up in the house."

Marty started toward the back door when Katie grabbed her arm.

"He's really nervous about seeing you, Mom. Don't tear him up too bad."

"I won't kill him tonight. I have all day tomorrow while you guys are gone."

Marty went outside and found Mike sitting on the back step. He was thirty-six, of average height and build, and his arms were muscular from almost two decades of carpentry work. His brown hair was thin and it receded considerably off his brow, but Marty thought him a handsome fellow.

Hurriedly, Mike flicked his cigarette into the back yard and stood, bracing himself for his mother-in-law's ire.

"I'm glad you made it, Mike." She shocked the young man when she took him in her arms and gave him a friendly hug. "Katie and Tyler have missed you."

"Thanks, Marty. I'm ... I'm glad I'm here too. I need to get a job, and ... we'll find a place to live, and ..."

"Don't worry about everything all at once. You guys have been down on your luck awhile so it's going to take a little time to catch up. But it'll all work out if you really want it to." She sat down on the top step and he followed suit. "I'm pretty disappointed in you, you know. When you asked me if you could marry my daughter, you promised me you were going to take care of her. You dropped the ball, and you're not allowed to do that—not ever, especially with Tyler because he depends on you."

"I know. I ... I don't have any excuse."

"That's right. You don't. And if you came down here to get back on your feet, I'll help you as much as I can. But if you turn your back on your responsibilities again, I'm going to hire Katie the best divorce lawyer I can find. You understand me?"

"Yes," he said meekly.

"Good." She sat and stared for a minute into the night. "Did your truck do okay on the trip? I couldn't believe I saw it here still in one piece."

"One piece is right. One piece of shit."

Both of them laughed.

"I want you and Katie to stay in my house this summer and get some money saved. It would help me out because I might be back and forth a few times. I don't want to have to close up and throw all the food out."

"Katie says you're seeing somebody."

"Katie talks too much. I'm going to bed." Marty stood up and squeezed her son-in-law's shoulder affectionately. "I really am glad to see you here."

"Come on, boy. Let's go see what we can find." Louise clipped the terrier's leash in place before opening her car door.

Marty had called earlier to cancel their lunch plans because her son-in-law had arrived last night from Michigan. It was family time, and Louise understood that family took priority over everything. She envied Marty her daughter and grandson. Those were choices Louise had never made, and she hadn't been able to have as close a relationship as she would have liked with her brother Hiram's daughters because they weren't in the same town.

Petie jumped across her lap to the parking lot at Tropical Point Park and shook himself vigorously to loosen up for their outing. Louise stopped first just in front of the car at the edge of the grass so Petie could do his thing, and she cleaned up his mess like any responsible pet owner would. Then she allowed him several minutes to explore the unfamiliar smells. When he appeared satisfied, she tugged him gently toward the shore for their walk.

She had been looking forward to lunch today. Marty had promised to introduce her to a hole-in-the-wall restaurant here in Saint James City that only the locals knew. She had found it on her own and gotten a grouper sandwich, eating at a picnic table with Petie outside the small establishment.

Despite their broken date, Louise was upbeat about where things stood between Marty and her. They would have dinner again tomorrow night at Louise's house and watch hockey on television—the sort of casual night they had been enjoying together regularly since the argument that day at the driving range.

In the back of her mind, Louise had stored that critical tidbit Linda had brought up: Marty would be leaving for North Carolina in three more weeks. That didn't leave much time for their relationship to progress. If they were going to—

Louise was yanked from her ruminations when Petie pulled hard on his leash, struggling to reach the outstretched hand of a woman who had dropped to her knee to pet him.

"I just love Boston terriers," the woman explained, smiling at the reception she was getting.

"Shhh ... he doesn't know he's a dog." Louise enjoyed the way Petie took to strangers, thanks to his upbringing around hoards of teenagers. He wasn't big enough to be a protector, but he barked at everything, making him a good watchdog.

The woman finished lavishing attention upon the pooch and went on her way.

"How are you doing down there, little man? Come here, Petie." Louise squatted and scratched the happy dog behind his ears. "You want to go spend a week or two in the mountains?" His ears went up and he jumped excitedly, just as he did every time she asked him anything at all. "Go ride in the car? See Marty?" He danced and spun around. "Go to the vet? Get a shot?" Still he twirled, and Louise laughed, her point proven.

Louise returned to her thoughts of Marty. She had no idea what their remaining time together would bring—but she was getting clearer on what she wanted. She had decided weeks ago that she didn't want things to go too far between them this spring; that they could begin anew when Marty returned in the fall. If the feelings were still there they could decide then what they wanted.

But even Louise, a perpetual planner, understood the futility of trying to plan a relationship. Plans meant nothing when emotions took over. And after their argument a couple of weeks ago, something had changed for Louise. That was a moment of truth for her, a moment when she had to imagine things might not work out and Marty Beck's walk through her life would be short-lived. Louise had realized then she wanted more than just a few fun-filled weeks, and more than just the companionship of someone special. She wanted to know Marty deeper, and the feeling she got when they kissed made her yearn for something more intimate.

The thought of having sex with someone new scared her, but it didn't diminish the attraction she felt. Even if they made it through the next three weeks without becoming lovers, Louise had a feeling that tight quarters in North Carolina—if she were to visit as Marty had asked—would prove too great a temptation. Either way she looked at it, she and Marty were likely to be lovers soon unless one of them willed it not to happen. Things were definitely moving in that direction, and with every minute they shared, Louise was more certain it wouldn't be her putting on the brakes.

She was finally ready to admit to herself that she was in love, and she deserved everything that came with it. Rhonda would have wanted her to be happy.

Chapter 18

LOUISE CHUCKLED TO herself as she felt Marty go still in her arms. They were lying together on the couch, Louise in the back and propped up on pillows so she could see the hockey game over Marty's shoulder.

"Marty." She nuzzled the soft hair behind Marty's ear. "Marrrr-ty."

"Hmmpf." Marty stirred and squeezed the hand on her shoulder. "Okay, I'm awake."

"You don't have to be. I don't mind if you go to sleep. I know you're worn out." Marty had asked to be awakened if she nodded off.

"I mind. I keep falling asleep on you. I hate to be so rude."

"It isn't rude. I'd rather have you falling asleep with me than not get to see you at all. But I worry about you driving home when you're so tired."

Marty shifted on the couch so she was flat on her back looking up into Louise's face. "You don't have to worry about me ... but I like that you do."

Louise dipped lower and helped herself to a soft kiss. "I like that I do too."

Marty's arms went up around her neck and pulled her back down. Their lips met gently at first, then more firmly as their tongues came into play. Louise's hand drifted to caress Marty's hip and waist.

"You make me half crazy, Louise," Marty whispered when their kiss ended.

"Is it a good crazy or a bad crazy?"

Marty smiled. "It's definitely a good crazy." She stretched her neck upward and delivered another kiss. "I guess I should get up and go home before I drift off again."

"Please stay here tonight." Louise saw the surprised look and quickly added, "You need some rest. I don't want you to drive home like this anymore."

"Do you think I'd get any rest if I slept with you?" Marty said it like a dare, and it felt like a moment of decision for Louise, one she hadn't expected quite so soon.

"I ... I don't ..."

"I was just teasing, Lou. I can sleep in the guest room if that's what you want."

"No, I ... you don't ..."

"Is there something in there trying to get out?" Marty asked playfully, her index finger dabbing at Louise's bottom lip. "Or are the aliens in charge again?"

Louise sighed and put the words together in her head first. "I want you to sleep with me, so I can hold you just like this. We will sleep."

"That's too bad." Marty's smile now held a bit of mischief. "I was just starting to get my second wind."

"Maybe we should sleep in our windbreakers." Louise smacked Marty's bottom and nudged her off the couch.

"Oh, that was bad, Lou."

Louise stood up and followed her prancing dog to where his leash was kept. "I need to take Petie out one more time." *And I need lots of deep breaths after getting all that out!* "Why don't you get ready for bed and I'll be there in a minute? There's a new toothbrush in the medicine cabinet."

Marty took the leash from her hand. "I don't have much to do to get ready. Let me take him and I'll lock up."

"Okay." Louise felt her panic rise. Her best hope of calming down—talking to Petie about what she was doing—was walking out the door with Marty, oblivious to his mistress's need. Louise went into the bedroom, her nervous eyes falling at once on the smiling face in the pewter frame.

It's just a picture, Louise. It isn't Rhonda. She isn't watching.

From the top drawer, she pulled out what she considered her most conservative pajamas—silk shorts with a button-up short-sleeved shirt. At least the shorts came to her mid-thigh and the top was long. She hurried into the bathroom to change and brush her teeth. Then she wrapped herself in a long robe and went back out to the living room just in time to greet the pair at the front door.

"All done," Marty announced. "Let me give Katie a quick call."

Louise could hear bits and pieces of the telephone conversation from the bedroom, and from the playful tone she gathered Marty was taking some ribbing from her daughter.

"I don't know how I managed to raise such a brat," Marty said when she entered the bedroom.

"She gave you a hard time?"

"Worse than I ever gave her back when she went out with all those boys. It isn't fair." Marty walked around the bed and set her wallet on the nightstand. "Are you finished in the bathroom?"

"Yes. I laid out your toothbrush and a comb." Louise was doing her best to sound casual, telling herself over and over this wasn't a big deal. They were only going to sleep. Never mind that she had never shared her bed with anyone but Rhonda.

"Okay. I'll be ready in just a minute. Is it okay if I sleep in what I have on?"

"Sure." Louise breathed an internal sigh of relief. Marty was wearing baggy knit shorts and an over-sized T-shirt. Louise would have offered something else, but she had nothing that would fit.

She watched as Marty disappeared into the bathroom. Then she folded the bedspread and turned down the sheet and light blanket on both sides.

We're just going to sleep.

"Come on, Petie." The terrier jumped onto the queen-sized bed and circled three times before curling up on his blanket. Louise laid her robe on the bedside chair and sat down on the side of the bed, her back to the framed photo on the dresser.

Marty emerged from the master bath with her bra folded in her hand and came around to sit on the other side of the bed. "Can you set the alarm for me? I guess I should get up about five-thirty."

"No wonder you fall asleep so early every night." Louise was grateful for this casual banter. It got her mind off the fact that they were actually getting into bed together.

"I usually get up at six but I have to give myself time to get home and change."

"Maybe you should bring some work clothes next time you come so you won't have to get up so early." *Next time?*

"Good idea. And maybe something to sleep in." She grasped the top of her shorts. "Is it okay if I take these off? The waistband is kind of tight."

"Sure." Louise turned away and switched off the bedside lamp. When she rolled back into her spot, Marty had turned off her own light and settled into bed. "Goodnight."

"Goodnight, Lou. Thanks for letting me stay."

Louise leaned over and found Marty's lips in the dark. "I'm glad you're here."

"Me too."

The women lay side by side on their backs, their hands connected beneath the covers. In only a few minutes, Louise could hear deep breathing that told her Marty was asleep. Carefully, she pushed the covers back and swung her legs out of bed. In the dark, she went to the dresser and picked up the photo. Tiptoeing through the house to the study, she deposited it in its new home on the bookshelf.

"We'll talk about this in the morning," she whispered.

Louise smiled to herself as she read the email from Michele, thanking her for their time together. She even remembered to ask Louise to pass on to Marty her appreciation for the visor. Louise answered that she was welcome any time, and she promised to lend career advice down the road.

Next, she took a quick look at the weather in Greensburg before shutting down her computer. When she spun around in her swivel chair, she was startled by the newly-placed picture in the pewter frame.

"Hey, sweetheart. I promised we'd talk, didn't I?"

Louise leaned back into the chair and sighed, rubbing her face with both hands as she searched for the right words. This wasn't as much about coming clean with Rhonda as it was Louise laying her sense of betrayal to rest once and for all.

"If you can't hear any of this, it doesn't matter much what I say. But if you can, you already know who you are to me. I guess I just need to tell you who Marty is ... or at least who I think she is."

Louise leaned forward and intertwined her fingers, resting her forearms on her knees.

"I remember back when I first realized I was in love with you. It wasn't an easy thing to figure out, because I didn't know the first thing about what being in love was like. I just knew I got sick to my stomach when I thought about you being with anybody else. That's when it occurred to me what kind of love it was, because I wanted to be with you that way."

She chuckled softly.

"You really made me who I am, Rhonda. You taught me so much about love, about life, about myself. And we gave each other so much over the years."

Louise leaned back and relaxed. This was turning out to be easier than she thought.

"Now Marty Beck's come along and she's making me remember all those feelings I had when you and I first fell in love. I want to spend all my time with her, and I've been thinking a lot lately about ... what it would be like to make love with somebody again."

With that admission, it became clear just what she needed to tell Rhonda ... and herself.

"You're always going to be my first love, and the first person I gave myself to. Nothing can change that. But I've still got love to give, sweetheart ... and you're not here anymore to give it to."

Louise leaned over and picked up the photo.

"You'd really like her, Rhonda. She's a good person, and I think we'll take care of each other. I don't know how this will all turn out, but right now it feels a lot like it did when you and I first fell in love ... and I got thirty-one years out of you."

Marty guided the cart to the right of the sixteenth green. It was a glorious day in Southwest Florida, seventy-five degrees with a soft southerly breeze. Everyone knew the stifling hot temperatures were right around the corner, and they were taking advantage of one of the last pleasant days to play golf.

In just two more weeks, she would be packing up to leave. She wasn't going to waste a minute she could be spending with Louise; so when Bennie offered to hold down the fort while she played a round of golf with her friends, she jumped at the chance.

"Let me out here, hon. Looks like I'm going to the beach," Louise lamented, spotting her ball in the sand trap. Shirley and Linda had just hit their approach shots and were right behind them coming toward the green.

Marty smiled as she pulled to a stop, waiting while Louise extracted a sand wedge and putter from the bag. Her own ball sat on the green, about eight feet from the cup. After ratcheting the parking brake, she grabbed her putter and strode to the top of the sand trap where she could watch Louise grapple with her predicament.

The picture of total concentration, Louise finally stroked, lofting the ball barely high enough to catch the fringe ... but not enough to keep it from rolling back into the trap, where it came to rest only a foot from where she started.

"Darn!"

Marty chuckled. "Lou, I think I know what your problem is. It's your vocabulary."

"My vocabulary?"

"Right. Now, you see, that was not a darn. That was at least a shit if not an all-out fuck."

"Martha Beck! I do not use words like that!"

"And you're still in the sand trap, right?"

Louise sighed and shook her head. Marty had a point.

On her next shot, she managed to roll the ball across the green, and thanks to a neat nine-foot putt, salvaged a double-bogey on the par-four hole. Linda and Shirley putted in and all eyes turned toward Marty, who was putting for birdie.

Like the pro she was, Marty walked the green back and forth studying the break. The greens were fast today, but she hated to leave it short. After what seemed to the others like ten minutes, she finally gave it a tap, only to lip out.

"Screw!"

"Perhaps there's a different vocabulary for putting," Louise said smugly.

Marty putted in and followed her friends to the carts. Sliding into the driver's seat, she released the brake and they lurched forward.

"Perhaps there's a different vocabulary for putting," she mocked in a snippy voice, causing both women to burst out laughing.

"So where's Pauline this week?" Louise turned and asked Linda and Shirley, who were in the cart behind them. All she knew was that Pauline had called Linda yesterday and canceled.

"You're going to love this. You remember that woman she went home with from the Valentine's dance?"

"Uh-huh." She was a chic woman in her early seventies. "Doris somebody."

"That's right. Pauline said Doris invited her on a Mediterranean cruise, all expenses paid. She said she loved us, but she wasn't crazy."

"Well, who could blame her!" Louise exclaimed.

"Yeah, I asked Linda how come I never met anyone like that," Shirley said. "And then she smacked me."

"No wonder! Even I know better than to say something like that, and I don't know a thing about what women want," Marty said.

"Don't listen to her," Louise said, poking Marty playfully. "She just doesn't want people to know she has a sweet side."

They sped ahead to the next green and Marty jumped out, grabbing her driver as she did. She offered honors to Louise, who teed up her ball and took a practice swing. Number Fourteen was a par five that angled to the right around a broad stand of pine trees about one hundred-fifty yards off the ladies tee. Another hundred yards past the turn was a lake that spanned the width of the fairway; a prudent golfer laid up for the third shot.

Louise shanked her drive, sending it into the woods on the right. She would have a tricky second shot. Marty, on the other hand, played her ball to fade, exploding off the tee with a powerful drive that disappeared past the turn. If she had a decent lie, her three-wood would carry the water on the second stroke.

"That was beautiful!" Louise exclaimed.

"Thanks." Marty was playing well today, enjoying the chance to show off for her girlfriend. And Louise was paying attention—of that she was certain. Twice already, Marty had caught her checking out her cleavage, prominent today in the scooped-neck top.

"That's nothing. Watch this." Shirley teed up and ripped one out past the dog-leg. Hers didn't go quite as far as Marty's, but it was a great drive nonetheless.

"That was beautiful, honey!"

Marty and Louise realized instantly that Linda was mocking them and they both snorted and returned to their cart. They waited for Linda to hit her drive and Marty said, "We're headed into the woods now, ladies. If we don't come out in ten minutes, play on without us." She gunned the cart and they took off in the direction of Louise's errant shot.

"I'm glad you hit over here, Lou. I wanted to show you something." She hopped out of the cart and headed into the trees with Louise following.

"What is it?"

"This," Marty answered as she ducked behind the low branches of a thick pine. Wrapping her arms around Louise's waist, she pulled her close, seeking out her lips for a passionate kiss.

"Oh, my!" Louise sighed when they parted. "You're sneaky."

"You're pretty hard to resist, Miss Stevens. I've been wanting to do that ever since you walked into the clubhouse."

"Hmmm," she studied her companion's face.

"What?"

Louise pulled a tissue from her pocket. "Not your shade," she remarked, dabbing red lipstick from Marty's lips and chin.

"Then we're going to have to find one we agree on, because I'm not going to have you giving me kisses and then wiping them off."

"Oh, that's smooth, Marty."

"Got a million of 'em."

"I bet you do."

"You should come spend the summer with me in North Carolina. Then you can hear them all." Marty pointed out Louise's ball amid a stand of trees. "If you keep it low, you can send it out the other side to the fairway."

"I can't just pick up and go to North Carolina all summer. What about the mail and the phone? And who'll take care of my house?"

"Lucky for you, you've asked an expert. You get the post office to forward your mail and you leave a phone message with another number. You pay your lawn service in advance. And this year Katie's going to be around, so she can check on your house if you want her to." She was almost amused at Louise's flustered look. "So now that those things are settled, will you ride with me or do you want to follow along in your own car?"

"How long a drive is it?"

"About fifteen hours. That's why you have to stay for a long time, so you can rest up for the drive back—in October."

"October? Listen to you! I promised to come see you for a week or two and you already have me staying until October." Louise smacked her ball hard and it cleared the woods.

"Good shot! You'll get there and you won't want to leave because it's so beautiful. Besides, you can't kiss me like you just did and expect me to manage on my own all summer."

"I've seen you in action, Marty Beck. You can manage anything whether I'm there or not."

"But I don't want to. I'd rather manage it with you." Marty took Louise's club from her hands and wiped it off before dropping it into the bag. "I'm wearing you down. I can tell."

June 1985

Louise scooted over in the hospital bed to make room for Rhonda to sit.

"This is a big bed, Lou. Maybe we should have a quickie since we won't be able to have sex for awhile."

"Shhh! Will you keep your voice down?" Despite her scolding tone, Louise appreciated Rhonda's lighthearted way of getting her mind off the hysterectomy she would have tomorrow morning. It wasn't her first choice for how to spend her summer vacation, but it was unavoidable. "Besides, I believe what he said was that I couldn't have sex. That doesn't mean I have to keep my hands off you."

"Oh, no. If you're going to be a nun, I'll have to be one too."

"You a nun? You haven't even been to church in three years."

"I'll be a heathen nun."

"What do heathen nuns do?"

"Whatever they want." Rhonda stroked Louise's breast through her hospital gown.

"You're so bad."

"You better believe it."

Louise caught the roaming hand as it drifted underneath her blanket. "Behave."

"I can't help it. Now that I know we can't have sex, I'm horny as hell."

"You'll have to take care of that tonight when you go to bed."

"That sounds like an interesting idea, but I'd rather do that when you're there to watch."

Louise fanned herself. "You really are bad."

"And maybe when you get home on Thursday I can put on a show for you. Would you like that?"

Louise just shook her head with a smile. "Bad!"

Rhonda leaned down and lowered her voice. "You like it when I'm bad, don't you? You like lying there with your head on my thigh watching me play with my clit."

Louise felt her temperature rise.

"When it stands up nice and tall and you lick your lips. When I won't let you touch it ... when I make you watch me come . . . watch me ripple while the juices trickle out. You do like that, don't you?"

"I think you need to go," Louise said with a flustered sigh.

"You're not trying to get rid of me so you can touch yourself, are you?"

"No, I'm going to wait for you to do it. But I'm going to watch you practice over and over again on this right here." Louise put her hand in Rhonda's crotch and stroked it hard through her pants. "I love you, you know."

"I love you too." Rhonda folded Louise into her arms and hugged her hard. "I'll be back first thing in the morning. They probably won't let me back there, but remember that I'm right outside. And I'll see you as soon as I can."

Chapter 19

"THIS COULD BE trouble, Lou." Marty was nestled in Louise's arms on the couch.

"Are you falling asleep on me again?" After dinner, they had moved to the living room for conversation, forgoing the usual sporting event or movie on television, neither wanting to divide her attention from the other.

"I'll try to stay awake. Just keep talking to me."

"What would you like to talk about?"

"It doesn't matter. I hang on your every word."

Louise's laugh was a low rumble. "Flattery will get you everywhere."

Marty shifted so she was facing Louise. "There is something I would like to ask you about."

"What is it?" Louise was suddenly concerned by the timid voice, and she knew Marty wasn't making a joke this time.

"I was wondering if you ever thought about"—Marty looked at her fingers as she gently outlined the collar of Louise's top—"making love with me." She quickly added, "But if you don't want to talk about it, we don't have to."

Louise felt her whole body shudder with Marty's words. "We can talk about it if you want to."

"I've been thinking about it a lot, Lou. Not just the physical stuff, but what it would feel like to be close to you like that ... close to your heart." She put her palm in the center of Louise's chest.

"You're already close to my heart."

"You're close to mine too." Marty gently stroked Louise's breastbone. "Is it hard for you to think about being with somebody like that again? It's okay to say so."

Louise grasped Marty's hand and squeezed. "Maybe a little ... but probably not for the reasons you think."

"What is it?"

Louise just shook her head, unsure if she could articulate her worries. "It's just that ... I've only been with one other person. And things aren't always easy for me."

"What do you mean?"

"We just get into habits ... routines." Louise blushed, but forged ahead. "I have trouble sometimes. It can be frustrating."

"Lou, I haven't been with anyone in a very long time. I don't know what's going to happen any more than you do. But it's the journey that matters—the one we take together—not the destination. Just being with you like that would be so special."

Louise forced herself to meet Marty's insistent gaze. It was time to lay the last of her fears to rest.

"Please don't be afraid. I won't push anything." Marty pulled Louise's face closer and gave her a gentle kiss. "But I've fallen in love with you, and I want more of you every day."

"You're in love with me?"

Marty nodded and smiled softly. "I am."

"I'm in love with you too." Louise felt that love surge as the words left her lips and she lowered her head to deliver a demanding kiss.

Marty answered with fervor, and in no time, both sets of hands began to wander in escalating passion. Louise daringly slid her fingers underneath the soft T-shirt, delighting in the first caress of

Marty's bare skin. Marty responded by grasping the soft behind she had admired the first time she ever saw Louise. They began to move against each other in a sensuous rhythm and Louise's hand moved up to squeeze Marty's breast through her bra.

"Can we move this to the bedroom?" Marty gasped.

Slow down, Louise! But something inside her had already tipped and opened the floodgates of her desire. "Yes."

Together they stood and walked across the living room, Louise turning out lights as they went. A glimmer of light from the bathroom cast a faint glow across the bed. Marty walked to the far side—the side that had become hers—and folded the covers back. Louise kicked off her shoes and maneuvered on her knees to the middle of the bed. Marty met her there and they came together in a tight embrace.

The next few minutes were filled with kisses—noisy, sloppy kisses—as they stroked one another freely over clothed backsides and thighs. Louise returned to caress Marty beneath her T-shirt, where she boldly released the clasp of her bra. She slid her hands underneath the elastic, following it to the front where she took both breasts in her palms. Now panting with excitement, she found the nipples and teased them with her thumbs until they grew hard. They formed large peaks ... just as she had imagined from seeing them stiffen against Marty's shirt in the breeze.

"God, Lou. Do you have any idea what you're doing to me?"

Louise was totally focused on her task and Marty's whispered words excited her even more. The heavy breasts felt wonderful in her hands and she closed her eyes to try to imagine them swaying gently above her face.

Again, they kissed. Marty moaned in her mouth as Louise squeezed and cradled the breasts in awe.

"You wouldn't believe how long I've wanted to hold your breasts like this," she murmured.

"You could have ... anytime you wanted." Marty drew her arms up and tossed both the shirt and bra to the floor.

"These are so beautiful." Louise continued fondling the large breasts as she kissed a line from Marty's ear to her shoulder. She could feel her own top being lifted and she paused just long enough to help. Her bra followed and she hurriedly pressed her naked chest into Marty's. "This feels so good."

Louise gradually leaned back and stretched her legs out, forcing Marty on all fours so as not to rest her weight on Louise's chest. It was exactly what Louise wanted, and she guided Marty forward until the breasts swayed above her face, just the way she had imagined. She brushed her cheeks and chin against them, languishing in their heavy softness. Then she took a nipple in her mouth, nibbling and sucking until Marty leaned to the side, shifting the neglected breast to her lips. She repeated the procedure, all the while kneading both breasts with abandon. "I love these."

"They love you."

Louise could feel Marty tiring from holding herself up and she scooted sideways to let her fall alongside. In an instant, Louise covered her, not yet willing to give up the sensation of the beautiful breasts in her hands and mouth. She could feel Marty's fingers running up and down her back, pushing at the top of the elastic-waist shorts she wore.

She followed Marty's lead and began tugging at her waistband too. Together, they pushed their shorts and panties to the growing piles on the floor. Marty's hands were on her backside now, her fingers teasing the groove.

Louise buried her face in the well between Marty's breasts and allowed her hands to wander the bare skin. "Tell me what you like."

"Anything. You've got me so hot."

Louise gently stroked Marty's thighs and edged them apart. Then she pushed her fingers through the thin patch of pubic hair, nestling her hand against the moist heat. "I want to put my mouth here … will you let me do that?" She had already scooted lower in the bed, her lips near Marty's navel.

"God, yes!"

Marty's plea thrilled her and Louise wrapped her arms around the thighs and plunged her tongue into the folds, savoring the new taste. The hands in her hair urged her on and she lapped and teased until she felt Marty's thighs clench each time she circled her clitoris with her tongue. Finally, she moistened a finger with her tongue and pushed it inside, just as she drew the swollen flesh between her lips. Marty's cries as she came made Louise grind her hips into the mattress, wanting to match the sensation.

"Come up here and hold me," Marty panted as the contractions slowed.

Louise crawled up and took the still-trembling woman in her arms, planting soft kisses at the corners of her mouth. "I love the way you taste."

"That was amazing." Marty gripped her hard around the shoulders as another tremor coursed through her. "As soon as I can move, you're in trouble."

Louise chuckled and tightened her hold. "You can rest. I have all I need right here."

"Oh, no you don't. There are definitely rules against this being one-sided." Marty slowly relaxed and ran her fingers gently across Louise's back. "Please tell me you're going to let me do that to you."

"I don't ... that usually doesn't work for me." Here was the part Louise had dreaded, the part where Marty discovered that her body would respond only to certain things, namely, a forceful touch.

"It's about the journey, Lou," she reminded. Gently, Marty tipped Louise onto her back. Her hand came up to cup a small breast, whose nipple had gone completely rigid.

"Not much there," Louise said nervously.

"These are perfect. Besides, I have enough for both of us … and all our friends."

Louise smiled, grateful for how easily Marty had dispelled that particular insecurity. She closed her eyes as she felt soft lips encircle her nipple. It was the most delicious sensation she could imagine. Marty took both breasts in her hands and pushed them together, slowly lavishing her attentions on each alternately.

"That feels so good," Louise moaned, concentrating on how her nipples fed the arousal between her legs. She wrapped her fingers in Marty's coarse hair to hold her head in place. She could feel Marty's hips pressing against her leg and her own hips rose to match the rhythm.

Marty's hand caressed her side from her breast to mid-thigh, finally coming to rest in the grayish curls at the top of her legs. Hesitantly, Louise opened to invite the touch. She could feel her own need and hoped for both their sakes that she would be able to reach her climax without the usual struggle.

Marty stroked her gently at first, then with more pressure, careful not to irritate the dry, tender skin. But no matter how hard Louise concentrated, the tingling sensations that preceded her orgasm wouldn't catch. She would last all night at this rate and still not have a climax. She would be frustrated, but not nearly as much as she knew Marty would be. That's what she had learned from talking with Rhonda about it.

"I need to use this cream," Louise said, stretching to reach into the drawer of the nightstand.

Marty held out her hand to receive the lubricant from the tube. She swirled it in her fingers and returned to her earlier task, coating Louise's folds with the slicking gel.

"You're so soft, Lou." Her fingertip passed over the swollen clitoris. "Except this part ... nothing soft about it."

"I need more pressure," Louise begged as she lifted Marty's hand and placed it exactly where she needed it to be.

Marty obliged and Louise started to rock her hips against the stroking fingers.

"Oh, yes. I love that." She grasped Marty's shoulder and began to squeeze it gently as the sensations started to build. Marty slid two fingers inside, and Louise lurched upward to drive them deeper. Faster they rocked, until Louise again grabbed Marty's wrist and brought her fingers back to the spot that needed them most. "Here." She was close ... so close.

When the first spasms started, she dug her fingers into Marty's back. "Faster!"

Marty moved her fingers up and down furiously as Louise's leg began to shake.

Even in the dim light, Marty could see that Louise's eyes were tightly closed, her face contorted in total concentration. When the orgasm took her, her mouth opened wide and she drew in a deep gasp, moaning loudly as she thrashed from side to side.

"Oh, baby ... you're so beautiful."

"Marty ..." Louise collapsed on the bed, exhausted from the effort. She pulled Marty into a tight hug and held her there, overwhelmed with both physical and emotional sensations.

Several minutes passed without either one speaking. Finally, Marty asked, "Are you okay?"

Louise nodded. "That was wonderful," she said, her voice barely above a whisper.

"You are wonderful." Marty covered her face with light kisses, her fingers still tickling Louise's folds.

"I'm sorry I made you work so hard."

"It wasn't work." Marty cupped her hand over Louise's soft mound of pubic hair and scooted as close as she could get. "Watching you come took my breath away."

"You should have been on this end."

"I was. About ten minutes ago."

Louise gradually relaxed. Light footsteps across her legs caused her to lift her head. "Petie wants to know where his blanket is."

Marty looked over and chuckled. "Should we pull up the covers?"

Louise leaned up and kissed her. "I need to wash up. I'm sticky." She sat up in the bed, scanning the dimly-lit room for something to put on. She had no idea where her clothes had ended up, and her robe was in the closet. She chided herself for the sudden attack of modesty. After what she and Marty had just done together, surely she could walk across the room naked.

It's done, Louise.

The face that looked back at her from the mirror after such a momentous event was surprisingly calm, despite the disquiet that simmered beneath the surface. Touching Marty had been exciting, and Marty had been very patient with her needs. Louise's body still hummed from her sexual release, which had seemed as satisfying to Marty as it had to her. It had happened just as she had hoped, with both of them declaring their love.

She had no regrets about it—none at all—and now, they were in a new place.

Louise soaped a washcloth in the sink, her eye catching movement behind her in the wide mirror.

"Hey." Marty's head appeared through the crack in the door. "I came in to peek at you naked." She was smiling, her intrusion unabashed.

"Are you getting your eyes full?"

"Sure am. You have a lovely ass, my dear."

Louise fought the urge to cover herself with a towel. "Turnabout is fair play, you know."

"Okay, but you have to promise not to laugh."

"Why would I laugh?"

"Remember when you made fun of my white feet?"

Louise smiled. "Yes."

"The rest of me is like that too." She finally stepped into the bright bathroom to stand beside Louise where both women could look at one another in the mirror. As promised, her naked white torso stood out against the tanned arms, legs, and neck. A thin red scar—the remnants of her gall bladder surgery—bisected her abdomen.

Marty wrapped her arms around Louise's waist from behind and stood on tiptoes to peer over her shoulder. "Look at your nipples stand up. They know they're being watched. Here, let me have that." She took the soapy cloth from Louise's hand and pushed it gently between her legs.

"Easy." Louise opened her legs to allow Marty to wash her and to rinse the soap away. It was amazing—and marvelous—how Marty's appearance in the bathroom had disarmed her nervousness. Louise couldn't have imagined she would be this comfortable.

"All done." Marty rinsed out the cloth and washed her hands.

Louise traded positions to stand behind her, her hands massaging Marty's soft belly.

"No playing with my fat rolls."

"Can I play with these again instead?" She took both of Marty's breasts in her hands, watching her movements in the mirror. "I just love these."

"You're going to wear them out ... but feel free."

"You have a beautiful body."

Marty's playful smile faded and her eyes met Louise's in their reflection. "I don't think anyone has ever told me that before."

"Then all the others were fools," Louise said, turning Marty in her arms to kiss her soundly.

February 1980

Eleven-year-old Katie Beck closed her science book and picked up her pencil and tablet. With her eyes aimed at the floor, she retreated to her bedroom in uncomfortable silence, knowing by the clipped tones in Sue's voice that an argument was brewing, and that she was likely the subject.

"Why can't she stay with your mother?" Sue demanded.

"She was there all last weekend," Marty said, bracing herself for Sue's tirade. The topic of Katie—or rather, of time alone for Marty and Sue—was the thing they fought about most. "I was thinking the three of us could do something together. I bet there's a movie we all want to see."

Sue rolled her eyes and pushed away from the kitchen table. "And when do the adults get to have their time, Marty? Why does a child get to run our lives?"

"She's not running our lives. But it's not fair to make her go stay with her grandmother every weekend."

"It isn't fair to either one of us that we hardly ever get any time by ourselves. I come over here one night a week and on the weekends. Surely to God you two can get enough of each other when I'm not here."

"What's so terrible about being with both of us? Katie's a good kid and she's always nice to you."

"There's nothing wrong with her, except that she's spoiled from too much of Mommy's attention. You know exactly what my problem is. We can't be lovers when she's around. I'm Mommy's friend. You won't even sit by me on the couch. How do you think that makes me feel?"

Sue's voice was escalating and Marty peeked around the door of the kitchen to see if Katie's bedroom door was closed. It wasn't. "Keep your voice down, please."

"That's exactly what I'm talking about. We can't even have a discussion about the biggest issue between us because Katie's little virgin ears might hear it."

"I'm not saying we can't talk. I'm just asking you to keep it down. There's no reason she has to hear this."

"Maybe she should hear it," Sue said loudly.

"Don't!"

"Maybe it's time she found out that you and I have sex when she isn't here. That's what grownups do!"

Marty's stomach dropped as her daughter's bedroom door slowly closed. Katie had heard it all. "I can't believe you'd do something so mean." Tears of anger and hurt filled Marty's eyes.

"It wasn't mean. You being dishonest with her is what's mean—hiding who you really are from your own daughter."

"It was my decision, Sue, not yours. You are so selfish."

"I'm not the one being selfish. We've been seeing each other for almost two years. I don't think it's asking too much for you to tell your daughter that I'm somebody important."

"Well, I'd say she knows now. Do you feel any better? I know I don't. And there's a little girl in the other room who doesn't know what to feel. But that doesn't worry you, does it? You get to just go home and let me deal with it."

"Going home sounds like a great idea."

Marty pulled in a deep breath. "You can stay there, Sue. I don't want to see you anymore."

"Don't worry, Marty. Next time I want kids in my life, I'll have my own."

Marty stood shaking in the small apartment as the front door closed. Sue wasn't all wrong about the things she had said. Marty knew her stubborn refusal to deal with this had put a strain on all three of them, and it was no wonder things finally boiled over.

But Sue was gone now, presumably for good. As Marty walked toward the closed bedroom door, she considered the irony of her new situation. Her secret about having a girlfriend was spilled, but now it didn't matter, because she didn't have one anymore.

She knocked softly and waited for her daughter's voice on the other side. After a few silent moments she tried the door and it opened. Katie sat cross-legged on her bed, seemingly absorbed in her science book.

"Hey, sweetie."

"Hi."

Marty walked over and sat on the bed. "I'm sorry you had to hear all of that, honey."

Katie shrugged, still not looking up.

"Do you want to talk about it?"

The girl shook her head.

"Is it okay if I talk just a little bit?" Marty looked desperately for a sign that her daughter didn't hate her. "Sue won't be coming over anymore."

Katie looked up for the first time. "Is she mad at me?"

Marty shook her head. "No, honey, she's mad at me. It was okay, though. I deserved it."

"What did you do?"

"It was more what I didn't do, I think. Sue thought I should have told you that we . . . that she and I were in love with each other. I was afraid it would upset you to know that I liked another woman that way, so I didn't say anything."

"That's why she said that other thing."

Marty sighed. "Yeah. She said that to punish me for not telling you. I wanted to, but I was afraid." She reached out and pushed her daughter's bangs aside. "I remember when I was your age. Your Aunt Betty and I used to giggle in our room at night when we heard our mom and dad . . . making love."

"I don't think I want to hear about Grandma and Grandpa doing that," Katie groaned in misery.

Marty chuckled, glad for the chance to lighten the mood. "Yep, that's exactly how we felt about it. I don't think any kid likes to think of their parents doing that. I always tried to convince myself that I was found in the cabbage patch or brought by the stork or something—anything but that."

Katie cracked a small smile.

"I'm still afraid, Katie. I'm afraid you'll be upset with me for finding out that Sue and I had that kind of relationship. I know that your friends—"

"Tanya's mom is gay."

"Tanya . . . your friend from gymnastics?"

"Yeah. They all live together, her mom and her girlfriend. Tanya says it makes her dad mad."

Marty nodded, dismayed that Katie had never told her this before, and glad that her daughter wouldn't feel totally out of place with her friends. "You can tell your friends about me if you want to, or you can keep it private. It's up to you how you want to handle it, and I'll do whatever you need me to do."

"Are you going to have more girlfriends?"

"I don't know. I just got rid of one. I think I need a vacation." Marty was still trying to lighten the mood, but Katie seemed to want a real answer. "One of these days I might be ready to meet somebody else, though. How would you feel about it?"

Katie's look said it all.

"That bad, huh?"

"It's just . . . weird."

"I know." Marty laid her hand on Katie's knee. "You won't have to deal with it for a while. And I promise I'll talk to you about it next time."

Katie nodded. "Does Dad know?"

"I don't know. I think he always suspected it, but he never said anything and neither did I. For what it's worth, I don't think your dad cares one way or the other who I go out with."

"Dad doesn't care about either one of us."

Marty couldn't argue, but she wouldn't let Wallace get away without some sort of admonition. "Your dad's the stupidest man in the world for not getting to know you. But I honestly can't complain, Katie, because I don't want to share you with anybody. Just like with Sue gone . . . there's more time for you and me."

For that, Marty got a hug from her stoic daughter.

Chapter 20

LOUISE PACED THE foyer nervously, peeking out each time she thought she heard a car. The invitation to dinner with Marty's family had been a surprise, and she was really looking forward to going. It was important that Louise get to know everyone.

Total acceptance. That's what Marty had promised from Katie, Tyler, and Mike. Louise admired them for forging that kind of relationship and couldn't wait to feel it from the whole family. That sort of family approval was mostly foreign to Louise, who had gotten barely a hello when she encountered Rhonda's kin. The most they had ever talked to her was the day they showed up in Greensburg to collect the family heirlooms after Rhonda's death.

It would also be nice to go out for a change, though being at home alone certainly had its merits. The two of them had practically holed up in Louise's house since last Friday when they had discovered their passion. Marty had gone to work each morning and returned to Louise's home in time for dinner. All the rest of their time had been spent in intimate pursuits—making love, giving each other massages, and soaking together in Louise's oval Jacuzzi tub.

A dark blue Subaru, Marty's brand new car, pulled into the driveway. She was giving the old one to Katie, she said. Louise didn't wait for someone to come to the door.

"Be a good boy, Petie."

She stepped onto the porch and turned back to lock the door.

"Hey, beautiful."

Marty's voice in her ear thrilled her and she caught herself before responding automatically with a kiss. The Subaru's headlights shone on the porch, and Louise knew there were three people watching them from the car.

"Let's see this new car of yours."

In the twilight, Marty proudly showed off the outside as they walked around—the bumper guards, the roof rack, and the off-road tires. Then she opened the front door on the passenger side and helped Louise into the seat.

As she buckled her seatbelt, Louise turned to see the three Comptons smiling at her from the back seat.

"Hello, Tyler, Katie. You must be Mike." She reached her hand between the seats and the young man took it.

"I am. And you must be Louise. Marty talks about you all day long."

Marty opened her door in time to hear that. "Now what did I tell you? No talking about me tonight in front of my girlfriend."

Louise blushed when she heard the moniker, but relaxed when she remembered what Marty had said. *Total acceptance.*

"But you're the only one we all know, Mom. Besides, we have lots of great stories. Don't we, Tyler?" Katie had never shown her mother any mercy and she wasn't about to start. "Tell Louise what Grandma said before we left."

"Don't do it, Tyler! Remember what I told you," Marty said playfully.

Louise turned around and looked at the boy seriously. "What did she say, Tyler? You can tell me. I'll protect you from her."

"She said kissing you was like eating candy," the six-year-old answered.

Louise looked over at Marty, who was peeking at the road through her fingers.

"She did, did she?"

"Uh-huh. And Mom said she was going to get fat."

Louise slid into bed and cuddled up to Marty's backside. Whether it was the newness of their relationship as lovers or Marty's looming departure, they couldn't seem to get enough of each other, even if it was just to snuggle together like this in Louise's bed. They had eight more nights together, and Marty wanted to spend every one with Louise, just as she had since the night they became lovers.

"I've already gotten used to this, Lou."

"Me too." Louise squeezed a little tighter. "You feel good right here."

"I have a king-sized bed up in North Carolina ... lots of room."

"You just won't give up, will you?"

"Not while there's just the tiniest chance you'll come with me."

"I said I would. And I'll even stay a little longer. But I can't just pick up and go for the whole summer. This is my home."

"I know, honey." Marty clutched Louise's arm, which was nestled under her T-shirt between her breasts. "Wouldn't you know I'd finally find something I've been looking for all my life, and now I have to leave it behind."

Louise kissed her softly behind her ear. "What have you been looking for, baby?"

Marty pulled Louise's hand over her heart. "This right here. Nobody but you has ever made my heart feel this way."

"You're not leaving that behind, Marty. That goes with you wherever you are."

"I know." Marty sighed.

"What's bothering you?"

Marty didn't want to answer, because what bothered her was that Louise wasn't dreading this separation as much as she was. "I just don't want to be away from you. That's all."

"We can email every day ... and talk on the phone."

"Maybe I'll kidnap Petie."

"He probably wouldn't mind at all." The dog sat up at the foot of the bed when he heard his name. "Go back to sleep, sweetie."

"Will you stay for the tournament I told you about?"

"The one with that girl you used to coach?"

"Yeah. It's the last week of June."

"I don't see why not. I've never been to a tournament before. And it's not like I have a schedule or anything."

That's what I've been trying to tell you, Lou! Marty was frustrated, but she suddenly realized that she now had a commitment through the end of June instead of just a couple of weeks around Memorial Weekend. Once she got to North Carolina, she could start lining up things for Louise to do in July and August too. By that time, maybe she would just decide to stick around for fall.

"Hey, I've got an idea," Bennie said. "Why don't you stay here this year and let me go to the mountains all summer?"

That was almost tempting, Marty thought. Pine Island Golf Club was relatively quiet through the hot summer months, and she wouldn't have to leave Louise. But she had other plans for the woman who had suddenly become the center of her life. She wanted Louise to have a taste of the mountains, and to fall in love with them as she had. For reasons she didn't totally understand, it was important to her that Louise feel at home in her mountain condo.

"I'm looking forward to getting back up there. It's always nice to play that course the first few times. You know ... it's familiar, but different."

"Which do you like better, that one or this one?" Bennie was proud of the Pine Island layout, which he had designed himself over twenty years ago.

"That's hard to say," Marty answered diplomatically. "This one is more challenging because of all the water, to say nothing of the alligators. But the one at Elk Ridge has a lot of hills and doglegs. You should come up and play this summer."

"Maybe one of these days I will." Bennie held a cardboard box while Marty dumped the contents of her desk drawer. "Aren't you going to miss your new lady friend?"

"Hell, yeah! But Lou's going to come visit, and I might try to get back down here to see her a couple of times, so don't be surprised if I pop in on you."

"It sure has been fun to watch you turn into a puppy dog over that woman."

"I have not!"

"You nearly drove us all crazy, trying to find out all about her … worrying so much because she didn't like you. And I thought we were all going to get our heads snapped off when you two had that fight. But now, you've got this lovesick smile on your face all the time and you're nice to everybody. It's not like you, but I'm not complaining."

"You think you're pretty funny, don't you?" Marty couldn't argue with him. Everything he said was on the money.

"I thought you might go for that redhead ... what was her name?"

"Pauline?"

"Yeah, Pauline Rourke. I haven't seen her in a while."

"No, she ran off with an heiress. I should get her number so I can call her over the summer." Marty opened the member directory and jotted down the phone number. "I liked Pauline, but she wasn't really my type."

Katie walked into the pro shop from the club in time to hear her mother's assessment. "No, Pauline's too easygoing. You need somebody like Louise to keep you in line."

"That's enough from the peanut gallery!"

"You should see her, Bennie. She irons her clothes now, and dries her hair with a brush so it fluffs up all nice and pretty."

"I'm positive they made a mistake at the hospital. My baby was that cute one, the one with the sweet disposition. She probably grew up to be a nun."

Katie snorted. "I'm clearly the product of my environment, Mom. You can't deny me and you know it."

"I can tell you two are related," Bennie said. "Marty's been dishing it out for years, so it's nice to see her on the receiving end."

"No fair ganging up on me! That's it, Bennie. I'm running away." Marty closed up the cardboard box and handed it to her daughter. Then she held open her arms and the other golf pro stepped into a robust hug.

"Take care of yourself, Marty. Come back and see us when you get tired of all that nice weather."

"I will. I'll see you back here in November. And I mean it about coming up to Elk Ridge. You should do it."

"I might just surprise you."

"All right. Take care, Bennie." Marty followed her daughter out to the old Subaru. Her new one sat in Louise's driveway, packed solid with summer clothes and golf gear. Marty had saved just a little room in case Louise changed her mind at the last minute.

"You know, I actually think I'm going to miss seeing you at work every day," Katie said, wrapping her free arm around her mother's shoulder.

"Are you serious or are you getting ready to say something smart?"

Katie laughed. "See, I really am your daughter. We're just alike."

Marty smiled and put her arm around Katie's waist. "I don't have to tell you how much I've enjoyed having you here these last few months. You have a knack for this kind of work that's good for the whole club. And I know Bennie likes having you too."

"So you're not disappointed about the nun thing?"

Marty shook her head and smiled. "I'm not disappointed about anything. I'm really proud of you, honey. You've come through the last few months in a big way, especially the way you put Tyler first."

"I had a good role model for that." They reached the car just in time to head off a mushy moment. "Take this box so I can get to my keys."

Marty took the box and walked around to the passenger side. "So what's this about me needing Lou to keep me in line? Are you implying that I don't know how to behave myself?"

"Nah, I was just teasing about that. But I do think she's good for you."

"How so?"

They both got into the car and Katie started the engine. "For starters, you've never stayed on a diet this long in your whole life. How much weight have you lost?"

"About fifteen pounds," Marty answered, slapping her midsection. "But I'm the one that's eating carrots every day. How come Lou gets the credit?"

"She doesn't get the credit. But she encourages you and helps you out by not tempting you with pizzas and ice cream like we do. I'm glad to know she's worrying about you."

"I guess losing her partner to a heart attack makes her pretty sensitive to something like that."

"Maybe so. But it's more than what she's doing. It's what you're doing for yourself, and I think it's because somebody cares about you. That's why Louise is good for you."

Marty considered her daughter's observations. "I don't know where it's all going to go, Katie ... but I sure am having a good time getting there. Lou might be the first woman I've ever been with who likes who I am already. Everybody else had a laundry list of stuff they wanted to change."

"You know what I like best about Louise? I like the fact that she loves my mother."

"And your mother loves her too."

"That was nice of Linda and Shirley to have us over," Marty said as she pulled the Sable into Louise's driveway. "You guys are funny together, especially you and Shirley."

"Shirley is so much like Rhonda. You should have seen them together. They just fed off each other, and Linda and I were in stitches all the time."

"It's great that you've had them as friends for so long."

"I don't know what I would have done when I lost Rhonda if they hadn't been there. I really didn't have anywhere to turn to let it all out. Unfortunately, they got to see that part of me more than everyone else, and I think that made it harder on all of us."

Marty jumped out and ran around the car to open Louise's door. "Sounds like it was hard for them to lose Rhonda too, so at least you all had each other."

"Yeah, Shirley took it hard. She and Rhonda were so close."

"I hope it was all right with you that I invited them up for a couple of weeks. When they said they remembered Tami, I thought they might like to see her play in the tournament too." Petie ran ahead to the porch and waited excitedly to go inside.

"Why wouldn't it be all right with me? It's your house."

"I know. And I know they're your friends and all, but I don't want you to feel like I'm dumping them on you."

"I wouldn't feel like that."

Marty opened the front door and they went in. Louise reached for the light switch, but Marty stopped her. "Don't bother, Lou. I'm taking you straight to bed."

The alarm chimed at six a.m. Louise tapped the snooze and shifted to the center of the bed to embrace Marty and stretch their last minutes together in bed.

"I don't want to get up," Marty murmured. She couldn't believe the day had finally arrived.

"Then don't. Stay right here and we won't tell a soul."

"I have to go to the bathroom." Marty pulled away and disappeared for a few minutes, returning just in time to hear the alarm chime again. "I need to get up for real this time, baby."

Louise wrapped her hands around Marty's neck and pulled her back into bed. "No."

They cuddled together for nine more minutes until the alarm sounded for the third time. Reluctantly, they climbed out of bed to begin what would be a difficult day for both. Louise silently fixed a breakfast of low-fat granola and yogurt with sliced fruit while Marty dressed and packed her toiletries.

"Will you try to stay on your diet?" Louise asked.

"Sure. It's hard to cook for just one, though ... especially if I'm the cook."

Louise chuckled. "Just keep it simple. Fish or chicken on the grill every night with a nice salad for dinner. You can eat bran cereal for breakfast with skim milk, and a turkey sandwich for lunch. Keep fruit and veggies handy if you want a snack."

Marty had dropped almost twenty pounds since February—only five pounds shy of what the doctor had ordered—but once she reached a plateau, the scale started to creep upward again.

The morning was like most others in many ways, except that both women were more subdued than usual. Marty had fallen into the habit of ushering Petie for his morning walk while Louise fixed their breakfast. Then they talked as always while they ate and drank coffee, but their conversation today was more serious.

When breakfast was finished, they eventually migrated to the door. It was time.

"I wish you weren't driving straight through. I'm going to worry about you being on the road that long."

"I do it every year, Lou. I'll be okay. But thanks for worrying."

"I shouldn't have kept you up so late."

"Oh yes, you should have. I wouldn't have wanted to miss a minute of last night, lady. That's what I'm going to think about when I get tired."

Louise smiled. "Call me when you get there."

Marty held out her arms for a hug. "I love you, Lou."

"I love you, too." For the barest second, Louise considered changing her mind and going along after all. "Petie and I will see you in a month." She leaned back and looked solemnly into Marty's sad eyes. Then she brought her head down in a hard kiss as they hugged each other tightly.

When they finally separated, both women were spouting tears.

"Goodbyes suck, don't they?" Marty said as she wiped her cheek on her shirt sleeve.

"Hellos are definitely better."

"I can't wait for you and Petie to get there."

"Neither can we."

Louise stood in the doorway and cried shamelessly as Marty walked to her car and got in. She picked up her dog and waved his paw as the Subaru rolled backward down the driveway. She continued her wave as it started down the street until it finally disappeared around the corner.

"Marty's right about goodbyes, Petie. They suck."

Chapter 21

THE WEEKEND BROUGHT summer's steamy temperatures to Southwest Florida with a vengeance. Seventy-percent humidity made the upper-eighties feel more like ninety-five. Shirley was finishing up the lunch dishes inside, but Louise and Linda were seeking an outdoor respite from the suffocating heat at the pool, which was enclosed within the lanai.

"No wonder Marty leaves in the summertime," Louise said, fanning herself with a magazine as her feet dangled in the water. Marty had been gone almost two weeks, and Louise was wishing she had gone as well, and not just for the cooler weather. "Will it be like this all summer?"

"No, it'll get worse," Linda answered. "We may get a break or two before June, but then it stays hot until late September."

"I guess I'll get used to it."

"I don't know why you didn't go with Marty. It's so much cooler up there. I can't wait for us to visit next month and stay a week or two."

"I don't know why I didn't go either. It was probably stupid, but I didn't want to rush into anything. I bet I end up staying up there longer than I planned though."

"I take it things are still going well?"

Louise nodded and smiled. "Things are going great. She calls me every morning before she goes to work."

"Aw, she misses her sweetheart."

"I miss her too. I call her every night to hear about her day." Louise took a long drink of lemonade. "I can't believe things worked out like this, Linda. I feel like with Marty I have a whole new lease on life."

"Sounds like you do."

"You know, the more things change, the more they stay the same," Shirley declared as she joined the two women poolside.

Louise and Linda exchanged quizzical looks, wondering where Shirley was headed with her pontifications.

"We have a dishwasher now to save time in the kitchen, but Linda makes me wash everything before I put it in there." She looked at her partner and winked. "And Angel's grown up now, but he still plays with Petie like a puppy."

The dogs lay together on the cool river rock deck, both engaged with their respective rawhide bones.

"And no matter what happens in Lou's love life, she still ends up over here moping around like a lost soul."

"I should have seen that coming," Louise said, splashing water from the pool in Shirley's direction.

"She's not a lost soul anymore, Shirl. This Lou is different from that one who went with us to the Valentine's dance."

"I'll say. This one smiles more."

"Boy, I really am different," Louise said. "I can't believe how much has changed in just . . . what's today?"

"The eleventh of May."

"The eleventh of May. How could I forget that day?" Louise's face went sad. "My father died twenty-three years ago today."

"I remember the day your father died," Linda said somberly.

"You do?"

"Yeah, I was at my brother's wedding in Chicago."

"You two were out of town?"

"No, just me. Shirley didn't go, but she told me about it when I got back."

The implication of Linda's words dawned gradually and Louise felt as though she had been struck in the stomach. *No!* She fought the bile that was forming in the back of her throat and turned slowly to look at Shirley. The woman was staring into the back yard, her face a million miles away—until she shot a nervous sidelong glance at Louise.

Louise pulled her feet out of the water and stretched for her sandals. "Come on, Petie. We need to go home."

"Wha—?" Linda was startled. "Are you okay?"

"I'm not feeling very well. I need to go."

"Do you want some medicine? Was it something you ate?" Linda jumped to her feet while Shirley sat frozen.

"No, I just need to go home. Now, Petie!" Abruptly, she scooped up the terrier and her purse, dashing through the house to the front door. She was afraid to say another word.

"Lou?" Linda called after her, but the door closed before she could catch up. She returned to the lanai, where Shirley continued to stare silently into the back yard.

Her hands shaking uncontrollably, Louise pulled three suitcases out of the closet in the guest room. It would take more than a walk along a windy beach to clear her head today. What she needed was to get away … from Linda and Shirley … and from Rhonda, whose specter engulfed her as soon as she entered the house.

It all made sense now, the mystery that had eluded her for years.

Louise had always known Rhonda's tryst was with someone she knew, since they both had all the same friends. She had assumed for years it had been a man, since Rhonda had always gone out with men before. She even had a few suspects among the single teachers at their school, but thought it best not to know for certain, not wanting to fix a face to the painful images in her mind. Never had she imagined it was a woman, let alone a woman who had pretended to be her friend for over twenty-five years.

Louise slammed the closet door in a burst of anger, causing a nervous Petie to skitter under the bed.

When she had forgiven Rhonda all those years ago, it was with the assurance that the affair had been a one-time mistake. But now she realized Rhonda and Shirley might have carried on for years right under her nose. They certainly had plenty of opportunities, because they often traveled overnight together to band workshops and competitions.

Louise spread her suitcases open on her bed and began filling them from her drawers. She would go to Marty's home in North Carolina ten days sooner than planned, and she would stay longer there or with Hiram and his family. Because of her plans to be in the mountains, she hadn't considered a summer vacation for this year, but she could take a driving trip somewhere—anywhere to keep from having to be here, from having to face the truth.

It shouldn't matter anymore, but it did.

Louise pushed her golf clubs deeper into the trunk of her Mercury to make room for the suitcases. She filled in the gaps with bags of shoes, dog food, and toiletries. She then spread her hanging clothes—a couple of dresses and skirts, blouses, slacks, and golf outfits, filling the trunk to the brim.

On her next pass through the house, she stopped in the study and glared at the photo on the shelf. "I ought to leave you here and not come back!" She snatched it up and took it out to the garage, opening a suitcase and stuffing it face down inside. "You can ride in here with my socks!"

"Petie!" She dumped his water and food bowls and wiped them clean before placing them on the floorboard behind the driver's seat with his leash. "Come on, baby. I'm not mad at you."

The terrier had learned his mistress's emotions and knew when it was best to steer clear. He sheepishly emerged from his hiding place and followed her into the garage.

"Let's go see Marty." Louise opened the driver's door and Petie jumped into the front seat.

Louise then went back into the house to double-check the locks on the windows and doors. She set her thermostat to eighty-two degrees. If she decided to stay gone for more than a few weeks, she would follow Marty's simple plan of forwarding her mail, changing the message on her voicemail, and paying the lawn service in advance. Maybe Katie would stop by to check on things.

She would take care of everything once she reached Marty's. All that mattered now was that she got out of this place.

Louise hit the red button by the entry to raise the garage door and got into the car, petting her dog to calm him down. "Easy, boy. It's going to be a long ride."

As she started backing out she was startled by a horn blast. Shirley sat directly behind her in her station wagon, blocking her exit. It was the last thing Louise wanted to see.

She lowered her window so Petie would have air and killed the engine. Before getting out of the car, she paused to take a few deep breaths and heard a car door close behind her. In her rearview mirror she could see Shirley come around to lean on the front of her station wagon, her arms crossed over her chest.

Louise opened her car door, got out slowly, and closed it. "What are you doing here?" she demanded, her voice shaking with anger.

"We need to talk." Shirley's face was desperate.

"I don't. I don't want to go through all of this again."

"Lou, please don't throw away our friendship over something that happened so long ago. I'm so sorry. I never wanted—"

"Never wanted what? For me to find out that you slept with my partner?" Louise snarled.

"What we did was awful, but it wasn't something we planned. It only happened that one time. We were so stupid … we didn't think. Believe me, I have paid the price with my guilt for the last twenty-three years."

"Does Linda know?" Louise asked, her voice still filled with ire.

Shirley shook her head solemnly.

"Then you never paid for anything, Shirley … and neither did Rhonda. I'm the only one who paid! I'm the only one who got hurt by what you two did."

"That's not true. Rhonda hated herself for it … and so did I. We even hated each other for awhile, but we had to work it out because neither one of us wanted to come between you and Linda. In all the time I ever knew Rhonda, I never saw her hurting more than she did then. She was so afraid you'd never love her again."

Louise was jolted by the words, remembering the tears she shared with Rhonda the night they finally put the ugly incident behind them. "I forgave her because she was my life. But you and I would never have been friends for all these years if I'd known it was you."

"I know that, Lou … and so did Rhonda. She always said she would tell you if you asked, but she was glad you never did. It was a secret I would have carried to my grave too because I never wanted to hurt you."

"Don't give me that … bull. You're only here because Linda doesn't know and you want to save your own skin."

Shirley threw up her hands in surrender. "I admit that's part of why I'm here. But it isn't to save my skin. It's to keep from hurting Linda. She doesn't deserve it any more than you did, Lou."

"Linda is your problem."

"Linda is your best friend. I know you don't want to see her hurt." Shirley began to cry. "We're sixty-eight years old, for

Christ's sake, and we've made our whole life together. Will it give you any satisfaction to destroy that for us?"

Louise tightened her lips. Just as Rhonda had done all those years ago, Shirley too was laying the burden of forgiveness at her feet. "Move your car."

"Lou, please!"

"Move your car!"

August 1987

Rhonda kicked off her shoes as soon as she entered the hotel room. "Would you unzip me, honey? I need to get out of these pantyhose before my legs turn blue."

Louise stepped out of her own pumps and moved behind her partner, kissing the bare back as it was revealed by the sinking zipper. "Why don't we turn out the lights and go stand by the window?"

Rhonda shook her dress to the floor, pushed the pantyhose off her hips, and started to scratch the red stripe around her waist. "I feel like I've just died and gone to heaven. Think we ever have to wear pantyhose in heaven?"

"I told you we have to turn the lights off." Louise located the button on the bedside lamp as Rhonda killed the switch by the door, plunging their room into total darkness. From their window, they had a spectacular view of Horseshoe Falls. "Isn't it beautiful?"

Rhonda, dressed only in her half-slip and bra, joined Louise at the window and wrapped her arms around her from behind. "It's almost as beautiful as you. I bet we can even hear it if we crank this window open." She did and the dim roar made its way up to their fifteenth-floor room. "What did you think of this evening, Lou? Wasn't it romantic?"

Louise thought a moment before answering. "Yeah, I suppose so."

"What do you mean you suppose so? You didn't like it?"

Rhonda and Louise had been invited to Niagara Falls by Shirley and Linda to celebrate their friends' twenty years together. Before dinner, the four women gathered in the privacy of Shirley and Linda's honeymoon suite, where the couple recited vows of devotion.

"I don't know ... it just seemed like we were in the middle of what should have been a private moment. I didn't expect that." Louise wasn't comfortable showing affection in front of others, even those few who knew how she felt about Rhonda. She was just as uneasy about seeing it from Shirley and Linda.

"But they don't always have to be private moments. I think they just wanted the chance to share how they felt about each other publicly."

"I know. I just felt sort of embarrassed about it, especially when they kissed."

"That was certainly some kiss. Made me want to grab you and do the same thing."

"Thank you for showing restraint."

Rhonda sighed and rested her chin on Louise's shoulder. "Sometimes I think you're ashamed of being a lesbian."

"You know better than that. I just don't think we have to shove it in people's faces. Not everyone is comfortable with that sort of thing."

"What sort of thing?"

"You just said it—lesbians."

"And that's exactly why I think you're ashamed of it, because you were embarrassed by our best friends, who happen to be lesbians too, talking about how much they loved each other. You don't act that way when it's a couple of our straight friends or family members getting married. You didn't act that way at Hiram and Janet's twenty-fifth anniversary party."

Louise squirmed out of Rhonda's grasp. She didn't like having her feelings examined under a microscope this way, and it spoiled for the moment any notion of romance she might have been entertaining for the rest of their evening. "I'm not ashamed of it. But how I feel about you isn't anyone else's business."

"No, it isn't. But I'd like to think that someday under the right circumstances we could have a little ceremony of our own."

"I don't need a ceremony to tell you how much I love you or that I intend to spend my life with you. We both convey that to each other every day, just by what we say and do."

"We do, but saying those things in front of witnesses makes them more ... I don't know, solemn. It's like sharing your love when you can tell other people how you feel. Isn't that what weddings are all about?"

"But it isn't a wedding. It's just pretend." Louise saw right away the impact of her harsh words on Rhonda, whose face fell as she sighed and turned away. "The fact that we haven't recited vows or poetry to each other doesn't mean what we have isn't real. I love you with all my heart. You know that."

Rhonda nodded. "I do, and I know you're a private person when it comes to things like that, so I've learned not to expect much in front of other people. But what I don't understand is how you can watch our two best friends talk about their love and devotion to each other, and all you can think about is how uncomfortable you are. Shirley and Linda wanted something really special for their twentieth anniversary, and I was honored that they asked me to witness it. You should have been honored too."

Louise slumped onto the bed as Rhonda disappeared into the bathroom and closed the door. She was irritated and hurt that Rhonda hadn't seemed to hear the part about loving her with all her heart. And since when were Shirley and Linda's feelings more important than hers? But as she sat there listening to the sound of the falls, she acknowledged the first inkling of guilt for her selfish thoughts. Rhonda was right ... as she usually was. At least she hadn't voiced her feelings out loud to Shirley and Linda. That would have ruined their night, a night that was very special to them.

She got up and walked across the room where she tapped softly on the bathroom door. "Rhonda?"

The door opened and the light spilled into the room. Rhonda was naked and washing her face.

"I'm sorry, baby."

Rhonda didn't answer but continued her ablutions.

"You were right about it being a special night for them. I should have felt honored just like you did, and I was being selfish."

Rhonda dried her face and turned around. "Louise Stevens, you drive me nuts, you know that? I love you so much that it's all I can do sometimes to hold it in. I'm surprised I haven't told everybody."

"I love you too, baby. I really do. If it means that much to you, I'll try harder to show you ... and to show the people that matter how much you mean to me. I'm not ashamed of loving you." She held out her arms and Rhonda stepped into them.

"I know you aren't, honey. And I won't ever ask you to do something you're not comfortable with."

"I know you won't. But I do love you, Rhonda. And I plan to be with you as long as I live."

Chapter 22

MARTY PLUNGED HER orange hand inside the bag of cheese curls, extracting a third handful to accompany the Italian sub she had picked up at the snack bar before leaving the club. She kept her promise of healthy eating for exactly two days until choosing convenience over weight loss. To her chagrin, she had already picked up five pounds in less than two weeks. She would have to lose that again before Louise arrived at the end of the month. Crunching two cheese curls at a time, Marty solemnly vowed to skip food altogether on Tuesdays and Fridays.

It was almost eight o'clock, the designated time for Louise's call. It was easily the highlight of her day, though Marty had to admit that the first couple of weeks back at Elk Ridge had been fun. She had already hooked up with a number of her clients from summers past, and the staff had even thrown a "Welcome Back" party in the clubhouse on her first day.

But talking with Louise at the end of her work day helped her relax. The down side was the loneliness she felt each time they said goodnight.

Right on time, the phone rang in Marty's condo and she hastily wiped her hands on her T-shirt and grabbed the cordless phone.

"Hello."

"Hi, baby."

Right away, Marty heard a tenor in Louise's voice that told her something was amiss. "What's up, honey? Is everything okay?"

Louise didn't answer at first, and Marty was sure she heard a sniffle before she finally spoke. "Are you ready for some company?"

"Of course." Unconsciously, Marty began to collect the remnants of her dinner in her first step toward straightening up the condo. "Is something wrong?"

"I can't talk long tonight. I'm just outside of Brunswick in a motel, and I think this is costing me a dollar a minute."

"Give me the number and I'll call you back."

"I really don't want to get into all of it over the phone. I'll tell you everything when I get there."

"Lou, you've got me worried. I'm not going to be able to sleep tonight and work all day tomorrow if you don't tell me what's got you so upset. Please give me the number for where you are."

Louise sighed and supplied the phone number for the motel, mumbling something about wishing they could be together tonight. When Marty called back, Louise told her what had happened earlier in the day.

"I can't even imagine how you feel. I know it must hurt like hell."

"I can't believe she's acted like my friend all these years. I feel so stupid."

"You're not stupid, Lou. You were lied to." Marty hated to hear the hurt in her lover's voice. "But I don't think Shirley just pretended to be your friend."

"People don't treat their real friends that way," Louise argued, her tone more exasperated than angry, as though she was trying to find a way to see past the deception.

"I know, and I agree with you that Shirley wasn't being your friend back then. But from what you're saying, it sounds like something that happened only once a long time ago."

"Why are you defending her?"

"I'm not, Lou. I just ... people make mistakes. And even when they feel bad about them, there just isn't any way to make up for it. Shirley's right about how much this would hurt Linda, and I know you don't want that."

"No, but I can't just pretend I don't know about it either."

"Then you're doing the right thing by coming here, Lou. Maybe after the shock of finding out wears off, you can figure out a way to deal with it. I know you'll do the right thing."

"I don't know if I can." Louise sniffed.

"You will. You just need a little time."

"All I know is that I want to be with you right now."

"And I want to be with you." Marty went over the directions to her condo again, guessing that Louise would probably arrive around four or five. She had a late lesson, but she would leave a key under the mat, and she told Louise to make herself at home. They would go out for dinner as soon as Marty could be ready.

"I love you, Lou. It's going to be okay." Marty knew Louise was strong enough to get past this, even if Louise didn't know it herself.

Louise laid one hand on Petie's head as she braked and started into another curve on the mountain road. "Almost there, baby. Sorry I'm slinging you around so much." Petie was accustomed to traveling in the car, but he was tired and restless from the swaying and turning. "We're going to see Marty."

With every mile today, it seemed to Louise that she felt lighter. Her talk with Marty last night had been good for her, and the issue of Shirley and Rhonda had finally begun to settle in her gut. It was clear what she needed to do, and the sooner she did it, the sooner she would begin to feel better about it all.

Louise spotted the sign for Elk Ridge and put on her turn signal. "This is it, Petie." Just past the entrance, the road forked, with markers pointing to the golf course to the left, the residences to the right. Louise slowed when she reached an electronic gate and entered the code Marty had given her. The gate arm rose and she went through, turning uphill past a small lake that bordered the course on one side and several condo buildings on the other.

"Marty was right—it's beautiful here." Petie was standing now with his front feet on the dashboard.

Louise followed the road into the woods, turning off one last time into a cul-de-sac that held two gray buildings, each with two units. Hemlocks, maples, and oaks towered all around, and rhododendrons lined the porches. The last unit on the end—a two-story condo—was Marty's, and Louise parked in a spot whose number matched the one on the door.

"Come on, Petie. Let's go see our new home away from home." She clipped on his leash and opened the car door, happy to finally stretch her legs after two long days behind the wheel. Petie pulled her right away to a bush, where he sniffed, turned, and relieved himself. Then they mounted the steps to the front porch where Louise retrieved the key from under the mat.

A wondrous feeling enveloped her as she entered Marty's home for the first time. The kitchen was to her right and opened up into a dining area and living room with vaulted ceilings. A massive stone fireplace stood on one wall, and sliding glass doors led out onto a large wooden deck. The floors were a combination of hardwood and taupe carpet, and the furnishings were worn leather or rustic wood, the latter matching the trim around the doors and windows. There were very few knickknacks on the furniture or the dark green counters, but there was clearly a golf theme present in the décor—the lamp bases were golf bags, and the throw pillows were embroidered with crossed clubs. The whole place had a simple, almost masculine elegance that said it belonged to Marty Beck. Louise loved it.

Petie followed her into what was obviously the master bedroom, given its king-sized bed, attached bath, and sliding glass doors onto the deck. The green and taupe color scheme continued with the bedspread and drapes, and the walls were adorned with golf-oriented art—misty, Scottish course landscapes and a few cartoons.

Back out in the main area, a small powder room was tucked beneath the staircase. Upstairs, a reading nook had been set up on the landing above the kitchen, and a guest bedroom suite and storage area stood above the master suite.

Back in the kitchen, Louise found a note instructing her to call the clubhouse and leave a message that she had arrived. But first, she wanted to make another call.

After two rings, Linda answered the phone. "Hi, it's me, Louise. I just got to Marty's in North Carolina ... I'm fine. I guess I was just missing her like crazy. But I wanted to let you know that I made it up here safely with Petie." Louise listened to a litany of offers from Linda to help out. "No, the house is locked up. It'll be okay. Thanks, though. Is Shirley there? I want to tell her something."

Louise drew several deep breaths as she waited for the woman to come to the phone. "Hey, Shirl ... I'm at Marty's. I forgive you … and I don't ever want us to talk about this again."

"Petie, I think you and I are about the two luckiest creatures in the whole world!" Marty loosened her grip on the plastic handle, allowing the Boston terrier another six feet at the end of the leash.

The little dog was investigating the clues that others had visited the pet area between the condos and the seventeenth fairway. Not that Petie minded the other dogs; on the contrary, he seemed to think this new dog walk was a very exciting place. And he obviously enjoyed his morning time with Marty, evidenced by his enthusiasm each time she climbed out of bed and picked up his leash.

"Your mommy loves us both, doesn't she?" In the week since Louise had arrived, Marty sensed a familiarity with her that hadn't been there in Florida. They had fallen into an easy routine, with her going to work in the morning while Louise explored the surrounding towns, the High Country, as it was called here. Each night, Marty came home to find dinner—low-calorie, low-fat—ready and waiting. They spent evenings relaxing on the deck as the sun set, or in front of the television, where Marty usually fell asleep.

Petie seemed at home here as well. He quickly adapted to sleeping at the foot of the king-sized bed, though his mistress had forgotten his favorite blanket. She made up for it by taking him on walks to new places where there were lots of friendly people.

Marty looked up and spotted the object of their affections on the back deck of the condo. Louise was setting the outside table for breakfast and stopped to wave in their direction.

"We've got it made, Petie." More each day, Marty marveled at her good fortune. It might have taken her almost sixty-two years, but by golly, she had found the woman of her dreams.

"Breakfast is ready," Louise called from above.

"That's our cue, boy. Come on, and I'll slip you a little piece of that extra-lean turkey sausage under the table."

Petie scuffed his hind feet to throw dirt and grass on the other dogs' territorial markings, and strutted with Marty up the hill to the condo.

"Yep, she loves us."

August 1999

Marty drummed her fingers silently on the tablecloth, asking herself one last time if she was doing the right thing. Most club professionals would give an eye tooth for the chance to shape the career of a promising young golfer, and here she was, about to give up Tami Sparks to Pat Shapiro.

"Here they come," she said, spotting Tami and her parents at the entrance of the restaurant. It was too late for Marty to turn back now. They had covered the preliminaries over the phone. Tonight's first meeting was just a formality before Mike and Cathy Sparks committed to moving to Tampa.

Pat and Marty stood nervously to await their arrival.

"Marty, good to see you again," Mike said, extending his hand.

She took it and quickly made the introductions, saving the fourteen-year-old for last. "And this is Tami. She learns very fast, so you have to watch her like a hawk, or she'll pick up bad habits." Marty cuffed the girl gently on the shoulder.

"Nice to meet all of you," Pat said.

The Sparks family scooted into the corner booth, while Pat and Marty took the seats on the outside. A waiter appeared to take their drink order.

"Two vodka gimlets and a Coke, please." Mike gestured to indicate that he was ordering for his family.

"A white Russian," Marty added.

"Ice tea for me," Pat said. "I've got a long drive back to Tampa tonight."

"Why don't we take care of business first? That way, we can enjoy our meal," Mike said. "And this is my treat."

"Thank you, Mike. That's very generous," Marty said. "Pat and I have a few ideas about what Tami should concentrate on these next couple of years."

"That's right," Pat said. "There are several youth tournaments we'll want to enter. Most of them are in Florida, but a couple are in Georgia. They're small, but we can get a good idea where Tami stands on the regional scene."

"And Pat says there's a good high school in the area for golf, one that's won a few state championships. You might want to consider looking for a house in that district."

Mike and Cathy looked at each other. "My goodness," Cathy said. "You really have this all worked out."

The waiter returned with their drinks, but went away when he saw the unopened menus.

"There's more," Marty said. "We'll need to hook Tami up with a caddy, somebody who's good enough to make the jump to the tour when she's ready."

"Do you have someone in mind?" Mike asked.

"There's a young man at my club, Jeff Hanley. He's caddied for me in a few senior tournaments. I think he'd be a good match for your daughter." Pat looked at Tami. "I bet you wish we'd stop talking about you like you're not here."

Tami laughed. "I'm used to it. Dad and Marty talk about me all the time."

"It's going to be different from now on, sweetheart," her father said. "We're making this move because Marty thinks you're ready for the next level." He looked seriously at Pat. "I don't want you to take any of this personally, but I'd like for Marty to tell us one more time why she thinks Tami needs a different coach."

Marty took a sip of her drink, cleared her throat, and looked directly at Tami. "I've really enjoyed working with you these past few years, kiddo. You know that?"

Tami nodded.

"I think you have a real gift, and you've worked really hard on your game. You have a chance to make it big, and I think Pat's the best one to help you get there, not me. She's coached two women who are now on the pro tour, and everybody in the league knows her. She'll open some doors for you that I can't touch."

Marty paused and took another drink. "From now on, the motivation's going to have to come from here." Marty put her fist on her heart. "You'll have to tune out everybody but Pat and Jeff ... only work on the things they tell you, and commit yourself to getting better and better. Your mom and dad are going to be cheerleaders now, not taskmasters."

Tami nodded. "Okay, I can do that." She lowered her head and said shyly, "But I'm going to miss working with you, because you always made it fun."

"I'm going to miss you, too." Marty leaned over and wrapped her arm around the girl's shoulders. "Remember that dream you told me about?"

Tami smiled. "Winning The Dinah and jumping in the water."

Marty nodded in Pat's direction. "She'll help you make that come true. But it's your job now to make the game fun, not Pat's. Do whatever it takes, but don't ever forget that having fun is what it's all about."

Chapter 23

BOB SEAVER STOOD behind the counter watching Marty peruse the rack of women's golf wear. "Something for your lady friend?"

"Yeah, where are those pink pullovers with the Elk Ridge logo?"

Bob gestured toward the sale rack. "Maybe the four of us should go to the club for dinner some night. Francine wants to meet Louise, but you should warn her first."

"You mean because your wife's a nut?" Francine was one of Marty's favorite people, an outgoing woman who never stopped celebrating life. "I think she and Lou would hit it off." She walked behind the counter with the new sweater just in time to catch the ringing phone. It was Tami's coach, Pat Shapiro.

"Hey, Pat. How's our girl?"

"Busy! You remember how summers used to be, driving all over the country from one little tournament to the next. Tami and I still have to hit all those places, but at least we fly now."

Marty felt a pang of jealousy. It wasn't longing for the old days, but for the chance to be back in the thick of the action like Pat. "How's Tami doing?"

"Incredible. She's playing the best golf of her life, Marty."

"That's great news. I hope she does well in Asheville. That'll give her confidence going into the qualifier."

"That's the plan. And if she makes the cut in September, she'll probably turn pro right away. Her mom and dad are pretty much maxed out and I think she's starting to feel a little anxious about it. That's not good for her game."

"We know that feeling, don't we?" Marty remembered sleeping in the station wagon, literally worrying about where their next meal was coming from. "It's hard to concentrate on golf when you can't pay the bills."

"I remember. That's one thing that's nice about this go-around. I get a lot more respect as Tami's coach than I used to as a player, especially from potential sponsors."

Marty envied her old friend, remembering again her tough decision to pass on the opportunity to coach the prodigy golfer. If she hadn't, she would be the big shot, the one booking tournaments and talking with sponsors. Tami Sparks was going to do something neither Marty nor Pat had done—she was going to hit the big time in the LPGA.

"So, the reason I called was to see if you could help me out at the tournament."

"Of course, whatever you need."

"I was wondering if you would walk with Mike and Cathy. I really need to focus on Tami's mechanics so I can get her ready for the qualifier."

Walk with Tami's parents? Marty was hoping for a bigger role than that. "Sure, I can help out with that. But I might help even more if I walked with you and looked at her game too. I'm pretty good at diagnosing problems."

"I know. You're the best there is," Pat said. "I just feel like I really need to concentrate on it, and you know how Mike and Cathy like to talk and ask questions. I wouldn't trust anybody else to handle them, Marty. And they really like you."

Marty bit the inside of her cheek and sucked in a breath. "Of course I'll do it. It'll be nice to see them again."

"That's great. They'll be glad to hear it, and it'll really help me out a lot."

"Good. I can't wait. Tell Tami I said to keep her head down."

"Will do. Thanks again, Marty."

"Sure."

A cool breeze rattled the mini-blinds in the master bedroom, a pleasant reminder for Louise of why so many people flocked to the mountains in the summer. The weekend crowd had jammed the shops and streets around Banner Elk, but Marty said things would quiet down during the week until the temperatures rose in August. The tourists would be back in droves for that.

Louise knew already that she was going to love Tuesdays. That's when Marty could take a break from giving lessons and working in the pro shop to join her for a round of golf. Not only was it a chance for them to spend an afternoon together, it was also a chance for Marty to relax and play the game she loved

Louise put the finishing touches on her makeup. Even after all this time, she still wanted to look her best on her days out with Marty. Also, she wanted to make a good impression on people at the club, especially those who knew she was Marty's guest. The members at Elk Ridge were more upscale than those at Pine Island—retired physicians, attorneys, and business executives.

"Wish me luck, Petie."

Louise drove to the clubhouse and dropped her clubs by the curb. By the time she parked, they were gone, presumably loaded into a cart that was now waiting for her by the pro shop.

She walked in and spotted Marty behind the counter.

"Hi, sweetie. I'll be ready in just a minute," Marty said.

Louise blushed and looked around, spotting two men talking with Bob Seaver. She doubted she would ever get used to Marty's openness about their relationship. Only in the past few years had she gotten comfortable just being in the company of other lesbians. That was a far cry from how Marty lived her life—she was out with practically everyone.

Louise stepped outside and waited in the cart. Marty joined her after a few minutes, strapping her heavy bag onto the back.

"You look nice, Lou."

"Thank you." She didn't mean for that to come out frosty, but she knew it had.

"What's wrong?" Marty stomped on the accelerator and the cart lurched forward to the first tee.

Louise sighed. "Nothing ... really."

"What?"

"I just ... you called me sweetie." That sounded stupid, she thought. "In front of people."

"That's Bob! He's known me forty years."

"But he doesn't know me. And what about those other men?"

"Lou, Bob knows you're staying with me. And that reminds me. I'm supposed to invite you for dinner at the club with him and his wife. They're good friends of mine, and I think you'd like them."

"Good friends are one thing, but what about those other people? What are they going to think?"

"I don't care what they think. If they have a problem with it, it's theirs."

"But I don't like total strangers knowing my private business."

"Lou"—Marty stopped the cart at the tee and got out, shaking her head—"I know you and Rhonda were discreet about your lives. That's the way it was back when you two first found each other, and I understand. But our life doesn't have to be like that."

For Louise, the argument was almost painfully reminiscent of the dozens she and Rhonda had about making new friends, and about the casual things they could say in conversations with their coworkers. In the old days, she might have dug in her heels, refusing to entertain another point of view. But over the years, she had learned to listen, and to compromise when she needed to.

"Tell me what you're afraid of, honey."

"I don't know, Marty." Louise sighed with exasperation, just as she had when Rhonda pinned her down with the very same question. "I know it's different now, but suppose one of the members here knows somebody back in Greensburg? Or what if one of my old friends came here for a visit? I can't very well tell a hundred people not to say anything."

"What would be so bad if your old friends found out? They can't fire you now. You don't even have to look at them every day anymore. Besides, if they're your friends, they'll stay that way."

"I know, but ... I just ... it would ..."

"What is it? What's bothering you?"

"I know what they all would say, Marty. Half of them would say 'Oh, I always knew those two were more than just friends. They didn't fool me.' And then the other half would be mad because we lied to them all those years."

"You can't do much about the know-it-alls. All of us had to deal with them at one time or another. I found that 'I always thought the same about you' clams them right up."

Louise chuckled and pulled her driver from her bag, hoping Marty's injection of humor would end this serious conversation soon. She didn't want to be at odds over this. She would try harder to see it from Marty's point of view. It really was easier not to worry all the time about what others would think, but old habits were hard to break.

"Eww! What happened to you?" Louise exclaimed as she took in the sight of the mud-covered golf pro.

"My three-iron behaved very badly on Seven, and I had to hit out of the water."

"No one hits out of the water, silly. It's a drop."

"But it wasn't all the way submerged. The top of it was just sitting there right on the edge."

"Well from the looks of things, you took a heck of a divot!"

"I needed to get it all," Marty explained seriously.

Louise laughed as she pictured the scene. "Who were you playing with that you had to impress so much?"

"A couple of new guys up from Winston-Salem. They come up on the weekends because they have second homes in the mountains. Both of them signed up for lessons after the round, so I guess they really were impressed."

"Well I hope they don't think everyone up here is as crazy as you are," Louise teased.

"I'm only crazy about you," Marty answered sweetly. "Let me grab a shower and we'll go to dinner." They were meeting Bob and Francine at the club.

Louise followed her into the master bedroom, picking up the discarded pieces of clothing almost as soon as they hit the floor. Neither of them was wholly conscious of this new routine, but it was a habit Louise had acquired over her last fifteen years with Rhonda, who tossed her clothes throughout the house whenever she had a hot flash.

Marty flipped the switch in the bathroom and stopped short. "Where'd these come from?" Her hand went out to brand new, colorful towels that hung in place of the ragged beige ones she had used for years.

"I bought them today at one of the outlet shops. I thought they'd look nice in here. What do you think?"

Marty ran her fingers along the plush terry, admiring the softness. They were definitely nice ... but Marty suddenly had a queasy feeling in the pit of her stomach. This was how it had started with Angela—tossing out her favorite coffee mugs, junking the golf trinkets, and relegating most of her furniture to the garage, where it was subsequently discarded.

"I'm sort of used to the beige ones," Marty said, bracing for an argument.

"Okay," Louise readily agreed. Apparently she hadn't even noticed Marty's hesitation. "They're in the dryer, though, so you'll have to wait. Go ahead and use these for now and I'll switch them when the others are ready. I can take these back to Florida. They'll look nice in my guest bath."

Louise proceeded to collect the rest of the new towels, but Marty stopped her. She had expected Louise to make a stronger case for her own preferences.

"Wait. These are really nice ... and they're soft."

"I know. That's why I like them. But if it's not what you're used to—"

"I can get used to them. I like the colors." This wasn't Louise trying to impose her tastes and decorating ideas. Nor was it a rejection of Marty's things. It was just new towels to replace the old ones that had worn out.

"Yeah, they look good with the bedspread and the tile. But we don't have to use them if you want yours."

Marty turned the shower on and tossed one of the new washcloths inside. "Too late! I've changed my mind." With a wide grin, she planted a kiss on Louise's cheek and stepped into the shower.

Ten minutes later, Louise was waiting with a towel when Marty finished. "Doesn't this feel good?" She patted the fluffy terrycloth over Marty's wet skin.

"Yeah." Marty decided then to tell Louise why she had reacted that way about the new things. "I'm sorry if I acted funny about the towels. I know the other ones are pretty ratty."

"That's all right. I feel the same way about my green bathrobe. You just get comfortable—"

"It wasn't that, Lou." Marty took the towel and continued to briskly dry herself. "I just got worked up about it because Angela used to do things like that. She didn't like any of my stuff, so little by little, she got rid of everything. When we split up, practically all I had left in Florida were the clothes on my back."

"Oh, Marty!"

"Thank goodness I still had this place. I guess I'm just a little possessive now when it comes to my stuff." She could tell by the fallen look on Louise's face that her words were causing unintended remorse. "I overreacted, Lou. It wasn't your fault."

"I should have known better, though. You told me how she was, and I should have realized what you'd think." Louise followed Marty into the bedroom where she began to get dressed for dinner. "I like it here. I like this place, and everything you've done with it."

"You do?"

"I do. Really! The second I walked in here, I knew that you lived here. And I happen to love you, so why wouldn't I love your things too?"

"I just thought ... well, your house is full of flowers and light and frilly things. I didn't think you'd really go for all the leather and dark colors. Not to mention all the golf stuff."

"The golf stuff? Are you kidding! I love the golf stuff." Louise sat on the bed as Marty continued to dress. "In fact, I have some things like that in the attic over the garage. I put them away for now because ... well, they reminded me too much of Rhonda. But I can put some of them out when I get back, since you like that sort of thing."

Louise's revelation turned the tables, and now it was Marty who felt bad. "No, you don't have to do that for me. I don't want you to do something that would make you sad."

"It doesn't make me sad like it used to, though. I mean, I still miss her, but I don't think about her as much as I did. I think about you instead," Louise said softly.

Marty sat down on the bed beside her and wrapped an arm around Louise's waist. "Do you have any idea how much I love you?"

Louise nodded and managed a feeble smile. "I think so."

"I hope so. I know I'm not ever going to take Rhonda's place, but—"

"No, but you have your own place. I don't think of you ... like I think of her," she stammered.

Marty felt her stomach drop, and her first reaction was to pull away. But Louise caught her arm and pulled her back.

"I didn't say that right. Let me try again." She drew in a deep breath and looked seriously into Marty's eyes. "I'll admit there are times you remind me of Rhonda, but that's usually when you've said something that made me laugh or you've made me feel happy. But I don't compare you to her."

"How can you not?"

"I just don't, Marty. It's as simple as that." She took both of Marty's hands in hers. "Holding you up next to Rhonda would be pointless. Linda made me see that back when I first realized I had feelings for you. I felt guilty about it and I was afraid to let go. But all of my feelings for Rhonda are just memories. I can't share them with her the way I can share my love with you."

"But you spent thirty years with her. How can I ever compete with something that deep?"

"You don't have to compete with her, Marty. She's dead." The blunt declaration came down like a hammer.

Marty sighed and shook her head. "Listen to me. I sound like a nutcase." She squeezed Louise's fingers and then worked her hands free to stroke her lover's face, a face that looked as though it might burst into tears at any second. "I'm sorry, Lou. I'm the one that makes the comparisons, not you. I just feel so"—she searched for the right word—"intimidated sometimes about the fact that you had such a happy life with one person for so long."

"Why are you intimidated by that?" Louise shifted on the bed so that they faced one another.

"Because I never had a relationship that worked right for more than just a couple of years."

"Did you ever have one with somebody you really wanted to stay with?"

Louise's question stunned her and Marty couldn't think of what to say.

"Rhonda and I stayed together that long because it's what we both wanted. We had to work at it—hard sometimes—but it was worth it because we loved each other."

"I love you, Lou. As a matter of fact, I don't remember ever feeling this way about anybody else in my whole life. But what if I don't have what it takes to make it last? What if I screw up like I always have?"

"Everybody screws up. Rhonda did, I did—all the time. But screwing up and giving up aren't the same thing. If you both really love each other, you just keep on going. And in the end, you get out of it what you put in."

Marty was struck by the simplicity of what Louise was saying. "So the key is just being willing to work at it?"

"No, the key is that both people are willing to work at it."

Marty sighed as her shoulders sagged. "So nobody really controls their own fate."

"I wouldn't say that. If you want to resign yourself to fail, there probably isn't anyone who could stop you."

"You're playing with my brain, aren't you?"

Louise chuckled. "What makes you say that?"

"Because no matter what I say, you have an answer for it."

Louise scrunched her lips as she seemingly searched for a comeback. "I don't know what to say to that."

Both women laughed.

"It's true what I said about Rhonda, though," Louise continued. "When I realized where my feelings for you were headed, I had to put that part of her away. I'll always miss her, but she's my past. You, Marty Beck, are my present. And the more time we spend together, the more I want you in my future."

Marty shook her head with amazement. "I told Petie the other day that I felt like the luckiest woman in the whole world."

"I'll remind you of that one of these days when I need a pass on something."

"You do that." Marty leaned forward and gave her a peck on the lips. "Let's go eat barbecued ribs."

"Nice try. Let's go eat broiled fish and a salad."

Louise laughed at the cartoon on Marty's computer, part of her personalized home page. It was funny, she thought, how well you got to know someone by staying in her house and using her things. Marty's condo was filled with reminders of her sense of humor, from the witty sayings on the coffee mugs to the bathroom scales that let out a scream whenever you stepped on them. Most certainly, Rhonda would have adored Marty, and Louise always found that comforting.

The familiar chime on her email program announced mail, another from Michele Sanders. Michele was probably home for the summer, Louise thought.

Dear Miss Stevens,

I don't know if you've heard the big news or not, but since we were talking about this sort of thing when I was in Florida, I wondered what you thought about it. The new superintendent just fired Mr. Ulster because he's gay. He didn't come right out and say that was the reason, but everybody thinks it is because there was an article in the paper about a guy that got kicked out of the army reserves for being gay and it mentioned his partner, Darren Ulster. So I guess if I want to

teach in Pennsylvania, I'm going to have to make sure nobody ever finds out about me. I just wanted to let you know, in case you hadn't heard. I hope you're having a nice summer.
Love, Michele

Louise read the note again, three times in all before she fully understood. She had always thought Darren might be gay, and even though she and the new band director had become friends at school, she had never pried into his personal life. These were things they all left at home—at least that's how she and Rhonda had dealt with it. But in this day and age, it seemed farfetched that just being gay would get a teacher fired. There had to be more to it than that, she reasoned.

Dear Michele,
I hadn't heard that news, but I wouldn't read too much into it if I were you. The contract forbids the discussion of personnel matters, so there may be another reason for Mr. Ulster being let go that we don't know about. Whatever it is, it's unfortunate that things didn't work out. I know that Mr. Ulster was well-liked by the band members and faculty, and I'm sure he'll find another position. I am having a nice summer, and I hope you are too.
Love, Louise Stevens

"Hey, Petie!" Marty squatted to greet the excited terrier at the door. "I'm home, Lou!" She could hear Louise talking in the bedroom.

"He can't do this, can he?" Louise was pacing the room as she talked on the phone. A scant look was all the notice she took of Marty's arrival, and immediately, Marty could sense something was wrong.

"This is just awful, Ted. What kind of message does that send to the kids who are starting to deal with this kind of thing? And what does it teach them about respect for other people?"

Marty tiptoed into the room and sat on the bed, reaching out to stroke the back of Louise's thigh as she paced.

"So when is the hearing?" Without a word to her, Louise lovingly ran her hand through Marty's wind-blown hair. "Who's going to speak on his behalf?"

Hearing? Marty couldn't piece together what the conversation was about, but she had never seen Louise so obviously distressed. Nor could she imagine which of Louise's friends or family would be getting a hearing.

"I don't know, Ted ... I need to think about this. I want to help, but …" Her voice began to quiver. "I'll think about it, I promise. When do you have to know?" Louise sat on the bed beside Marty. "I'll call you tomorrow, then. Thanks for talking with me."

"What is it, Lou? What's wrong?"

Louise related the news of her email from Michele. "I didn't think Ted would let something like that happen, so I called him to see what the issue was. I still can't believe it, Marty."

"What? Was she right?"

"I'm afraid so. Ted says the superintendent called him in and told him he wasn't going to renew Darren's contract. He said the voters made it clear they weren't ready to accept any so-called alternative lifestyles. He thinks that gives him authority to go digging around in people's personal lives."

"All because of a few little words in the paper? I'm surprised anyone even noticed."

"It wasn't just that. Apparently, somebody from the superintendent's office followed up with Darren and he confirmed that he was living with another man."

"Still, I don't see why they're making such a big deal out of it. Are you sure there isn't something else?"

Louise shook her head. "Ted says no. Darren's a good teacher. He took over the band when Rhonda died. It was hard for him, because the kids liked her so much. They resented him at first, but he worked hard and won them over. He doesn't deserve to be treated like this."

"Doesn't Ted have a say in this? I thought principals made decisions like that."

Louise shook her head. "The superintendent has the final authority. But Darren has appealed the decision and he's going to speak at the school board meeting. Ted says he's going to say a few words, and there are a couple of band parents who'll stand up for him too."

Suddenly, Marty realized what Louise was considering. "What sort of decision do you need to make by tomorrow?" She took Louise's hand and squeezed it.

"Ted asked me if I'd come and speak on Darren's behalf."

"What does he want you to say, Lou? Surely he doesn't—"

"I think he knows, Marty. He's been my friend for forty years. He was the one who introduced me to Rhonda, and he stood there and held me while she died." Her eyes filled with tears. "If there was one person at Westfield who really knew both of us, it was Ted. But he never said a word."

"If he really knows you, then he knows how difficult it would be for you to do what he's asking."

Louise nodded and looked at her shaking hands. "But this hatred and bigotry has to stop, Marty. The only reason people get away with it is because we don't stand up when we should."

October 1999

Ted Meyer sat at Louise's kitchen table, nursing his fourth cup of coffee since returning from the hospital, where Rhonda's body had been taken to await pickup by a funeral home. All afternoon, he had talked quietly with Louise about what had happened today. Louise admitted she had been nagging Rhonda for the last few days to see a doctor about her red face and shortness of breath.

"I should have insisted."

"You didn't know, Louise. And Rhonda must not have thought it was serious either, or she would have gone. It was just one of those things."

Off and on into the evening, the phone rang with calls from Linda and Shirley, from Rhonda's relatives and Hiram, and from other teachers who just wanted to know Louise was all right.

"I want you to come stay the night with Dottie and me, Lou. You shouldn't be at home alone at a time like this."

"Thank you, but I need to be here."

"Then why don't I stay here too? Or if you'd rather have Dottie, I'll call her."

"I appreciate it, Ted, but I'll be all right. I have so many things to do. And Rhonda's sister and her husband are on their way from Wilkes-Barre right now. I'm sure they'll stay with me tonight."

"I can wait with you until they get here."

"It's okay. I'd ... if you don't mind, I think I'd just like to be alone for a while." Louise could read the reluctance in his face, but she kept up her strong visage. The longer he stayed, the more anxious she grew about the state of things upstairs.

"Are you sure?"

"I am. I really appreciate everything you've done today."

"If you need anything ..."

"I know. Thank you." She followed her old friend to the door where they embraced, both fighting back sobs for just an instant. Then he was gone, and Louise closed the door. The clock on the mantle said nine-thirty. Rhonda's sister Helen would be here in about an hour with her husband, Jack. That wasn't much time.

Louise scanned the living room and study for any stray notes or pictures. It was rare for people to drop by unannounced, but it happened on occasion, so they were always careful to keep their personal things in their bedrooms upstairs.

There were only two bedrooms in the old house. Helen and Jack would probably want to stay in "Rhonda's room." Louise hurried into the room and opened the dresser drawers on the right side. She scooped out all of her underwear and nightclothes and carried the armload to "her bedroom," where she dropped it in the middle of the bed. Rhonda's jeans and sweatshirts were in the bottom drawer of the bureau, and Louise deftly made the switch. That took care of their clothes ... except for her robe and house slippers in the closet of the other bedroom, which she retrieved and stored in her own closet.

Next, she swapped the contents of the nightstands so all of her personal items were now in the seldom-used room, and all of Rhonda's were in the room they had shared. That left only the boxes in the closet—the boxes that held their mementos of thirty-one years together. Louise climbed onto the stepstool and pushed aside stacks of sweaters to reveal two large gray strongboxes. One was heavy, jam-packed with birthday cards, Valentines, anniversary and holiday cards, and the love letters they sometimes wrote to one another to heal a hurt or to celebrate a happy occasion. The other box held souvenirs and their private photos, like those Linda and Shirley had taken of the two of them together during rare carefree moments. These were moments in which they had dropped their guard to stand arm in arm, or to lounge in a loving embrace.

Over their years together, Louise and Rhonda had talked many times of these boxes, beginning most conversations with that ominous phrase, "If anything ever happens to one of us ..." With Rhonda's family totally in the dark about their relationship, it was imperative that Louise fulfill her partner's wishes.

One at a time, Louise carried the boxes to her bedroom. Locating a key beneath a lamp, she unlocked a trunk at the foot of her bed and removed two quilts, creating enough space for the boxes. When they were secured, she pushed the key into her pocket. No one would ever know their memories.

Last, she stopped in the hallway to pick up fresh linens for their bed, the one Helen and Jack would sleep in. As she folded back the comforter, the faint scent of Rhonda's perfume wafted up from the sheets. Louise jumped back, fighting the hard knot that formed in her throat as the horrible reality jolted her. Taking a deep breath to steady her resolve, she stripped the bed. With quiet determination, she replaced the sheets, added the quilt and bedspread from the other bed, and swapped the pillows. She then remade her other bed with the old sheets ... the ones that smelled of Rhonda.

Chapter 24

LOUISE FINALLY RELAXED as the toll booth came into sight. She was almost at the end of her journey, and she was relieved to have survived the West Virginia Turnpike one more time. Rhonda had always thought it was amazing that they took your money for driving on this treacherous roadway instead of the other way around.

It was only three more hours to her brother's house in Wheeling, where Louise would spend the night. She had calculated along the way that the past nine months—since she left Pennsylvania to move to Florida—was probably the longest she and Hiram had ever gone without seeing one another. Hiram and Janet wanted her to stay longer on this visit, but Louise felt much like she had when she learned about Shirley and Rhonda—she needed to get this over with and go right back to Marty, who, in just a few months, had become her source of strength.

The more Louise thought about her escape to North Carolina, the more she knew staying there for the rest of the summer was the right thing for her to do. It wasn't just that she didn't want to be away from Marty now that they had found something special. It was more that she needed Marty in her everyday life. That's what had fed her relationship with Rhonda and made it grow—

being with her every single day, first as roommates, then as lovers. There was no way to avoid having to deal with all of the ups and downs, or having to face the gamut of moods and emotions. That's what had given them the experience to see their relationship through the tough times. And that's what she needed with Marty.

Louise paid the toll and continued onward, her thoughts shifting from Marty to what awaited her in Greensburg. She had hoped to make a trip later in the summer to visit some of her friends, but she doubted now that she would be back anytime soon. If she went through with what she had planned, she wouldn't be able to face anyone else.

"Come on, boy. Let's go eat junk food!" Marty tugged on Petie's leash and headed back for the condo. They were on their own for the next three nights, and Marty was expecting delivery of a large pepperoni pizza any minute. She came through the door just in time to catch the ringing phone. It was Louise, calling from Wheeling to say that she had made it safely.

"Petie and I miss you already, you know."

"I miss you too. I wish you were here with me."

"I'm really sorry, honey. I just couldn't leave with Bob out of town." She felt guilty, even though it wasn't her fault. Louise really needed her support right now, and she hated that she wasn't there to lend it.

"I know. But I guess this is something I ought to do by myself anyway."

"Have you decided what you're going to say?"

"Not really. I might chicken out and just say that I think Rhonda would be rolling over in her grave if she saw them getting rid of somebody as good as Darren."

"Maybe that's all you have to say, Lou."

"Maybe … but if they go ahead and fire him after that, I'll blame myself for not saying more."

"It won't be your fault, Lou. This isn't your battle."

"This battle belongs to all of us, Marty. People like you have been fighting this kind of bigotry all along, just by being brave enough to be yourselves. I never was, and now Darren's paying the price because nobody had the nerve to stand up and show people that we're worth something."

Marty didn't answer, since she was concentrating on paying the pizza man without letting Louise know about it.

"I really am proud of you, you know," Louise said seriously. "You've got more personal integrity than just about anyone I've ever met."

"Wow, Lou. That's quite a compliment coming from somebody like you." Marty made a dismal face as she set the pizza box on the edge of the trashcan. How could she cheat on her diet with Louise talking about her great integrity?

"I can't wait to get back. You take care of my little boy, okay?"

"I will. Call me tomorrow night." Marty reached into the refrigerator for a crisp, fresh, healthy … tasteless head of lettuce.

Louise pulled into the parking lot at the school board building at a quarter past six, relieved to have the drive from Wheeling behind her. At least the steady downpour had kept her distracted from the contentious meeting that lay ahead. But now that she was here, it was time to focus her attention on what she would say to the board.

She spotted Ted's car and pulled in next to it. Before she could even get the window down to say hello, he got out of his car and slid into hers, closing the door quickly to keep out the rain.

"It's so good to see you again, Ted." Ignoring his wet jacket, Louise reached out to embrace her old friend.

"It's good to see you too, Lou. You look great. I'd say retirement agrees with you." He took her hand and set a manila folder on the dashboard, not yet ready to talk about why they were here.

"It does, believe me. You and Dottie should give it a try."

"We plan to, starting next summer when I turn sixty-five."

"That's great news! Congratulations." Louise squeezed his hand and shook it at the same time. "It feels so good to be sitting here with you again. I can't believe how much I've missed seeing you nearly every day."

"Me too. I don't know what I'd have done this last year without having you to talk to on email."

"So how come you didn't write me about Darren? You wrote me about practically everything else."

Ted shrugged, clearly at a loss for words.

"Did you find the pictures I wanted?"

Ted nodded and handed her the folder. Inside were the agenda for the meeting, three scanned photos, and a CD. "I put them in a slide presentation so you can put them up on the big screen."

Louise shuddered and looked at her watch. She had about twenty minutes to change her mind. "Am I doing the right thing?"

"Only you know the answer to that, Lou. But I think your words will carry more weight than anyone in the room."

She nodded and looked at the agenda again, reading through the list of names of those who would bear witness to her message tonight.

"I just hope I can help Darren. This isn't right."

"No, it's not." Ted took the folder back and closed it. "So why don't you tell me what you're up to. The Lou Stevens that left here a year ago was sad and lonely, and I don't believe I see her this time."

Louise knew she was blushing, but she smiled nonetheless. "I'm happier now."

"And does this happiness have a name?"

"Marty." She knew from the look on his face that her answer hadn't helped him much. "She doesn't like to be called Martha."

The principal smiled. "I'm really glad for you, Lou. May I tell Dottie? She'll be happy for you too."

"Of course." For the next few minutes, Louise told her oldest friend about her new life in North Carolina and Florida. The more she talked, the more she relaxed. It was oddly comforting to be able to speak so openly with someone who knew her so well.

"You'll have to bring Marty with you on your next visit," Ted insisted.

"I might just do that. But you and Dottie also have a standing invitation to come see me in Florida."

"The rain's finally stopped." Ted looked at his watch and picked up the folder again. "Are you nervous?"

"Are you kidding? I just hope I don't get up there and forget how to speak."

"You'll be fine. I couldn't get you on the agenda without knocking someone else off, so I'm giving you my time. But I want to use about thirty seconds of it to introduce you, if that's okay. This new superintendent doesn't know Louise Stevens, and I think he should."

Louise nodded, shaking in anticipation as they got out of the car. As they walked to the building, she spotted a familiar young woman getting out of an SUV with her parents.

"Ted, will you excuse me? I'll meet you inside."

"Sure."

Louise walked quickly to catch up with the family. "Michele?"

The student turned at the familiar voice, her eyes wide with surprise. "Miss Stevens!"

Louise greeted the whole family like old friends and turned to face Michele. "I just learned that you're going to speak tonight."

"That's right. I talked it over with my mom and dad, and we agreed I should come and say something for Mr. Ulster."

"We're very proud of Michele," Will Sanders spoke up, placing his hand on his daughter's shoulder.

"I'm very proud of her too," Louise said. Her voice filled with emotion, she pulled the girl into a strong hug and told her, "Michele, I think you're one of the most courageous people I've ever known."

They marched into the small auditorium with determination. The noisy room quieted when the meeting was called to order.

Louise recognized the chairman … Donald … Donald Sumter. He graduated in one of her first classes, back in … 1964. It wasn't that he was memorable in high school; she knew him because he had been on the school board for almost four terms, now in his tenth year. And the third one from the left was Annette Hartig, whose name was now Mowrey. She graduated back in the mid-70s, and Louise distinctly recalled that she had been in the band.

For more than an hour, the board dispensed with other business as Louise fidgeted nervously in her seat. Finally, they reached new business, an open forum to hear from the community regarding the announced decision not to renew Darren Ulster's teaching contract.

Sumter began with the ground rules: "There are five people on the agenda for this discussion, and each will be given the allotted four minutes to deliver their remarks. No additional remarks will be heard at the close of this forum. Following these speakers, the board will adjourn to discuss the issue in private, as all issues pertaining to personnel are not subject to open review."

Taking the podium first was Darren Ulster himself, who spoke not of his sexual orientation, but of his love for teaching. He implored the board to continue to allow him to live his dream as a band director in a top school district, and he promised to always perform his duties in a professional manner.

The next two speakers were band parents, the first who told of how involvement in the band had awakened in his teenage son an interest in school. He attributed this new zeal for learning directly to the influence of Darren Ulster. The second parent spoke of Ulster's dedication to his work, obvious by the consistent high marks in regional band competitions. Her daughter had parlayed her first chair clarinet status in such an excellent band into a college music scholarship. This too, she said, was a product of the encouragement and guidance provided by Darren Ulster.

Finally, Michele's name was called. The girl nervously approached the podium and began.

"Hello. My name is Michele Sanders, and I used to play in the band at Westfield High School, but I graduated last year. Thank you for letting me come tonight to speak on behalf of Mr. Ulster. There are three things I want to say."

It was obvious to Louise that Michele had written down her remarks and practiced saying them over and over. Now realizing how nervous she had grown as she waited her turn, she wished she had done the same.

"First, I want to say that I think Mr. Ulster is a wonderful teacher. He was friendly to all of the students, and he always encouraged us to do our best."

She looked at the smiling band director and blushed.

"Second, I want to say that, as a student who discovered in high school that I was gay, I would have liked it if I could have had someone like Mr. Ulster to talk to. I have a bunch of gay friends at college now, and all of us felt like outsiders in our high schools because there wasn't anyone there to talk to about our experiences. We didn't fit in, no matter how hard we tried. One of my friends at college even said she tried to kill herself back then because she felt so all alone. I think the schools should do more for all of the students, not just the ones who are straight. They already get all the breaks."

The young woman's words weren't polished, but they were nonetheless from the heart. Her remarks held just a trace of that youthful defiance that Louise had come to appreciate over the years.

"And third, I want to say that I have an interest in how all of this turns out because I am studying at Slippery Rock State to become a math teacher. I want to teach because I love working with numbers, and because a math teacher at Westfield High inspired me. But I also want to be able to be who and what I am, without worrying that I can be fired just because I happen to be gay. That's all I have to say, and thank you very much for listening."

Michele came back to her chair as several of the observers clapped. Her mother and father both stood and hugged her briefly before sitting back down. Louise leaned over and patted her arm as Ted Meyer made his way to the podium when his name was called.

"Good evening, Mr. Superintendent, Chairman, and board members. I'm Ted Meyer, the principal at Westfield High School. With your permission, I'd like to yield my minutes on the floor to Miss Louise Stevens, a former teacher of mine who retired a year ago. Since you're new to this area, Mr. Superintendent, I'd like to point out that Miss Stevens was the 1979 and 1991 Teacher of the Year in Westmoreland County, the only teacher to hold that honor twice. The best part of my job is leading dedicated faculty like Louise Stevens and Darren Ulster."

Louise anxiously took her place at the podium as her former boss turned on the slide show. Behind her, a large picture of Rhonda Markosky directing the high school band graced the screen.

"Thank you, Mr. Meyer. Mr. Superintendent, Chairman Sumter—it's nice to see you again—and board members, hello and thank you for hearing me tonight."

Louise laced her fingers together and leaned on the podium.

"I came so I could tell you a little about the woman in this picture. She was Rhonda Markosky, and she held the position of band director at Westfield for thirty-two years. As many of you know, Miss Markosky died in 1999, at the front of her band room doing what she loved most. Mrs. Mowrey, you were in Miss Markosky's band, weren't you?"

The board member nodded, smiling at the high school memory.

"I could tell you about the thousands of students she inspired over the years, and the hundreds of awards she garnered for the school. But here was one of our proudest moments at Westfield that I think says it all."

Ted Meyer changed the screen to a front-page headline from the local newspaper: *Westfield's Markosky named Pennsylvania State Teacher of the Year.*

"That was in 1986. Rhonda Markosky is the only Westmoreland County teacher to win that state honor, so I don't have to say anymore about what kind of teacher she was." She nodded toward Meyer, who changed to the final slide, a yearbook picture of her with Rhonda, both of them bundled up warmly as they cheered their football team.

"What I also want to tell you is that Rhonda Markosky was a lesbian." Her voice began to shake and she squeezed her fingers so tightly that her knuckles began to turn white. "I know that because she was my partner for over thirty years. Throughout our teaching careers, we kept that private, afraid we might lose our jobs. Obviously, we had good reason to worry. Now that I've retired, I don't have to hide from people's prejudices or unfounded fears. I can stand here now and speak on behalf of the dozens—maybe even hundreds—of staff, teachers, and administrators in the school system who are gay but who are afraid to come forward and live their lives in the open. I ask you to let them do their jobs as they do every day, without the risk of being fired because of things that have nothing to do with their skill and dedication. Let them make their contributions to the education of your children as Rhonda Markosky did, and as Darren Ulster does. Make it part of your county-wide policy to end discrimination against gays and lesbians, as much of the country has already done. Take this opportunity to teach the children of this county that no one deserves to be thrown away. You and the students will be better for it. Thank you."

Louise stepped down amid sporadic applause that erupted into a sustained chorus of cheers. Red-faced, she walked with Ted back to their seats, where Michele sat with tears streaming down her face.

"I'm sorry I never told you, Michele," Louise whispered, misreading the emotion as betrayal.

"It's okay, Miss Stevens. I understand. It's just … I'm so proud of you for saying all of that."

"I'm proud of you too, sweetheart. What you did took a lot of guts."

The board then adjourned and returned to chambers to discuss the issues and vote on the personnel moves. Louise was inundated with a steady stream of people offering their congratulations and support. One was Darren Ulster.

"Thank you, Lou. It means the world to me that you came all this way to speak up for me like you did."

"What they're doing is wrong, Darren. Rhonda and I shouldn't have had to live like that, and you shouldn't either." She was still shaking as she spoke. It wasn't as easy to talk with people she didn't know well as it had been to talk with Ted. But she stood her ground and greeted everyone who came by.

"I have to go call Dottie," Ted said, pulling out his cell phone. "I think what you said was exactly what they needed to hear, Lou."

"At least I didn't faint."

"Will you come by tomorrow and have lunch with us at school?"

Louise shook her head and guided him off to the side so they could speak privately. "I don't think so, Ted. Not everybody's going to be okay with this, and I don't think I want to deal with it just yet."

"What do you mean, Lou? Everyone at Westfield likes you. They'll be disappointed if you don't stop by."

"Maybe next time, after this has had a little time to sink in—for all of us." It might be a year or two before Louise could face her fellow teachers. Perhaps by then, her relationship with Rhonda might not be the only thing on their minds.

When the well-wishers had come and gone, Louise found herself sitting alone with a still-sniffling Michele Sanders.

"Are you going to do that all night?" she teased.

Michele chuckled and blew her nose. "No, I hope not. But it makes me sad that Miss Markosky is gone and now you're all alone."

Louise put her arm around the young woman's shoulder. "It broke my heart to lose her, and I was sad for a long time. Now I haven't told many people this …" She hesitated while making eye contact, astonished at how far she had come in just a few hours.

"If it's a secret, I won't tell anyone."

"It's not really a secret, but I only share important personal things with people I really like."

The girl brightened.

"I'm not alone anymore."

"You're not?"

Louise shook her head and gave a hint of a smile. "No, I met someone when I moved to Florida, and I was lucky enough to fall in love again."

"Really?"

Louise nodded.

"Miss Stevens! That's so nice." Overcome with happiness, Michele reached out to give her former teacher a hug. "I hope I get to meet her the next time I go see my grandmother."

"You've already met her."

The girl thought for a moment before her eyes grew wide with surprise. "Your friend at the golf course?"

"That's right," Louise answered grinning. "Marty Beck."

"Aw, Marty's so cute!"

Louise laughed aloud. "Yes, she certainly is. And the next time you come down, the three of us will spend some time together. I think you and Marty will like each other a lot."

The small group of Darren's supporters waited in the auditorium for what seemed like hours to Louise. The superintendent was the first to emerge from the closed meeting, and he didn't look happy at all. Louise took that as a very good sign.

Chapter 25

MARTY TAPPED THE alarm clock on the bedside table and rolled over to wrap her arm around a still-snoozing Louise, who was worn out after her long drive back from West Virginia. Petie stood at the foot of the bed and stretched, eventually sneaking up to walk across their pillows, his usual morning greeting.

"I'll get breakfast," Louise mumbled, shifting beneath the covers.

"It's okay. You're tired. Stay here and sleep some more. I can eat cereal." Marty kissed her bare shoulder and pulled the blanket up. "Let's go, Petie."

She got dressed and took the terrier out for his morning walk, just as she did every morning. After breakfast, she peeked in to find her companion still asleep. The last few days had been very emotional for Louise, but her visit back to Greensburg had been a success. Something about her manner seemed a little different from when she left to go up north, but Marty couldn't put her finger on what it was. When they had made love last night, Louise was quieter, more serious than usual. It wasn't like there was anything wrong ... just different.

Or maybe it was just Marty's perception, colored by her own ruminations of the past week. Left with so much time to think, she had let her mind wander about what might lie ahead for the two of them. She had keenly felt Louise's absence, even more than she had a few weeks ago when she left Florida on her own. And she was already dreading the day Louise would pack up to return to Cape Coral, though Louise hadn't talked at all about leaving. Being together in North Carolina seemed right for them and Marty hoped that Louise would decide to stay a little longer.

It was all that talk about Rhonda a week ago—about what Louise thought it took to make a relationship last—that had gotten her thinking well past their time together in North Carolina. Marty began to ask herself what kind of future she wanted with Louise. Given her abysmal experience with relationships, it was hard to look so far ahead, but she knew one thing for sure: she didn't want to think about them not being together.

That raised tough questions for Marty about how they might make it work, something she and Louise approached with different philosophies. Louise seemed to think two people just decided to stay together, and that's all there was to it. Marty figured they would have to work through it a little at a time, both of them asking themselves over and over if being with each other was what they wanted. And then one day—presto! A few years have passed, and both of you realize that it's going to work out.

Then, a couple of days before Louise got home, it suddenly struck Marty that her way of thinking had failed her every time, while Louise had spent thirty-one years with the same woman. What if having so many doubts was what had sabotaged all of her past relationships? Even if those doubts were well-placed with the people in her past, she didn't have those doubts about Louise.

Maybe Louise was right, and all she had to do was make up her mind that she wanted it badly enough to work for it.

Marty stood behind Louise, watching the familiar station wagon pull into the parking space in front of the condo. "Are you sure you're going to be okay with this?"

Louise nodded. She was nervous about seeing Shirley again, but she had firmly settled the issue of her anger at the betrayal by her friend. "She's probably more nervous than I am."

"I wouldn't doubt that."

Together, they walked out to the parking lot to meet their friends. Louise hugged Linda first and was almost overcome with feelings of fierce loyalty and protectiveness. With crystal clarity, she reaffirmed her decision to bury what was past—she never wanted to see Linda hurt.

"Hi, Lou."

"Shirley." She held out her arms and her longtime friend stepped into the embrace. "I'm glad you're here."

"Me too."

Louise was sure she heard the woman's voice crack. "I love you, you know," she whispered.

"I love you, too."

"Good gracious! They're moving in, Lou," Marty shouted when Linda opened the back of the car to reveal four large suitcases.

"We didn't know what we would need. Louise said it was cool at night. We have golf clothes ... going-out clothes ... and a little extra room to take back what we buy."

Each woman took a suitcase and climbed the stairs to the front door. Louise turned to face their guests. "Pay no attention to Marty. She'd wear the same thing every day if I let her."

"You look good, Marty," Shirley said. "Have you lost more weight?"

"Lou makes me eat vegetables."

"She's good for you," Linda said. "Maybe we really ought to move in, Shirley. I could stand to drop a few pounds."

"And I could probably stand to dress a little better."

"Hey, you two! I'm retired. Didn't you get the memo?"

After putting the suitcases away, the women gathered at the table on the back deck to relax.

"Boy, this is really nice. I can see why you like it here," Linda said. "I don't know why you'd want to go back to Florida while it's still so hot and muggy, Lou. I'd stay here all summer if Marty would let me."

"I don't know why she'd want to go either," Marty echoed, scooting her chair close so she could hold Louise's hand. "Petie wants to stay here, don't you, boy?"

The terrier stood to be lifted into Marty's lap.

"She's stolen my dog."

"He likes it here. If you aren't going to stay for yourself, you should at least consider his feelings."

Louise had no inclination to head back to Florida any time soon. In fact, when she got back from West Virginia, she began to think she might stay all the way to the end of October when Marty packed up to return to Florida. As long as Marty was here, there wasn't anything in Florida to go home to.

"What's wrong with Lou?" Shirley asked when Marty finished hitting her approach shot on Number Twelve.

"She's having a bad hole. We call that BIPSIC."

"You call it what?"

"BIPSIC. Ball in Pocket, Sitting in Cart."

"Is she done for the day?"

"Nah, just this hole." The women stepped aside as Linda grappled with her lie in the high grass just off the fairway. "She gets mad at herself when she doesn't play well."

"Does she ever! I saw her throw a pitching wedge into a lake once."

Marty's jaw dropped. "No way!" She looked over at Louise in the cart, unable to imagine the prim woman capable of an outburst like that.

"Oh, yeah. She used to have an awful temper. She's really mellowed a lot over the years. Lucky for you."

"I'll say. What do you think did it?"

"Rhonda. She stopped playing with her for a while. She said it wasn't fun if Louise was going to act like that."

"I had no idea she could go off that way."

"She doesn't do it anymore."

Marty nodded. She had seen a glimmer of Louise's temper the first few times they met, and again when Louise thought she was flirting with that woman on the driving range. But not since, so it never occurred to Marty that a bad temper was a basic part of her personality.

"She's always been easy to rile, though. But what I like about Lou is that she calms down right away and she isn't afraid to admit when she's wrong." Shirley lowered her voice to be certain that neither Linda nor Louise would hear the next part. "And when she does admit it, you be sure to forgive her right away, because she's forgiven more than anyone I know."

"She's a good soul."

"No, Marty, she's more than that. She's special. Hold on to her if you can, and you'll never be sorry a day in your life. I know Rhonda wasn't."

Marty looked over at Louise sitting in the cart and smiled, her heart suddenly swelling with love. She turned back when she heard the thump of Linda's ball as it dropped softly onto the green and rolled toward the flag ... and rolled ... and rolled ... and disappeared into the cup!

The trip to Asheville for the golf tournament took them two hours along the Blue Ridge Parkway. "We'll have to walk from here, ladies," Marty said as she pulled Louise's car into a shaded spot in the parking lot. "Everything closer is handicapped."

"Does being tired and lazy qualify?" Shirley asked.

"Come on, Shirl. We have to keep up with the kids," Linda chided.

Marty grinned. "I like hanging out with you two. I feel young again."

"Well, you are the youngest," Louise pointed out.

"But only by two years."

"Two years is a lot at our age!" Shirley grasped Linda's outstretched hand to pull herself up from the back seat.

Marty took Louise's hand as they walked toward the gate. "Sorry I can't walk with you today." She had explained to all of them that she was doing a favor for Pat. "If Mike and Cathy go into the clubhouse for lunch, I'll come find you." Without warning, she stood on her tiptoes and planted a kiss on Louise's lips. Then she was gone.

Louise shook her head as Marty disappeared into the crowd, well aware that she was blushing furiously from such a public display. If Shirley and Linda noticed—*they had to have noticed*—they never said a word. "Why don't we sit up in the stands and watch everyone tee off? Maybe we'll see somebody we want to follow," she suggested.

"That's fine with me," Linda said. "I wish we could walk with Tami. I remember the first time I saw her play at Pine Island. She was something else!"

"Yeah, I guess Marty's worried that having a gallery will make her nervous. But if she plays well, she'll draw a crowd anyway tomorrow and we can join in then."

"I'll go get us a program," Shirley offered as the other two women scouted for seats in the bleachers.

Linda sat down next to Louise, saving a spot for her partner. "Can I say that I think you and Marty Beck are about the cutest couple I've ever seen?"

Louise grinned through her embarrassment.

"I can't get over how you've mellowed."

"What's that supposed to mean?"

"Well, you seem more comfortable with things ... like holding hands in front of people. You hardly ever did that with Rhonda, even when it was just the four of us."

Louise shrugged. "Marty's a whole lot more open about things than any of us ever were. It's still hard for me sometimes, but I try not to make a big deal out of it."

"I'm really proud of you."

"I wish I could have been more that way with Rhonda. It would have meant a lot to her."

"You can't second-guess any of that now. Besides, Rhonda knew how you felt. It just wasn't the right time for you two."

"That's what Ted said, that we were probably right to keep things secret at school, so the wrong people wouldn't find out. At least no one has to worry about that any more."

"I'm proud of you for that, too."

Louise waved her off. "It wasn't just me. Besides, I'd like to think they would have done the right thing anyway."

"Maybe, maybe not. But you really gave them food for thought, and I bet Rhonda would have loved it."

"Here you go," Shirley said as she returned with the programs. "There's a girl from Pittsburgh in the next-to-last group. Why don't we walk with her?"

"I missed you again today," Louise said as Marty closed the door to their motel room. They were staying in Asheville during the tournament to avoid the long drive back and forth.

"I know. I missed you too." Marty gave her a quick kiss and sprawled across the bed. "But you should be able to walk with us tomorrow. Tami's going to have a gallery whether she wants one or not. That's what she gets for playing so well."

Tami Sparks had a scorching third round, finishing the day at five under, only four strokes back of the leader.

"And just think—she owes her career to Marty Beck."

Marty snorted. "Not to me. To Pat Shapiro, maybe. All I did was hook them up with each other."

"That's not all you did." Louise had gotten the feeling over the last few days that Marty was feeling down about this tournament, but she couldn't figure out why. It was almost as though she was jealous of Tami's success. "You're the one that noticed her talent to begin with."

"I wonder what's on TV tonight." Marty jabbed the remote and scooted back against the pillows.

Louise sighed and kicked off her shoes. Whatever was eating Marty, she obviously didn't want to talk about it. "Let me in behind you and I'll rub your shoulders."

"That would be great. But I can't promise I won't fall asleep."

Louise chuckled. "When do you ever not fall asleep?" She took her position behind Marty and began her massage, pausing to drop a kiss on Marty's neck. "Honey, have you thought about when you're going to retire?"

"Not really. I'd probably just play golf all day anyway, so what difference would it make?"

Louise felt a surge of anger that Marty wasn't even taking her seriously. "The difference is that you wouldn't have to get up so early every day. I worry about how hard you work. Some mornings, you're already tired when you walk out the door. I'm afraid you're going to work yourself to death."

Marty sat up and turned around. "You don't have to worry about me like that, Lou. I had a checkup when I had my gall bladder out and everything else was fine."

Louise nodded, fighting back tears that suddenly filled her eyes. She lunged forward and wrapped Marty in a tight hug. "The thought of losing you is more than I can stand."

"I'm not going anywhere, sweetheart. I promise."

More than anything, Louise wanted to believe that. But she had seen firsthand how quickly tragedy could strike.

The soft buzzer sounded at six-thirty a.m. on Sunday, the last day of the tournament. Marty tapped the snooze alarm and snuggled into Louise's long body. "You feeling any better this morning, Lou?"

Poor Louise had eaten something yesterday that made her sick, and had been in the bathroom half the night. Around midnight, Marty had gotten dressed and gone in search of an all-night pharmacy, finally coming back with a bottle of pink stuff to settle her stomach.

"I think I'm going to live," she mumbled.

"You must be better then. Last night, you didn't want to live."

"What do you think it was?" Louise struggled to sit up, gently rubbing her stomach in small circles.

"I don't know. Maybe your dinner was bad. Or it could have been that sausage with peppers and onions you picked up from the wagon for lunch. That stuff sits out a long time. It's a wonder more people—"

"That's enough, Marty." Louise's face had gone gray. "Sorry I asked."

Marty chuckled and stroked her l back. "All things must pass, eh?"

Louise smacked her playfully, warning, "The next time you feel like this, I'm going to show you the same sympathy."

"Sorry, babe. Speaking of being sick … are you okay about where we left things last night?"

"Yeah," she answered with a sigh. "I don't know what came over me. I just got scared all of a sudden."

"Don't be scared, okay? I promise if work gets too hard, I'll hang it up."

Louise nodded. It wasn't exactly what she wanted to hear, but it was all she could ask.

"So do you feel like going today?"

"I wouldn't miss it for the world." She managed to smile, and forced herself out of bed. They all needed to be out the door by seven to get the good seats at the first tee.

Marty fell back onto the bed to watch Louise get ready for the day. Louise had laid out her clothes the night before and was dressed in no time. Next, she rummaged through Marty's suitcase and pulled out one of her favorite outfits.

"Will you wear this today?"

Marty eyed the dark blue shorts and blue and white striped golf shirt. It was one of her favorites, too, but she suspected that Louise liked it because the neck scooped low. "You just want to look down my shirt."

"And what's wrong with that?"

Marty pulled her T-shirt over her head to expose her breasts. "And what's wrong with the real thing?"

Louise crawled across the bed and buried her face into Marty's chest. "We're going to be late if you keep teasing me."

"And I thought you were sick."

"I'd get off my death bed for this," Louise mumbled as she pulled one of Marty's nipples into her mouth.

Marty shuddered and let out a groan. "We can't be late."

Louise let go of her prize. "We'll finish this later. But put on the striped shirt."

An hour later, the four friends were walking into the tournament, eager for the last round to begin. Tami was tied for third and playing in the last threesome.

Marty took Louise's hand and pulled her aside. "Are you going to walk with us again today?"

"Yeah, I want to be with you when she wins it all."

Marty grinned. "She has a chance."

"I know." After watching the young golfer yesterday, Louise had found herself profoundly interested in Tami's game. Some of the nuances of her approach to the ball showed Marty's influence, even after all these years.

But the most intriguing aspect of following Tami Sparks was watching Marty watch Pat Shapiro. As they walked between holes, the elder pro made notes on the young golfer's performance, and it was as though Marty strained to see what she was writing.

Suddenly, Louise understood. Marty wasn't jealous of Tami, or thinking about her collapse at the Open almost forty years ago. She was kicking herself for her own lost opportunity to coach this rising star.

The four friends sat perfectly still in the stands as Tami Sparks lined up her tee shot on the first hole. Yesterday's leader, Shelley Coleman, had bogeyed the last two holes, dropping into a tie for first with Tia Johnston. Tami was four back, in a tie for third, but her hot round on Saturday had prompted the tourney officials to place her in the final group.

Marty understood the pressure that was on the young golfer, just as it had been on her at the Open in 1966. But Marty hadn't had someone like Pat in her corner. Sure, Wallace was there with her, but as her caddy, he had grown to be more concerned about how they lived day to day than what was best for her future in golf. Looking back, she could have used his encouragement that day rather than his scolding. She longed for the chance to give that same encouragement to Tami Sparks, but that job belonged to her caddy, Jeff Hanley, and to Pat.

All three of the golfers in the last group started off solid, each making par on the first five holes. The co-leaders seemed to be holding back on this final day, playing their most conservative game, each hoping the other would make a mistake. That was exactly the opportunity Tami Sparks needed, and Jeff pushed her through it. Number Six was a long par five, the entrance to the green narrowed by sand traps at the front on both sides. A prudent golfer laid up for the best position from which to loft one onto the green. From there, a solid putt would net a birdie.

Tami crushed her drive, and boldly went for the green on her second shot. The crowd erupted in cheers as her ball inched onto the fringe near the trap on the left side. If her putting game held, she would likely birdie the hole; putting pressure on her opponents to do the same.

As expected, both of the leaders laid up, finding the green on their third shot. Tami was away, and shocked the crowd by sinking a twenty-foot putt for eagle. Just like that, she had closed the gap to two.

But the leaders weren't conceding. Johnston parred, and Coleman birdied; Tami remained in third place, but had netted one stroke on the leader.

Two holes later, she picked up another stroke on a par three; and on the ninth hole, moved into second place as each of her playing partners dropped a stroke. Heading into the back nine, she was tied for second, one back from the leader.

The gallery had almost doubled since their start. When the electronic leader boards around the course showed the movement in the last group, fans abandoned their old favorites to see if an amateur might capture this tournament title for the first time. Intent on staying close to Pat, Marty was barely aware of the others around her, and was startled when Louise whispered in her ear. "I can't believe how well Tami's playing, Marty. She's got a real chance to win it all."

"Yeah, she's doing great. But she's got to keep pushing herself," Marty agreed, hustling ahead to see if she could catch what Pat was studying. She hoped Jeff would be able to keep Tami focused. They had to seek the advantage and seize it, keeping pressure on the leader to force a mistake.

On Number Twelve, Shelley Coleman reminded all those in attendance why she was out in front, and why she was the leading money-winner on the tour this year. From eighty yards out, she dropped a wedge shot within four inches of the hole. Her birdie, combined with Tami's par, stretched her lead to two strokes.

But the young golfer reached deeper into her resolve, returning the favor on Fourteen. She tightened the screws even further when she chipped in from the sand trap on the fifteenth hole. With three holes remaining, the two were tied. By this time, Tia Johnston had fallen back three strokes and was pretty much out of the race.

Marty was astounded at the way Pat and Jeff had kept the golfer on an even keel throughout the day. At twenty years old, Tami was handling the pressure like an old pro. But the real test came on Sixteen, when the young golfer's tee shot caught the treetops on the right, falling into the rough well behind Johnston's lie in the center of the fairway.

Hanging back, she looked for signs that Pat would give a word of encouragement to soothe the player's frazzled nerves. This was no time to come unglued. Looking ahead, she watched Tami circle her lie, studying the trees in her path and the angle of the incline. There was a narrow opening to push it into the fairway if she nailed it precisely between two stands of trees. But if she caught one of the trees, the ball might careen to an unplayable lie.

From the corner of her eye, Marty caught another image, that of Louise squatting low to study the golfer's approach. She smiled to herself as she noticed the flat-brimmed hat with the black band. It was the same one she had worn to the driving range two days after their initial prickly meeting; the day Marty had felt something inside her click. Suddenly, this profound longing she felt from seeing Pat and Tami on center stage seemed trivial and misguided. She didn't want to be in Pat Shapiro's shoes, running off to one tournament after another. She wanted exactly what she had with Louise.

The crowd exploded in applause as Tami's second shot sailed from the trees into the fairway. But Marty had missed it; she had been watching her partner. *Partner...* Out of the blue, her thoughts wandered back to the night before, when she had climbed out of bed to go in search of something that might help Louise feel better. No doubt about it, Louise Stevens brought out the best in her, and her best had nothing at all to do with playing golf.

As the gallery shifted forward, Marty left Mike and Cathy and pushed her way through the crowd to catch up. Without a word, she suddenly caught Louise's left hand, wrapping their fingers together tightly.

"That was some recovery, wasn't it?" Louise asked.

"Oh, yeah," Marty agreed, though she wasn't thinking about golf right that instant. "I love you, Lou."

Louise smiled, clearly pleased at the sudden display of affection and declaration of love. "I love you too."

Chapter 26

YOU GUYS BE careful, and call us when you get home," Louise said, stepping back from the car into Marty's arms so they could wave goodbye to their friends.

"You were great with Shirley and I'm really proud of you."

Louise sighed. "I couldn't have stood losing them, and that's what would have happened if Linda had found out."

"You have a good heart, Lou." They turned and walked back inside the condo as their friends disappeared down the road. "It was nice having them here, but I have to admit I'm glad to have you all to myself again."

"I know what you mean. Two weeks is a long time to have to share you," Louise said, folding Marty into an embrace. She wanted to understand whatever it was that had caused Marty to draw close to her yesterday afternoon at the tournament, and to hold her so tightly as they went to sleep. "I wish you didn't have to work today."

"Me too. There's nothing I'd like more than to stay home and do this all day." She pulled Louise's mouth toward hers and delivered a deep kiss.

Louise sighed. "You curl my toes when you kiss me like that."

"And don't you forget it." Marty pulled away and grabbed her visor off the hook by the door.

Louise held onto Marty's hand and tugged her back. "I think you should take a sick day."

"You mean call Bob and tell him I have to stay in bed all day?"

"Something like that." Louise began to loosen the buttons on her blouse. "I'll make it worth your while."

Marty swallowed, studying the lacy outline of the exposed bra. "I guess it wouldn't hurt to go in an hour late."

"Or two."

Marty hurried into the pro shop, but it was mostly cleared out, the early golfers already underway. "Hey, Bob. Sorry I'm late."

"Marty! Welcome back. You've got a customer out on the range, been here since I opened."

"I didn't have any appointments ... at least not any that I knew of. Did you schedule somebody for me?"

"No, he doesn't have an appointment. Or should I say, they don't have an appointment."

"They?"

Bob nodded. "His name's Clifton Meriwether. He's got his daughter with him. He said he talked with your friend at the tournament yesterday afternoon and she gave him your name."

"He talked with Pat?"

"Yeah. Oh, congratulations on your girl, by the way. It's in the paper. She played great ... and she even mentioned you."

"You're kidding!" Marty grabbed the paper and pulled out the sports page, smiling at the photo of Tami hoisting the winner's trophy. Scrolling down the article, she found it—*credits her solid fundamentals to coach Marty Beck.*

"That's cool. I'll have to let her know I appreciate that." She folded the paper and stuck it under the counter to take home and show Louise. "Did this Meriwether guy say what he wanted?"

"I'd say he wants lessons for his daughter. She was the one with the golf bag."

Marty thought about what he was saying—a father with his daughter. If there was one thing a club coveted, it was a young player who could build a reputation in the state and region. If the kid ever got a shot at the tour, the club would gain notoriety as one of the sponsors. It was prestigious, and it attracted more talented players who wanted to make it big.

"I guess I ought to go out there and have a look."

Marty approached the range from behind, carrying her driver, a seven-iron, and a handful of ball tokens. The girl in question looked to be about fourteen years old, and she was driving the ball over two hundred yards … nice loft, good mechanics … even better than Tami Sparks had shown at that age. Her father stood nearby twirling a putter, and they talked and laughed as though oblivious to what they were doing.

"Good morning."

Both of them stopped and turned, suddenly serious. "Are you Marty Beck?"

"I am."

"I'm Clifton Meriwether, and this is my daughter, Hannah. I hope you don't mind us showing up without an appointment."

"Not at all. What can I do for you?"

"We were at the tournament over the weekend, and I talked with Pat Shapiro because we were both so impressed with Tami Sparks. Pat was nice enough to give us your name as someone who might be able to help us out."

"Pat's a good friend of mine. We used to play on the tour together."

"That's what she said. She also said you were the one who coached Tami when she first started out, and Hannah and I were hoping you might do the same for us."

"She looks like she's had a good bit of coaching already." Marty looked directly at the girl, who just smiled shyly.

"She's worked with a lot of club pros, and she practices all the time. But she's never had a real coach to pull her game together."

Marty directed her question to Hannah. "You like this game?"

"Yes, ma'am."

Marty cringed. That would be the first bad habit to go. "Why?"

The girl shrugged. "I can't really say. I just know that I'm happier when I'm playing golf than when I'm doing anything else."

That was an answer Marty understood. She turned back to Clifton. "Did Pat tell you that I live in Florida through the winter?"

"That's not a problem for us. Hannah's mom and I are divorced. She lives up here, and I'm willing to move to Florida if it means Hannah gets the right coach."

Marty looked from the father to the girl and back. "I just turned sixty-two a couple of weeks ago. I'm probably going to retire before too long, so even if this works out, I'm not going to be the one getting Hannah on the tour—assuming she trains hard enough to go that far."

"We'll cross that bridge when we come to it. I just want her to have the kind of foundation Tami Sparks has."

Marty dug in her pocket for a ball token. "Let's see what you've got, Hannah."

"I think this kid could be really good—if she sticks to it, that is." Marty finished her dinner as she filled Louise in on the events of her day.

"It's really something that her father is willing to move to Cape Coral. That says a lot about your reputation, Marty."

Marty waved off the compliment. "He's just looking for the right fit for his kid. If it's working out with her by the time I head back, he'll make the move and it will be worth it for Hannah to get what she needs from somebody who's dedicated to her goals. That's the kind of commitment it takes to make it in this game."

"She's really that good?"

"She's the best I've ever seen at that age."

"I bet you were that good."

Marty snorted. "Not even close. But who knows? If I'd gotten some coaching, things might have been different."

"And you would have made it big on the tour." Louise stood up and gathered their empty plates.

Marty picked up the few remaining items on the table and followed Louise into the kitchen. "Maybe … but if I had it to do over again, I don't think I would change a thing."

"Why not?" Louise put the plates into the dishwasher. "I thought the tour was what you always wanted."

"So did I. But I was wrong. Because if I had made it on the tour"—she took Louise's hand and pulled her back into the living room where they sank onto the couch—"I might not have ended up here with you, Louise Stevens. And I wouldn't change anything about my life if it meant not having you in it now."

Marty put a finger to Louise's lips before she could reply. "I'm not finished. I want you to do something for me."

Louise nodded, her face now serious.

"I want you to say you'll stay here with me."

Louise leaned back so she could look Marty in the eye. "Do I act like I'm in a hurry to go back to Florida?"

"No, but you haven't said you'll stay, so I worry every single day about you leaving. I don't want to have to worry about it anymore. I want you to stay with me until October."

"And then what?"

"And then we go back to Florida—together."

"You to your house and me to mine?" Louise took both of Marty's hands and squeezed them tight. "I'll stay here with you, honey—no matter what your answer is."

"You will?"

Louise nodded. "But that's just three more months. I want more than that."

"So do I. I want you to come back every—"

"When we get back to Florida, I want you to move in with me." This time, she stopped Marty from interrupting by holding up her hand. "I know that's not an easy thing for you to do. But you can bring all your things. We'll make room for it if we have to put my stuff in the attic."

"But your things are so nice."

"I don't give a damn about any of it. All that matters to me is that you're there, and if you need your things, you can have them."

Marty was flabbergasted. *Louise just said damn!* "I'll probably give most of my stuff to Mike and Katie. And I can have the rest of it shipped up here. Then you won't have to change a thing."

Louise shook her head as if to clear her confusion. "Was that a yes?"

"Yes. It was a yes." Marty began to grin. "If I could marry you, Lou, I would. But since I can't, all I can ask is that you spend your life with me."

Louise's eyes sparkled with surprise and her lips turned up in the beginning of a smile.

"I know I don't have a lot going for me in the relationship department, but I promise that I'll work hard to make you happy—"

Louise cut her off with a kiss that sealed their promises.

June 1999

Louise peered over the dashboard as she squeezed her new Mercury Sable into the parking space. "You have enough room over there, sweetie?"

"Plenty," Rhonda answered.

"Stay put. I'll come around." Louise turned off the lights and wipers and reached behind her for the umbrella. By the time she made it to the other side, Rhonda was already out of the car. "I told you to wait. That silk will spot if it gets wet."

Rhonda stepped under the umbrella and wrapped her hand around Louise's so that they could carry it together. "I couldn't wait. I saw this gorgeous chick in a slinky black dress coming around the car and I had to jump out to meet her."

"Listen to you. You're the one that looks sexy tonight. That pantsuit makes your eyes so bright."

"The better to see you with."

"You're in a silly mood."

"You better watch out for me tonight. I'm feeling very romantic toward you."

"I hope you save some of it for when we get home."

They entered the restaurant and the maitre d' immediately took their umbrella and placed it in a stand. "Good evening."

"We have a reservation," Rhonda said. "Rhonda Smith." She winked at Louise, who was shaking her head. "Nobody can spell Markosky," she whispered.

"Right this way." He led them to a table in the center of the room, but Rhonda had other ideas.

"Could we have that one?" She indicated a table for two in the corner.

"Of course."

"I told you I was feeling romantic," Rhonda said as she picked up the wine list. "Are you in the mood for red or white?"

"Why don't you choose, since this year's an odd number?"

"That's right. You booked the cruise last year when it was your turn. I feel like a cheapskate. I better go with champagne."

Louise smiled. "A perfect choice."

"For the perfect night." Rhonda called for the waiter and placed her order. As he walked away, she slipped her hand beneath the tablecloth and found Louise's in her lap. "Maybe we should skip dinner ... go back home and devour each other instead."

"If you keep looking at me like that, we may not even make it out of the restaurant," Louise answered, her voice low.

The waiter brought their champagne and made quick work of pouring each of them a flute before placing the bottle in the ice bucket.

Rhonda held out her glass. "To the most beautiful woman in the world."

"I'm looking at her," Louise replied, clinking their crystal. "Happy anniversary, sweetheart."

"I don't know how you've put up with me for thirty-one years, but I'm glad you have, Lou."

"My life wouldn't be worth living without you."

Chapter 27

LOUISE RETURNED FROM her car, where she had loaded the last of their things. Mike had flown up earlier in the week to drive Marty's Subaru home, so they would have a leisurely trip back to Cape Coral, stopping in Savannah and St. Augustine to see the sights.

"Marty?"

"In here."

Louise followed her voice to the master bedroom, where Marty was emptying the contents of her nightstand into a tote bag.

"I almost forgot the stuff in here. I would have been blind without my reading glasses." Marty zipped up the bag and carried it into the living room.

"I guess I should check mine too. I didn't keep much in there." Louise opened her drawer and stopped short. Rhonda Markosky smiled up at her from the pewter frame.

"I'm going to take this out to the car and walk Petie one last time," Marty called from the front door.

Louise picked up the photo and sat down on the bed. "Oh, dear. We haven't talked in a while, have we? Not since I told you about going up to Greensburg and blabbing to everybody that you were a big ol' lesbian." She laughed softly as she ran her finger along the smooth metal frame. "I have so much to tell you, but I suppose you already know the important parts … especially about that woman out there." Louise sighed. "I really love her, Rhonda. Marty's a good soul and we've promised to spend the rest of our lives together. If it's even half as wonderful as my time with you, I'm going to die a very happy woman."

Louise heard a sound in the doorway and turned to find Marty watching her.

"You know, you don't have to keep that in the drawer, Lou. When we come back next year, you should put it out there on the table where I keep Tyler's pictures."

"I almost set it out there one day, but I wasn't sure how you'd feel about it."

"I'd feel fine." Marty came to sit on the bed beside Louise. "I know that she'll always be important to you. I won't ever ask you to put away those memories."

Louise nodded and looked at the photo. "I think I will put it out next year, if it really is okay with you."

"Sure. Maybe you and I can get one made too—together. I'll even comb my hair … put on a clean shirt."

"I love you, Marty Beck." Suddenly overwhelmed with emotion, Louise enveloped Marty in her arms and hugged her fiercely.

"I love you too, Lou, like I've never loved anyone in my whole life." Marty planted a noisy kiss on her cheek. "And I'll love you for as long as you let me."

"I usually average about thirty years."

"And then what?"

"And then we'll take another Mulligan and start over."

Books by KG MacGregor

Shaken (2005) – When a powerful earthquake strikes LA, two strangers are trapped in a crumbled shopping mall. Luxury car dealer Anna Kaklis and family attorney Lily Stewart join forces to escape the rubble; and the friendship that follows grows into the strongest connection either has ever known. *Shaken* is a story of chance and courage, loss and triumph, strength and family.

Malicious Pursuit (2005) – Ruth Ferguson wants a new life for her daughter and herself, and she's willing to risk everything to get it. Spencer Rollins wants to stay alive long enough to bring her friend's killers to justice. When their desperate lives collide on a rainy night, each one's fate is delivered to the other's hands.

The House on Sandstone (2005) – Twenty-five years ago, Carly Griffin left Leland, Kentucky, sure that it held nothing for her future. Now weary of living overseas for one consulting project after another, she's glad to have two months back in Leland to relax with her aging parents. What she doesn't count on is running into old friend Justine Hall, now divorced and walking a fine line between sanity and hell. But Carly's biggest surprise is Leland itself.

Mulligan (2005) – The days are long and lonely for Louise Stevens, whose retirement plans did not include facing the sudden loss of her life partner. Nor did she anticipate meeting sixty-year-old Marty Beck, a fun-loving golf pro with no experience in making relationships last. Too bad they didn't hit it off.

Undercover Tales
Coming Soon

Here are three new short stories from popular authors, now available under one cover

From **Blayne Cooper**, author of *Unbreakable, The Last Train Home, Madam President,* and many others, comes ***Quicksand***, a story about sinking into trouble so deep, there's no way out. Deceit, betrayal, and resisting sexual temptation were never part of private investigator Belinda Blaisdell's daily life. Until now.

KG MacGregor, who brought us the thriller, *Malicious Pursuit*, weaves ***Stolen Souls***, another tale of intrigue. Vonne Maglio signs up to spend two weeks on a working ranch, an adventure vacation where things – and people – are not as they seem.

From **S X Meagher**, author of *I Found My Heart in San Francisco*, comes ***Narc***. The dark side of Chicago is a cauldron of crime. Drugs, sex, blackmail, bribery and corruption so deep you can swim in it. And that's just the cops. How does an honest detective wade through this muck to do her job?